MW00412461

THE DARK
TETRAD

THE DARK TETRAD

A KORI BRIGGS NOVEL

A.P. RAWLS

The Dark Tetrad

A Kori Briggs Novel

A.P. Rawls

FIRST PRINTING

ISBN: 978-1-7372613-0-8 (paperback)
ISBN: 978-1-7372613-1-5 (ebook)

Library of Congress Control Number: 2021910392

© 2021 A.P. Rawls

All Rights Reserved

No part of this book may be reproduced or transmitted in
any form or by any means without the written permission
of the publisher.

UWS
Upper West Side Press, LLC

This is a work of fiction. Names, characters, places, and incidents
either are the product of the author's imagination, or are used
fictitiously. Any resemblance to actual persons, living or dead,
businesses, companies, events, or locales is entirely coincidental.

A NOTE FROM THE AUTHOR

"Do you have to leave so early?" Ronald Strickland watched as his girlfriend rose from the bed and moved toward the bathroom, her taut, naked figure silhouetted against the early morning light from the window. At least he *thought* she was his girlfriend. They'd been seeing each other for a few weeks now. This would mark just the second night they'd slept together. Ronald assumed the lovemaking signaled a commitment, but there was something about Kori that gave him pause. She was, well, it was hard to describe. *Distant*, he supposed was the right word, even during sex. Just what kind of relationship did they have, anyway?

Ronald wished he knew, but the only thing he could be sure of was that he was falling for her. Hard. There was something about her, something mysterious, something alluring. He wanted more emotionally from her, but he sensed that this was the kind of woman from whom one didn't make demands.

And so we are introduced to the fiercely independent Kori Briggs—highly trained special agent, expert in martial arts, dedicated Scotch drinker, and drop-dead beauty whose closest friend is her Glock nine-millimeter Luger. From this passage, excerpted from within these pages, we will ride along with Kori as she leaves Ronald's Washington, DC apartment and makes her way to the headquarters of Rampart, the most secretive intelligence agency in the world, unknown to even the CIA (but, oh, how they would love to prove its existence!). There, she discovers she is wanted in the Oval Office. It's a matter of national security and the president wants nobody else handling the ominous crisis but "the girl."

And then we will continue riding along with Kori, around the world, through thick and thin. And danger. Always danger.

I hope you enjoy getting to know Kori as much as I have enjoyed writing of her exploits. I continue writing. Rest assured, we will be hearing much more from Kori Briggs in the coming months and years. She has some amazing adventures that need telling. So, pour yourself a drink, strap yourself in, sit back, and savor the ride.

—APR

CHAPTER 1

"Mr. President?"

"Yes, come in, Randall." The president waved his chief of staff Randall Crawford into the Oval Office. "What's wrong? You've got that look on your face. You know I don't care for that look."

"Sorry, Mr. President. But I'm afraid I have some unsettling news."

The president, a sturdy man with a high forehead and dark, thinning hair, raised his eyebrows. "Unsettling? Randall, you know I never like to hear that word."

"Of course not, sir."

The president especially didn't want, or need, anything unsettling now. So far, it had been a fairly lazy summer and he'd been enjoying the relative quiet. Midway into his second term, his poll numbers were high, the world seemed at least temporarily stable, and Congress was in recess. The following week, he was scheduled for a weeklong retreat to his vacation home in the Poconos. For being the most powerful person in the world, his plate was surprisingly light just now.

"Well? Out with it, Randall."

"Apparently, we have a situation in Russia, Mr. President. Our man Blake, in Moscow, is on a secure line for you, sir."

The president saw the blinking light on his phone and reached for it. Crawford knew that Blake was one of the few operatives in the world with clearance to call the president directly. Most every other agent had to go through proper channels, relaying intelligence to officers above their paygrade. Anything POTUS needed to know was typically funneled through to the agency director who would report it to the president. But Blake was in a unique position. After thirty years in Russia, with a network of former KGB agents and current high-level Russian military officers at his disposal, he had intelligence nobody could touch. To the president, he was the second-most valuable intelligence agent he knew.

The president picked up the phone, placed his hand over the receiver and gave Crawford a look that said, *I've got it, thanks. You can leave now.* Crawford knew the look. He'd seen it many times before. He bowed his head slightly and left the room.

"Blake, what's going on over there?" What he wanted to say was, *Please don't jeopardize my trip to the Poconos.*

"Hello, Mr. President. Sorry to bother you, sir."

"It's all right. What's the situation?"

"Well, I've been given a little disconcerting news," replied Blake, whose first name the president could never remember. "And it comes straight from my top source."

"Kovalev?"

"Yes, sir."

"Good to know that son of a bitch is still out there. He might be getting a little long in the tooth, but he still works hard, doesn't he?"

"Yes, sir."

"So what's our favorite ex-KGB agent have to say for himself?"

"Well, it seems, sir, as if there's been a bit of a theft."

"Theft? What kind of theft?"

"In Bayanovka, sir."

"Bayanovka … Bayanovka … " the president said thoughtfully. "I've heard that name."

"Yes, sir, it's a small town in the Ural mountains. It's where about twenty tons of enriched uranium left over from the Soviet days are warehoused."

"Yes, Bayanovka, of course. I remember being briefed about that place during my first term. It's their main nuclear repository, if I'm not mistaken. Good Lord, what are you saying? The uranium?"

"About a hundred pounds of it, sir. Gone."

"Clerical error. It's happened before, as I recall. Their methods of record-keeping aren't exactly top-notch. In some respects, they're still working with twentieth-century technology. A week from now they'll tell us they did another inventory and all is right with the world."

"Not this time, Mr. President. There was a clear break-in. Alarms were disabled. So were video cams. This was a professional job."

"From the inside?"

"That's my initial instinct. Obviously, it was someone who knew the grounds well. But the fact is, it's just too early to speculate. We don't know if it was an individual, a group, somebody with terrorist ties ... we just don't know. Naturally, as always, the Russians are being pretty tight-lipped."

"Of course. Like those bastards would ever admit to anything. Thank God for Kovalev. If he still worked for their government, they'd shoot him dead for leaking this to us. They might anyway."

"If they could ever find him, sir. Which, of course, they won't."

"No, of course not. Listen, Blake, what can a hundred pounds of uranium do?"

"It's sufficient for a single bomb, sir. Enough, I would say, to take out a ten-mile radius of wherever it's detonated. But of course, the radiation from the bomb would affect a much larger area, covering a swath roughly the size of, say, Baltimore. I would suggest that we put Homeland on high alert."

"Of course. What did you tell Crawford?"

"Just that there was a serious problem in Russia. Just enough to get him to put me immediately through to you."

"Okay, good. He'll remain on a need-to-know basis. So will everybody else around here. I'll talk to Homeland personally. Nobody needs to know what you're up to over there, Blake. Everyone thinks you're with the CIA, after all. In the meantime, what's being done over there?"

"Kovalev promised to get back with me once their investigation yields some more clues as to the thief or thieves. I'll hear more later today and then we'll be able to make some better-informed decisions."

"Okay, Blake. I'll be waiting." The president hung up, spun his chair around, and gazed out of the Oval Office windows. Damn the luck. It looked like the Poconos would have to wait. The first lady would be disappointed, that was certain. And that would be the best case. The worst case? Who knew? But enough uranium to take out a major city, stolen and in God-knows-whose hands was downright frightening.

He spun his chair back around, picked up the phone again, and called for Crawford. "Get Cooper and Foster in here. ASAP!"

Darren Cooper and James Foster were the top intelligence officers assigned to the White House. Crawford and everyone else in the executive department assumed they were secret service. They weren't. Not anymore than Blake was CIA. Cooper and Foster and Blake all belonged to an executive intelligence agency so secretive that its existence was unknown to both the

Secret Service and the CIA. And to the FBI, for that matter. "Rampart" had been set up during the Kennedy administration during the height of the Cold War when double agents were not uncommon and even long-time intelligence officers could not necessarily be trusted. Payoffs were huge and loyalties were often compromised. It was determined that a higher echelon of agents was needed, a kind of super-group, but a small, tight-knit one. At any given time, there were no more than eighteen or twenty members. There was no red tape, no time-wasting levels of approval to climb through. Rampart could turn on a dime, its agents ready at a moment's notice to deploy anywhere in the world.

The Cold War ended, but the need for Rampart hadn't. The world was no less dangerous, and in many respects, more so. And so Rampart continued, most of its agents more or less hiding in plain sight. Nobody questioned Blake's affiliation, or lack thereof, with the CIA. He had all the credentials, just as Cooper and Foster had all the credentials of secret service agents. Such was the level of muddling bureaucracy that the agents' status of employment was simply taken for granted by everyone. They even drew their paychecks from their ostensible employers. The fact is, however, the agents of Rampart answered to no one but the president.

Now, sitting in the White House Oval Office, Cooper and Foster were being grilled by him.

"How long do we have, gentlemen?" he asked them. "How long does it take before somebody can make a working bomb out of a hundred pounds of uranium?"

"A few weeks, at least," answered Cooper. "And even then, they'd really have to know what they were doing." Cooper was lean but muscular, and with short, dark hair. Foster looked the same and the president often had trouble differentiating them. To him, they were interchangeable. If there were a way to tell them apart, it was probably Cooper's wire-rimmed glasses. Still, the president never trusted his memory and was careful never to call either one by his name, preferring to ask questions to both and look from one to the other until one of them answered.

"Okay," the president said, with a slight sigh of relief. "We're not in imminent danger. We have a little breathing room. Good. Next question: how could they deliver such a bomb? If it's a terrorist cell or even a rogue state, they wouldn't have the capability of launching it, would they?"

"That's correct, Mr. President," said Foster. "But they wouldn't necessarily need to."

"No? How else would they hit a target?"

"Overlord," said Cooper and Foster in unison.

"Say again?"

"Overlord, sir," said Cooper. "It's a scenario we've modeled quite thoroughly."

"Operation Overlord," explained Foster, "was the code name given to the Normandy invasion on D-Day, Mr.

7

President. The amphibious assault on the German-held French coast."

"Yes, thank you for the history lesson. I'm aware."

"Of course, sir. Well, anyway, the Overlord scenario, as we call it, involves an amphibious assault on the United States by terrorists. Of course, they can't storm our beaches with thousands of men from troopships and landing crafts all supported by battleships and aerial bombardment."

"But they wouldn't need to," said Cooper. "The fact is, all they'd need is a single boat."

"A single boat with a homemade nuclear bomb on board," said the president, thoughtfully.

"Yes, sir. A single boat with a homemade nuclear bomb. It could even be a small pleasure craft. And you wouldn't have to land it."

"All you'd need," said Foster, "would be to sail such a boat into New York Harbor. Or underneath the Golden Gate Bridge."

"Or into Chesapeake Bay and up the Potomac," added Cooper.

The president frowned. "I get the point. How prepared are our ports for such a scenario?"

"Not prepared enough, I'm afraid," said Cooper. "US Customs does what it can. So do the respective port authorities and, of course, there's the Coast Guard. Vessels are checked once they dock. Inventories and cargoes are routinely inspected, but you can't realistically catch everything. Billions of pounds of cargo come into this country every day."

"As far as nuclear material," Foster added, "radiation detectors are in place, but if you carried the uranium within a lead container, it probably wouldn't set them off. Even a hundred pounds."

"And if a boat doesn't need to dock …" said the president.

"Yes, sir. A small boat could slip in unnoticed," said Cooper.

"And of course that's just the ports, sir," said Foster. "Someone could conceivably fly it in, although our air defenses are a little better at spotting unidentified aircraft that approach our borders. But, again, the sheer numbers …"

"How is the uranium activated?" asked the president. "How, in other words, does one make a bomb out of it?"

"Well, that's the thing, sir," said Cooper. "The uranium itself isn't enough.

What you need to do is build two small containers or canisters, each housing half the uranium. Then you slam the canisters together. This compresses the uranium and creates what's called a supercritical mass. A nuclear chain reaction ensues. That's essentially how the bomb would work."

"But the slamming of the two canisters really needs to be hard," added Foster. "You more or less need to fire one at the other. So you need to rig up something like a small cannon to propel one canister at the other, achieving enough velocity to basically fuse the two together and start the reaction."

"Right," said Cooper. "And you need a detonating device to activate the cannon. So you need a small second bomb as well. That would be easy enough because all you'd really need for that is gunpowder. But all of this takes time, which is why it's safe to assume we have a few weeks."

"But what if all of that has already been built?" the president asked. "In anticipation of acquiring the uranium?"

"Well, that's possible," said Foster. "But unlikely. The hard part is getting the uranium. Why go to the trouble of building the structure for a nuclear bomb unless you know for sure that you have the actual nuclear material? You might even give yourself away if someone gets wind of what you're constructing. You start shopping around for lead and gunpowder and someone's liable to take notice."

"Yes, I see what you're saying."

"The other part of the equation, Mr. President," added Cooper, "is that to successfully pull it off, you'd need someone who really knows his way around uranium, especially how to handle it. You could irradiate yourself if you're not careful. When it gets right down to it, it's a pretty specialized discipline. Anyone can make the detonator bomb, but the nuclear part is another thing entirely."

"So there are a lot of hurdles," said Foster, which alleviated the president's concern, but only slightly. He knew intuitively that this was the kind of crisis that could make or break a presidential legacy. Foster continued, "Now, naturally, sir, our Overlord model is based on US security, but a small uranium bomb, depending on its owner, can be at least as much of a threat to France, England, or any number of countries."

"Including Israel," Cooper added. "Maybe especially Israel."

"Depending on its owner," repeated the president. "That's what we need to know. That's the million-dollar question, isn't it? So how do we find that out?"

"Sir, I'd suggest that Russian inefficiencies might work to our advantage," said Foster.

"Explain."

"The thieves are probably counting on the fact that a hundred pounds of uranium out of twenty tons won't be missed, at least not right away. After all, Bayanovka has been known for its inventory inaccuracies."

"I said the same thing to Blake."

"The thieves might think they have more time than they do. We know the Russians won't leak anything. This would be a tremendous black eye for them on the world stage. If the thieves believe they've gotten away with it, they may not feel the need to be as careful with their next steps. Surely, they'd have no idea that *we* know about the break-in."

"And so they won't be as inclined to be looking over their shoulder," added Cooper.

"Maybe they'll get sloppy," said Foster. "Make a mistake. Give themselves away. Interestingly, eighty-two percent of crimes are thwarted in just this way."

The president frowned. Clearly, he wasn't interested in statistics of other crimes.

Cooper jumped in. "There's another thing working in our favor, sir. Say what you will about the Russians, but putting their uranium storage in the middle of their country—in the mountains, no less—is at least one smart thing they did. Kazakhstan is about a thousand miles away from Bayanovka, and that would be the closest border."

"And the Barents Sea to the north is even farther away," added Foster. "That would be the closest water escape. Either way, it's a long ways to lug a hundred pounds of nuclear material."

The phone buzzed.

"Mr. President," came the voice of Crawford, "Blake is back on the line, sir."

"Put him through. Blake? I've got Cooper and Foster here with me. What have you got?"

"Well, sir, nothing definitive. But Kovalev is telling me the theft has all the earmarks of an Alfawda raid."

The president grimaced. "Of course. Alfawda! Damn. Well, I guess we shouldn't be surprised. Those terrorist bastards are making al-Qaeda and ISIS look like boy scouts. What's it going to take to be sure?"

"I'm going to Bayanovka tonight, sir. I'll be meeting with Kovalev. Of course, the Russian Foreign Intelligence Service is on the case, but Kovalev will already know everything they know. I'll rendezvous with Kovalev and get a full briefing and report back to you, sir."

"No matter what time of day or night, Blake," said the president. "Contact me the moment you have news."

"Yes, sir."

Hanging up the phone, the president turned again to Cooper and Foster. "We need to be ready to mobilize. We need to be prepared to take whatever action might be necessary and we need to be ready to go immediately. We need the best field person we've got to be on top of this, to be ready to go wherever the need dictates."

Rampart agents Darren Cooper and James Foster knew who the president meant before he even said it out loud. "We need the girl," the president declared. Then he pounded the desk to emphasize the sense of urgency. "Bring me the girl!"

CHAPTER 2

"Do you have to leave so early?" Ronald Strickland watched as his girlfriend rose from the bed and moved toward the bathroom, her taut, naked figure silhouetted against the early morning light from the window. At least he thought she was his girlfriend. They'd been seeing each other for a few weeks now. This would mark just the second night they'd slept together. Ronald assumed the lovemaking signaled a commitment, but there was something about Kori that gave him pause. She was, well, it was hard to describe. *Distant*, he supposed was the right word, even during sex. Just what kind of relationship did they have, anyway?

Ronald wished he knew, but the only thing he could

be sure of was that he was falling for her. Hard. There was something about her, something mysterious, something alluring. He wanted more emotionally from her, but he sensed that this was the kind of woman from whom one didn't make demands.

"You know they're expecting me first thing," Kori said. "I have to give a report on the quarterly sales numbers. All part of the job, you know."

"Yes, I know, I know. You said so last night. But couldn't we spend just a little more time in bed together? Just another half hour. Fifteen minutes? I feel well-rested and … ready to go, if you catch my drift."

Kori smiled and walked over to Ronald's side of the bed and kissed him on the forehead, her long, straight black hair cascading down her shoulders. "I have no doubt," she said, "but it wouldn't look good for the East Coast VP of sales to be late. I have responsibilities. People are counting on me. Plus, I have to stop by my place to shower and change." Then she turned and slipped into the bathroom.

"Call me later?" Ronald called after her, but the door was closed and he imagined she didn't hear him. She soon came out dressed, and stopped once more to give Ronald another peck on the forehead before turning for the front door. "See ya," she said.

"Call me later?"

"Busy day," she said over her shoulder, "but I'll try. I really will."

Then she was gone and Ronald lay there naked under the sheets wondering when he'd hear from her again.

Outside Ronald's apartment building, Kori Briggs stepped into her Tesla Model S and headed for I-395, stopping at a coffee shop for her morning cup—black, no sugar, and—why not?—one of those blueberry scones. The interstate took her to Army Navy Drive, then to South Eads Street to her high-rise condominium. From her fourteenth floor balcony overlooking the Potomac, she could see the Washington Monument. But Kori didn't spend much time on her balcony gazing out across the Potomac. Her work afforded her precious little time. She didn't really have time for Ronald, either, if she were to be honest about it. But a girl needs her distractions. Nobody would ever confuse Ronald with Albert Einstein, but he was not without his charms. Every now and again, he'd say something that would make her laugh. Plus, there was that well-toned body of his. Those upper arms, those broad shoulders. He kept himself in shape, she'd say that much for him. And the dark brown puppy dog eyes were hard to look away from.

After a quick shower, Kori changed into her black Burberry suit with one-button blazer and a crisp but simple white blouse unbuttoned halfway down. Then it was back in the Tesla for the drive to the office on L Street. Along the way, she called her mother. Joan Briggs, sixty-four, lived twenty minutes away in Alexandria, with Baxter, her Jack Russell terrier. Her husband, Kori's father, had left when Kori was three. Kori had only a vague memory of him. She seemed to recall a day when he'd punched a hole in the living room wall with his massive fist. It might have been her very first memory. He had a volatile temper, Joan would later tell Kori. And a habit of straying to other women, spending nights away from home, sometimes whole weekends. Then one day, he didn't come home at all. Joan had never remarried. There were no other children and although Joan had a small circle of friends, Kori often felt as though she was all Joan had in the world, with the exception of Baxter.

"Hi, Mom."

"Hi, honey. Whatcha doing?"

"I'm just on my way to work. Wanted to check on you and say hey. What's new?"

"Well, that stupid Mr. Schiller next door has reported Baxter to the homeowner's association again. I could just wring that man's neck."

"Mom, I told you, you can't just let Baxter run loose."

"But I only let him out in the backyard."

"Which would be fine, Mom, if your backyard was fenced in. But it's not. Have you looked into the idea of an electric dog collar, like I suggested? That way you don't even have to build a fence."

"That just seems so cruel."

"It's not, Mom. Once he gets a shock for leaving the backyard, he won't do it again."

"Hmm … I don't know."

"Well, what did he do this time, anyway?"

"Well, that's just it. Nothing! Although Mr. Schiller seems to think he dug up some flowers in his flowerbed out front. But that doesn't sound like Baxter at all!"

"Mom, that sounds *exactly* like Baxter." The two talked about Baxter some more and then about a problem Joan was having with her dryer. Apparently, it had begun making a terrible noise. Finally, Joan got around to asking about Kori. It was always this way. Joan seemed to be getting more self-absorbed as she got older, asking about things in Kori's world almost as an afterthought. For this, Kori was grateful. She couldn't talk about her work and she never much cared for the advice Joan would give her about her social life. She hadn't told her about Ronald, for instance, knowing that Joan would want to invite the both of them for dinner, and then, afterward, call Kori to tell her why Ronald was all wrong for her. He probably was, but Kori didn't especially need to hear that from her mother. She knew Joan's overprotectiveness was sourced in love, but she also knew that it was partly fear; fear of losing her only daughter. Kori thought that even if she were allowed to tell her mother what her job entailed, she'd still keep it a secret. Otherwise, Joan would worry constantly about her.

The two hung up after Kori promised to come over that weekend for brunch. She completed the half-hour drive to the office in her typical twenty minutes and entered the parking garage. Bypassing the arrow that pointed right directing everybody up the ramp, Kori turned left down a narrow aisle with a security gate that rose as the front end of her Tesla approached. The aisle wound around toward the back of the garage and into a secretive inner building where three other cars were parked. Kori got out of the car and walked through a private entry door that operated by way of a facial recognition system. Once inside, she walked down a narrow hallway and into a private elevator that took her to the seventeenth floor of the building—the headquarters of Gladstone Conveyor.

"Ours is a highly competitive business," Kori's boss had explained to the landlord when they'd moved into the building and requested the alterations. "Lots of company secrets."

That boss, Richard Eaglethorpe, was munching on a donut when Kori entered the small, plain office, nothing more than an open collection of metal desks and networked computers. "Morning, Briggs," he said. "Donut?"

Eaglethorpe was in his sixties. A black man with short, bristly gray hair, he was tall and thin with a kind face that belied his serious nature.

"Thanks, Chief, don't mind if I do. What kind?"

Eaglethorpe handed her the box. "Bunch of different kinds in there."

Kori grabbed a Boston cream. The blueberry scone hadn't quite done it for her.

"I'll never know how you do it, Briggs. You can eat anything you like and you never seem to gain an ounce."

"I guess it's my metabolism, Chief. Just one of those lucky ones. Besides, you cut a pretty good figure yourself."

"Yes, but I suspect I have to work a little harder at it than you. You don't even have a gym membership."

"Well, I've been meaning to get one."

"I'm sure."

"So what's going on today?"

"It's pretty quiet, actually. Gibson is in the back room on the phone to London. Vasquez is still putting that report together for the president on the Venezuela state of affairs. Oh, and we're thinking of sending you to Brussels."

"Brussels? What in God's name for?"

"We have our reasons. You'll know when you get there."

Gibson came out into the lobby from his back office. "Chief, Cooper's on the private line."

Eaglethorpe grabbed the red phone from the lobby desk. "Coop?" Kori and Gibson listened intently, trying to decipher Eaglethorpe's curt responses to whatever it was Cooper was talking to him about. All they knew for sure was that if Darren Cooper was calling from the White House, it was important.

Finally, Eaglethorpe hung up and turned to Kori. "C'mon Agent Briggs, you and I are wanted in the Oval Office."

"How come?" said Kori.

"There's a situation in Russia. Something about stolen uranium."

"Yikes."

"Yikes is right. I think it's safe to say you can forget Brussels for now."

"It's already forgotten, Chief."

Then the two slid out of the headquarters door of Rampart, walking past the large plastic sign out front that marked the lobby entrance of Gladstone Conveyor. *Simply the best* read the motto at the bottom of the sign.

CHAPTER 3

Wladyslaw II Jagiello was the Grand Duke of Lithuania and the King of Poland towards the end of the Middle Ages. In 1939, a large bronze statue of King Jagiello riding a horse and wielding a sword was created for the Polish pavilion at the World's Fair in New York City. The statue rested on a large granite pedestal, and a plaque on the monument read: "Founder of a Free Union of the Peoples of East Central Europe, Victor Over the Teutonic Aggressors at Grunwald." In 1945, King Jagiello's monument was moved to Central Park where it rests to this day, at the east end of Turtle Pond behind the Metropolitan Museum of Art.

Kori sat on the short stone wall that encircled King Jagiello's monument and tried not to look like she was waiting for someone. She and Eaglethorpe had met with Cooper and Foster in the president's office the day before and had been briefed on Russia. Later that night, Blake had reported back from Bayanovka. He and Kovalev had calculated a ninety percent chance that the theft of the uranium had, indeed, been carried out by Alfawda. The Russian countryside was now being scoured, but Blake likened the chances of finding the thieves in the vastness of Russia to finding a single flea resting on a blade of grass somewhere on a football field.

Alfawda had started out as a splinter group of al-Qaeda. Led by Safwaan el-Hanif in Yemen, the group's core belief was that al-Qaeda and other militant Sunni groups were not doing enough to bring about the war that would ultimately mean worldwide victory for Islam, a caliphate of a thousand years that would spell the doom of Western civilization and give all power to Allah's true chosen people. Toward that end, Alfawda had undertaken the terrorist attacks on Paris, London, New York, and elsewhere over the past few years. The group had built quite a name for themselves, and they were gaining more and more support from other radical Islamists. Their numbers were growing in alarming increments.

One of those numbers was Hasan el-Sadek, a forty-year-old swarthy, muscular man from Saudi Arabia who had been radicalized in his early thirties. El-Sadek thought he had the stomach for terrorism but learned early that he did not. College educated, he'd been given an officer's position and sent to the Netherlands to oversee a series of car bombings in Amsterdam. When he saw firsthand the carnage his suicide soldiers had wrought, something changed inside of him. The single image he would never get out of his mind was the sight of a small child, probably three years old, lying dead on the sidewalk several yards from where one of the cars had exploded. Her face, el-Sadek thought, was peaceful and angelic, perfectly unharmed. Her hair was fine and golden and strands of it floated on the summer breeze, giving her a sense of animation, even as her eyes remained still and shut as if she were in a deep, innocent sleep. But el-Sadek knew those eyes would never again open. From then on, he decided that the geopolitical problems of the world would have to be resolved without him. He didn't know anymore who was right and who was wrong, but he knew that the killing of the little girl was an act of evil, one he imagined he would spend eternity paying for.

El-Sadek had made his way to Belgium and, with his fake passport, had managed to take a flight from Antwerp to London, but he didn't feel London was far enough away so he then took a flight to New York. His idea was to melt into the crowd of the city and live a simple anonymous life. The vision of the little girl never left him, however. He slept little and ate less. Finally, close to madness, he called upon the FBI, telling them he knew secrets about Alfawda. Maybe, he thought, he could somehow atone for his wickedness. He never told them about Amsterdam, certain they'd put him away for life, but instead described his former position as that of a high-ranking officer with inside information.

The FBI turned him over to the CIA. There, he caught the attention of Rampart. Eaglethorpe was always nosing into the latest activities of the CIA and he had contacts there who helped keep him informed. He and Gibson interrogated el-Sadek, determined that he was sincere, and worked toward making a double agent out of him. It had been a year since he'd left Alfawda headquarters in Yemen bound for Amsterdam, and Rampart sent him back with a long, convoluted story about his capture at the hands of the Dutch, his interrogation and torture, his imprisonment, and finally his escape. As the concocted story went, the Dutch had turned him over to the CIA because several Americans had been killed in the suicide bombings. The Dutch had resisted, but enormous political pressure had forced them to concede their prisoner. Hasan el-Sadek escaped while being transferred at JFK airport and had been living in New York in the shadows. He managed to get yet another fake identification and was sure he could go back there and remain unseen. Alfawda could have a man on the ground in New York who could gather intelligence that they could never get access to from Yemen. Maybe he could even get a job at the United Nations. The Alfawda leaders believed the story and agreed to support el-Sadek's idea. Now he was living in an apartment in the Bronx, ostensibly gathering intel for Alfawda, but in reality, working for Rampart.

Kori had flown to New York that morning to meet with him, breaking a date later that evening with Ronald and telling him something about a trade show that she'd "completely forgotten about." Ronald had laughed. "Just like you, Kori," he'd said. "It's a wonder you get anything done with your absent-mindedness."

And now, Kori saw the swarthy, muscular man approach from behind the monument of King Jagiello. Right on time. He walked casually, as if on a Sunday stroll. Kori concentrated on not looking at him. She scrolled through her cell phone, she watched the movement of a group of pigeons, she gazed at the monument. She was just a woman sitting on a park bench on a summer afternoon. Hasan took anything but a straight line to her, finally arriving a few yards from her where he sat down, careful not to make eye contact.

"No good here," he finally said in a low murmur, all the while looking straight ahead. "I'm being followed. Tonight. The Plaza Hotel. Eight o'clock. I have news." And then he rose and slowly strayed off. Kori remained seated for twenty more minutes, then rose and walked down Fifth Avenue toward her hotel on 63rd. She pulled out her cell phone to call Eaglethorpe and noticed several missed calls from Ronald.

She made a call.

"Hi, it's me," she said.

"Briggs, it's about time," answered Eaglethorpe. "We've been waiting. What was Hasan able to tell you?"

"Not much. Only that he was being followed. He seemed worried. He pushed the meeting off until tonight. I'm supposed to meet him at the Plaza Hotel at eight. He knows something, though. That much is for sure."

"Okay, well, I guess we'll just have to wait. I'm a little concerned about his being followed, though. Why would he think that? Who would be following him? Is his cover blown?"

"Don't know. I didn't see anything. I hung around the park for a while afterward. If someone was following him, they were pretty good. I didn't see anybody else walk through that park but an old woman and a young couple. Maybe it's just his imagination."

"Hasan does have a bit of a paranoid streak to him. He's been through a lot over the years. Maybe the stress is just getting to him. At any rate, call me tonight, Briggs. As soon as you know something."

"Roger that, Chief." Kori hung up and walked into the lobby of her hotel. She knew she probably ought to call Ronald but decided to stop in at the hotel restaurant first for lunch. She was starving and the restaurant had a butterfly pasta dish with rock shrimp and baby zucchini that hit the spot, along with an especially refreshing chardonnay.

Finally, she pulled out her cell phone and called Ronald.

"Hi," he said when he answered. "How's New York? Nice, I hope. That's a place we should go to together sometime, huh? How's the trade show? Making a lot of sales?"

"You bet," she said. "I think I might get a raise."

"Wow, babe, that's terrific!"

Kori winced at the word "babe," but decided to let it go. "What have you been up to, Ronald?"

"Nothing much. Just missing you. I know you're only in New York, but it just seems like you're a million miles away. Strange, huh? You know, I tried calling you a few times. Guess you've been busy."

"Yeah," she sighed. "Just one thing after another here. Setting up the booth and doing little meet and greets. You know, that kind of thing."

"Sure, sure. Oh, by the way, a couple of guys stopped by here earlier today asking about you. Guess they're going to meet you there."

Kori perked up. "Guys? What guys?"

"I don't know. They said they worked with you. Nice fellas. They seemed to think they'd find you here. I guess you've been telling people about us, huh? I must say, I'm kind of flattered. Well, I've been telling people about you, too. Say, when do I get to meet your mom?"

"Ronald, listen to me carefully," said Kori. "What did you tell these guys that stopped by?"

"I told them you were in New York for the trade show, of course."

"Anything else?"

"Well, I told them where you were staying. That was okay, wasn't it? They said they had some stuff for the show and that they needed to get it to you. Some samples or something."

"Okay, Ronald. Yes, yes, the samples. Of course. Well, listen, I better get going. I'm on a break here but I better get back to our booth. And Ronald, please don't talk to anybody else about where I am or what I'm doing."

"Why? Is something wrong?"

"Oh, no, of course not. It's just that, well, there's a lot of competition in this business, you know? We never want our competitors to know what we're really up to. Understand?"

"Okay, babe. I understand. Well, good luck with everything. Will I hear from you later? If you get another chance to call, I'll just be hanging around today, so … " But the line was quiet. Kori had hung up.

"I'm sorry, but I need to check out immediately," she was saying to the front desk clerk. Five minutes later she was in a cab heading to another hotel on Broadway and 55th. Stepping out of the cab, she called Eaglethorpe, explaining the strange visitors at Ronald's apartment.

"They weren't ours," Eaglethorpe said. "I can't imagine who they were. Think, Briggs. Why would someone be looking for you? Who could possibly know anything about your work with us?"

"Nobody," Kori answered. "Nobody outside Rampart. Cripes, Chief, even my own mother doesn't know. You know that."

"Yes, of course. Well, this is disconcerting to say the least."

"Tell me about it."

"Stay low, Briggs. Keep your appointment with Hasan tonight but stay out of sight. We'll try to do a little digging into this on our end."

"Right, Chief."

"And, Kori ... be careful, okay?"

"I will, Chief. Don't worry."

Kori hung up and smiled at the thought of Eaglethorpe's concern. A former FBI man, he'd been head of Rampart for the past fifteen years, taking over when the previous head had retired to Arizona. The chief was some thirty years older than Kori and over the course of their working together, he'd become something of a father figure. Not that she needed one. After all, she'd gotten by her whole life without a father figure. But the concern felt good, just the same.

Kori loved being a Rampart agent. The agency employed the best of the best. They had recruited her out of the Air Force Academy in Colorado Springs, but it wasn't for her academic record. In class, her scores were average. She'd had some disciplinary problems, too, mostly for disobeying orders she disagreed with or talking back to superior officers. But her military training performance was second to none. She beat out all of the cadets, male and female, in every single exercise. The dean of the faculty, a brigadier general with forty years of military experience, said she was the most impressive cadet he'd ever seen. Eaglethorpe, who had contacts at all the military academies and who was always on the lookout for future talent, took notice. The grades didn't bother him. Neither did the discipline issues. Eaglethorpe was a lifelong student of history. He knew that great leaders like Ulysses S. Grant and Dwight D. Eisenhower had had similar problems at West Point. Eaglethorpe had no interest in the straight-A kids who never got into trouble. In his mind, to be a good agent, you needed a little rebelliousness.

Kori had jumped at the chance to join Rampart, although initially she thought she was being trained for the CIA. But the training, which lasted eighteen months was far more rigorous. Only one in fifty recruits ever made it through. Those who did, like Kori, were hired to be part of the most elite intelligence agency in the world—but only after pledging, with their lives, that their true employer would remain secret. No one was ever to mention the word "Rampart." Kori moved to Washington DC, telling her mother that her hitch in the Air Force was up and that she was taking a job as East Coast VP of sales for a conveyor company. Joan was thrilled, happy for her daughter to be a civilian again and in a safe, secure job.

After the call with Eaglethorpe, Kori whiled away the afternoon in her hotel room, streaming old TV shows and taking a long hot bath. She called room service for dinner—roasted, wild-caught salmon in a tarragon shallot butter sauce. Finally, she dressed: split-sleeve, plum-colored top; dark, bootcut jeans; and black leather ankle boots. She grabbed her small, Tory Burch crossbody purse that she kept only her essentials in. Those essentials included her Glock G43 nine-millimeter Luger. Then she walked out of her room, rode the elevator down to the lobby, and exited the hotel, all the while looking warily around her. She took a cab to the Plaza Hotel, instructing the cabbie to take a circuitous route, and then waited inconspicuously in the expansive lobby in an overstuffed chair by a window. She looked at her watch: 7:55. At 8:10, she rose and began walking around the lobby, seeing no sign of Hasan. By 8:20, she was poking her head into the several restaurants and bars off the lobby, most of which were crowded with people, none of whom were Hasan.

At 8:30, she called Eaglethorpe.

"It's not like Hasan to be late," Eaglethorpe said. "That guy operates like a Swiss watch. And he hasn't contacted anybody here."

"I don't like it, Chief," said Kori. "I could wait around longer, but it's been thirty minutes already. Maybe I should check out his apartment. What do you think? It's in the Bronx, isn't it?"

"Yep. I'll text you the address. Check it out and report back. If he happens to call here in the meantime, I'll give you a call. Otherwise, get back to me when you know something."

"Roger that, Chief. I'm on my way."

Hasan's Bronx apartment was a modest studio on Pelham Parkway. Rampart had offered him a housing allowance that would have afforded him a much larger place in a nicer neighborhood, but he'd refused to take it. Nobody knew why; nobody knew of the guilt he'd harbored, the face of that little girl haunting him in his sleep. Nobody but Kori, that is. A year before, he'd confided in her. They had met in another part of Central Park where he'd given her some intel on a potential Alfawda attack in Istanbul. Rampart was able to alert local authorities and stop the attack. It was only the third time Kori had met Hasan el-Sadek. She'd never know why he confided in her and why that particular day, but he did. Maybe he just needed someone to spill his guts to. "Everything I do, I do because of that little girl," he'd told Kori, after telling her the story of the Amsterdam car bombings. "It's the only reason I go on." Kori promised him that his secret was safe with her. What good would it do to turn this man in? she thought. Who could benefit? His demonstrable guilt was punishment enough and, besides, his intel was too valuable. She hadn't told a soul. Not even Eaglethorpe.

Kori took a cab to the nondescript apartment building, a forty-minute drive into the Bronx, once again directing the driver to get there in a roundabout way. She exited the cab and walked the opposite direction from the building, ducking into the entryway of another building one block down and across the street. From the shadows, she could see the lighted front entrance of Hasan's building and she stood and watched for several minutes until she was confident no one had followed her. She thought of the visitors to Ronald's apartment and knew it would be bad enough if her cover were blown; she couldn't stand the thought of blowing Hasan's.

Finally, Kori darted across the street and entered Hasan's building, bypassing the elevator and taking the stairs up to the third floor where his apartment was. She looked up and down the hallway. Nobody was around. She tapped lightly on Hasan's apartment door and, as she did so, the door opened ever so slightly. The apartment was dark and she instinctively reached into her purse to pull out her Glock. She stepped to the side of the door and felt her pulse quicken. With her boot, she pushed the door open, remaining to the side of it. The light from the hall was enough to illuminate the entranceway and she could see a switch on the wall. She listened for a few seconds, heard nothing, then burst into the room, flicking on the light and pointing her gun ahead of her.

Inside the apartment was stillness. She moved through the living room and then, out of the corner of her eye, she saw something lying on the floor just outside of the kitchen. When she turned toward it, the something became the body of a man, a pool of blood underneath of it. She knelt down at the man's head and saw the unmistakable face of Hasan el-Sadek. She felt for a pulse and found none. His skin was cold and Kori could tell he'd probably been dead for a few hours. His throat had been cut, most likely from behind as there were no signs of a struggle. Whoever the killer was, he was good at what he did.

Still kneeling, Kori took a moment to compose herself before pulling out her phone to call Eaglethorpe with the news. Waiting for him to pick up, she leaned in toward Hasan. "I hope you can find some peace now, my friend," she whispered.

CHAPTER 4

"Well, there can be no doubt now that it's Alfawda," declared the president. In the Oval Office once again were Darren Cooper and James Foster.

"It would appear so," said Cooper. "Hasan el-Sadek knew it and paid for that knowledge with his life."

"Ironic," mused the president. "Had he lived, he no doubt would have told Briggs that Alfawda swiped the uranium. But his death tells us the same thing."

"Unless it was someone else who killed el-Sadek," said Foster. "But that seems highly unlikely. El-Sadek kept to himself. Outside of Alfawda, he had neither friends nor enemies. Clearly, they had discovered his betrayal."

"And from what Briggs reported," added Cooper, "this

was no doubt a professional hit job. Not a botched robbery attempt or anything of that sort."

"I guess it's not surprising that there are Alfawda operatives working within the borders of this country," said the president, "but it's a little disturbing. The person or persons who killed el-Sadek are still out there, gentlemen. Walking around like everyday Americans. Who knows what they're planning? And now we've lost our best source of intel on Alfawda. Worst of all, we know they have a hundred pounds of uranium somewhere. But where?"

"We believe it's in Kazakhstan by now, Mr. President," said Cooper. "That would be the logical route. Our computer simulation models confirm this."

"Greater than an eighty percent chance," said Foster.

"But it's a long ways from Kazakhstan to their base in Yemen," said the president. "So how will they get there?"

"We think they'll start out by boat," said Foster. "They can sail down the Caspian Sea and put in at Azerbaijan, Turkmenistan, or even Iran. There's a lot of coastline. Lots of options, which, of course, is unfortunate for us."

"But we think Turkmenistan most likely," said Cooper. Foster nodded. "From there they can enter Afghanistan. That's where we think they'll operate from. You see, we don't think there's a need for them to take it all the way to Yemen. Afghanistan can give them plenty of cover. And there are sympathetic elements there to help them."

"Then we have to stop them before they get to Afghanistan," said the president.

"Would that we could, sir," said Foster.

"What are you saying? We can't stop them en route?"

"Well, technically," said Cooper, "we could stop them if we could find them. The problem is finding them. Our computer models—"

"Blast your computer models!" bellowed the president. "You're telling me we have no way of finding them?! With all of our intelligence? With all of our technology? Our satellites and ... and ... all of our technology!?"

Foster took his turn. "Yes, sir, I'm afraid that's an accurate assessment. Unfortunately, Kazakhstan is, well, it's big. Damn big, sir."

"Over a million square miles," said Cooper.

"And finding a single boat in the Caspian Sea," continued Foster, "comes with its own set of problems. Meanwhile, the Turkmenistan coastline is long, running all the way down to Iran. And then there's Afghanistan and we all know about the inherent difficulties of Afghanistan's terrain. Geography just isn't on our side, sir, I'm afraid. To be blunt about it."

The president leaned back in his chair and looked up at the ceiling and was quiet for a while. Finally, he said, "You know, when you take this job you go into it with the assurance that our intelligence capabilities are so good that nothing can ever get by. You think that we've got every square inch of the globe covered. But it's a big, fat, porous world, isn't it? Holes everywhere. So many ways and so many places to hide. Whoever said it's a small world clearly hadn't looked at it from the perspective of this office, I can tell you that. A hundred pounds of uranium? Christ, you could hide it in a suitcase. So what now?"

"Well, sir," offered Cooper, "the thing we have on our side is the time we know it will take to turn the uranium into something workable as a nuclear device."

"So we hope," said the president. "Go on."

"Well, once Alfawda gets to where they're going with the uranium, they'll be there for a while. A couple of weeks, probably."

"Before, you said a *few* weeks," said the president.

"Well, we might want to consider that they may be able to move faster. Just to be on the safe side."

"There's nothing that seems safe about any of this at all, gentlemen," sighed the president.

"Yes, sir," nodded Cooper.

"Anyway, go on."

"Well, sir," continued Cooper, "we think our best chance is not in finding them en route, but in finding them when they get settled in somewhere."

"And just how will we do that?"

"Well, sir, the fact is that they're going to need help making the bomb. Technical help, even scientific help. Having uranium is one thing. It's the most important thing, for sure, but making it into a workable device isn't something you learn how to do from a YouTube video. Alfawda will need to enlist the help of nothing less than a nuclear scientist. Our guess is that they've already done so. Instead of following Alfawda, sir, we suggest following the scientist."

"There are a finite number of them," added Foster. "So we've cross-referenced the world's capable nuclear scientists with those who may have some reason to be sympathetic with the radical terrorism of Alfawda. We have a couple of matches, sir."

The president smiled. "I'll say one thing about you guys. You might bring me terrible problems, but you also seem to come with solutions. Bravo. So tell me about the matches."

"Well, one of them is French," said Cooper. "Luc Courbet. He's a researcher at the Grenoble Institute and he's been on our radar for a while. He's a top-notch nuclear physicist who married a Middle Eastern woman whom we believe has a brother that's been radicalized. So far, we haven't found anything Courbet has been doing to be suspicious, however. Our sources tell us it's been pretty much life as normal for him over the course of the last several weeks."

"Who's the other match?"

"A Russian. Ivan Yanovich. He used to be with the Ministry of Atomic Energy, headquartered in Moscow."

"Used to be?"

"He left under mysterious circumstances. We believe he was forced out. He's living alone now back in St. Petersburg where he grew up and we think he may be harboring a grudge. And, he's taken several recent trips to the Middle East, mostly to Israel. His movements there have been unclear."

"Hmm … that seems like kind of a longshot. People lose their jobs all the time and don't build nuclear bombs. And lots of Russians visit Israel. No specific ties to any terrorist groups?"

"Well, sir, not that we know of. But on one recent trip to Tel Aviv, his whereabouts were undetermined for several days."

"Undetermined?"

"We've run a complete analysis of his spending," said Foster. "Credit card charges for restaurants, hotels, rental cars, etcetera. It was a ten-day trip. For four whole days there were no charges at all and no records we could find of any activity whatsoever. Not so much as a charge for a cup of coffee. We couldn't even find that he'd made a phone call or checked his email in that time. It was as though for those four days he just fell off the grid."

"Strange. So you think maybe he took a little side trip while he was in Tel Aviv?"

"Perhaps. Here's the most interesting thing, sir," said Cooper. "For six days now, he's been completely missing. Our contacts in St. Petersburg tell us that nobody's seen him. He came back from Tel Aviv and then more or less disappeared."

"And you think he's on the way to meet the terrorists."

"Possibly, sir."

"Recommendation?"

"We could send Blake to St. Petersburg, sir," said Foster. "Have him nose around Yanovich's apartment, try to find some clue as to his whereabouts. Yanovich has a sister somewhere close by, too. He could talk to her. We think they were close. Maybe Blake can dig up a lead on where Yanovich went."

"And if we find Yanovich, we find the terrorists and the uranium."

"That's the idea, sir."

"And I assume we have no better line of investigation?"

"Not at this moment, I'm afraid sir," said Foster.

"Okay," said the president. "Then let's follow this one. But as for Blake, well, Blake's a good man when it comes to forensics and crime scenes. But when it comes to nosing around looking for clues and talking to others, I'd rather have someone with a little more … intuition. And a little more grit and gumption."

"Yes, sir," said Cooper. "We understand. We'll have her on the first plane to St. Petersburg."

CHAPTER 5

"But you promised that this weekend we'd go to the National Gallery of Art," Ronald said, frowning. "You said you wanted to see that Georgia O'Keeffe exhibit."

"I know I did," said Kori, "but can I help it if the boss orders me to Montreal?" The two were sitting on Ronald's bed. Kori had been unbuttoning Ronald's shirt but had inadvertently broken the mood with her news.

"But you just got back from New York. And why Montreal, anyway?"

"I told you. We have a huge installation there and it's not going very well. The company needs me to take control of it. It's a very important customer." Kori was only mildly concerned about the risks of being back in

Ronald's apartment. She'd taken an indirect course to get there, parked three blocks away, and entered the building through the back door. That door was typically locked, but Kori had little trouble picking the lock, quickly identifying it as a Schlage F-40 Plymouth-knob, keyed-entry model. Difficult to impossible for most. Easy for her.

She wasn't worried about Ronald, confident that if the visitors he'd had when she was in New York had wanted to hurt him or, perhaps, kidnap him to get to her, they would have done so then. Most likely, they had rightly ascertained that he was clueless about her and had moved on. But she knew they were still out there. Who were they?

And it brought up another point. Whether Ronald was in danger or not, what right had Kori to potentially expose him? Maybe she was too dangerous to be around. It wouldn't be the first time. In fact, it was a hazard of the job. All of this struck her suddenly and it made her realize what she needed to do. *Before or after?* she thought. *No, it has to be before.*

"Listen, Ronald," she said, reaching over to the nightstand and switching on the lamp.

"What's wrong?"

"We can't do this anymore."

"Do what? What do you mean?"

"Ronald, you don't really want to be with me. I work too much and I'm always traveling."

"Oh, that's okay, babe. This thing in Montreal? I'm okay with that. Disappointed a little, sure, but I know your work is important to you. We'll go the National Gallery when you come back. I'm sure the Georgia O'Keeffe exhibit will still be there. It's okay. Really it is."

"But it's not fair to you, Ronald. You deserve someone who can give you more attention. Someone ... someone who *wants* to give you more attention." She reversed course on his shirt, buttoning it back up. "You know what I mean?"

"But I ... I see." Ronald was quiet for a moment, the realization sinking in. "Okay. Well, I mean if you don't ... but ... but I thought we had something special, Kori. Didn't we?"

"We did, Ronald. Very special. Of course. You're a sweet guy. It's just not good timing, you know? One of those things that's just not meant to be."

"Well, I must say, I wasn't expecting this tonight. I thought ... well, I guess ... Well, I'll miss you, Kori." He sniffed, feeling tears welling up in his eyes. That was the *last* thing he wanted her to see. He looked away.

Kori pretended not to notice the tears and rose from the bed. "Take care, Ronald," she said, gently kissing him on the forehead and turning to leave.

"Yeah, you too," he said, forcing an awkward grin. "Maybe I'll see you around."

"Sure, you bet."

Kori closed the apartment door behind her, imagining Ronald sitting on the edge of his bed crying for the loss of a woman he had never even known. Certainly, it was for the best for him, she thought. Besides, he'd had no right to allow himself to have become so emotionally involved. Still, maybe she should have stopped things before they'd gotten this far. But that toned body. Those brown eyes. I really have to exercise more self-control, she thought to herself, stepping into her Tesla. And then Kori's mind shifted to the business in front of her.

She stopped by her apartment and packed a carry-on bag and two hours later, she was at Ronald Reagan airport, ready to board a flight to St. Petersburg, Russia. The flight was scheduled to go through Montreal and then Frankfurt before landing in St. Petersburg, a fourteen-hour extravaganza in total including layovers. That was okay with Kori. She had a first class seat and a lot of work to do. Cooper and Foster had emailed her a complete dossier on Ivan Yanovich, everything known about the man, including the names and addresses of family, friends, and anybody he'd ever interacted with. As usual, their work was impeccable. Within fourteen hours, she'd know more about the man than he knew about himself. The only information missing was where in the world Yanovich had been for the past week.

Before takeoff, Kori made a quick phone call to her mother, apologizing for not being able to come by for brunch that weekend as planned. She used the same excuse she'd used with Ronald. It was her go-to. An installation somewhere that was going poorly and needed her attention. A trip her boss ordered her to make, giving her no say in the matter. But she promised she'd call every day she was gone.

Apparently, the crisis with Mr. Schiller had abated. Joan had promised, although grudgingly, to keep a closer eye on Baxter and not let him wander. "That sounds like the right thing to do, Mom. But don't forget to consider that electric dog collar. Now, I gotta hang up. The plane is about to take off. Love you, Mom."

The Corinthia Hotel was a luxury hotel on Nevsky Prospect in the heart of St. Petersburg, a half-hour taxi ride from Pulkovo Airport. It was 10 p.m. local time when Kori checked in. Nothing could be done until the morning. Yanovich's flat was in the borough of Petrograd Side, forty minutes from the Corinthia. Breaking in at night had its risks. Kori preferred daytime. People don't expect break-ins during the day and so people don't guard against them. Plus, the chances are greater that people aren't around during the day. Yanovich's neighbors would probably be working. She could better sneak into Yanovich's place unnoticed.

The minibar in Kori's suite had a bottle of vintage chardonnay from the Fanagoria winery in the Krasnodar region of Russia. The Russians might not have been known for their wines, but Kori knew the region was on par with some of the better wine regions of France. She opened the bottle and poured herself a glass while running a hot bath. She took off her clothes and slipped into the steaming water. It felt good to stretch out and feel the warmth on her tired body. And the wine was delicious. She soaked for a good while before realizing she hadn't eaten anything since a small meal on the plane. She got out of the tub, stepped into the plush hotel robe, and called room service. Fifteen minutes later, she was enjoying a ceviche of yellowfin tuna with light soy sauce. Twenty minutes after that, warm and fed and relaxed, she dropped the robe and slid into bed.

Yanovich's flat on Bol'shaya Monetnaya Street was a modest two bedroom, part of a five-story apartment building that spanned a block. The area was populated by older, gray buildings that reminded Kori of the type of urban section you might find in an American rust belt city. The sky was overcast and there was a slight chill in the air that made Kori grateful for the Veronica Beard Scuba Hadley jacket she'd decided to bring.

She walked through the front entrance of the apartment building as though she made her home there and strode past the elevator to the stairs. She walked up two flights and found Yanovich's flat at the end of the hallway. She'd been right about the daytime. Nobody was around.

She knocked on the door to make certain the flat was unoccupied and then pulled a lock pick out of her purse and in seconds found herself in the apartment's small foyer.

She pulled her Glock, just to be safe, and moved quietly through the apartment. Nobody home.

The second bedroom had a large oak desk and some bookshelves. Yanovich's home office. Kori started rummaging through the drawers of the desk looking for … well, what *was* she looking for? She had no idea. Anything that might shed some light on the whereabouts of Ivan Yanovich, former scientist with the Russian Ministry of Atomic Energy and now presumed member of Alfawda. There had to be a clue, a hint.

She flipped through files and papers, but nothing especially illuminating presented itself. Looking around the room, she made note of the conspicuous absence of a computer or any components thereof. No laptop, no thumb drives, not even a power cord or charger. Yanovich must have taken everything with him. On top of the desk was some mail, but it was mostly just ordinary bills. The most recent was dated a week before. At least that narrowed the time frame. Yanovich had probably been on the move since that day or the day after.

In the bedroom, she noticed a lack of clothes in Yanovich's wardrobe. Rifling through his dresser she found nothing in the drawers where one might expect underwear or socks. But everything looked neat and tidy around the bedroom. Yanovich hadn't left in a hurry. He had packed, deliberately and carefully. He hadn't been kidnapped from his apartment, and he apparently hadn't left in a rush. This was a man who knew where he was going.

Kori looked around the small living room and even went through the kitchen cabinets, but Yanovich hadn't left a single hint of his current whereabouts. She walked back to his office to take a final look. There was a stack of books and old magazines in the corner of the room and as she turned to look through them, she heard the turning of the apartment's front doorknob. She reached for the Glock and kneeled behind the desk. She had a view of the living room, but the foyer was just out of her sightline.

Whoever the intruder was, he had apparently stopped in the foyer. If it had been Yanovich, he would come right in, thought Kori. For several seconds, there was no sound. Then Kori heard footsteps as the intruder began walking slowly from the foyer into the living room. Kori stepped quietly toward the door of the office, gripped the Glock a little tighter, then wheeled around the corner and out into the living room.

"Hold it right there!" she commanded, leveling her gun.

CHAPTER 6

"Kori Briggs, I presume," said the intruder, a petite but athletic-looking woman, mid-thirties, Kori guessed, with short, blond hair. Her accent was unmistakably Russian.

"Who's asking?" said Kori, keeping the Glock trained on the woman who was suddenly smiling.

"Kovalev," the woman said. "Agent Anya Kovalev."

"Kovalev? Impossible. Kovalev's a man."

"Are you sure about that, Ms. Briggs?"

"Well, I—"

The woman laughed. "Blake knows that I am a woman, but we always figured we would keep it a secret. Your fellow Rampart agents, while having never seen or talked to me, apparently have assumed that, all this time, I was a man. It has become our little joke, Blake and me. You won't spoil it for us, will you?"

Kori lowered the Glock. The woman was clearly who she said she was. Nobody else would know Blake's name and even if they did, they'd never know the name Rampart. "Well," said Kori, "I'll be damned. A woman. I thought I was the only femme badass around. No, of course I wouldn't think of spoiling the joke."

Anya reached her hand out and shook Kori's. "Pleasure to meet you, my American friend. I have appreciated your work from afar."

"And I yours." Then she shook her head and said once more, "I'll be damned." They both laughed. "Well, how did you know I'd be here?"

"Blake said you were flying in. He is still back in Moscow, but he thought maybe I could provide some help. I thought of going to your hotel, but I was not sure where you would be staying."

"The Corinthia."

"You have good taste."

"Thanks. I like to be comfortable when I travel."

"I understand. Well, anyway, I knew you would be coming here, so I decided this would be as good a spot to meet you as anywhere. What's that you have there? A Glock?"

"Yes," Kori replied, realizing suddenly that she was still holding it. She slipped it back into her purse. "You?"

"I use a Sig Sauer."

"Nice. Not as rugged though, is it?"

"Perhaps not, but smaller to carry. Plus I have the fifteen-round extended magazine."

"Sweet," said Kori. She looked around the room. "So, you've gone through this place?"

"Oh, yes. Several times. There is a small bottle of vodka in the kitchen. Will you join me?"

"Yes, I saw that. The only thing of interest in the whole place, so far as I could tell."

They walked into the kitchen and Anya reached into a cupboard, pulling out the bottle and two shot glasses. She filled both glasses and handed one to Kori.

"To your health," she smiled.

"Cheers," said Kori. They clinked each other's glass and downed their shots. "That's the ticket," said Kori.

They moved into the living room and sat down.

"The fact is," said Anya, "there are no clues here. Yanovich left nothing of himself behind."

"Yes, he seemed pretty thorough in his packing. So what do you know about him?"

"Probably not much more than you. I assume you were briefed. Ivan Yanovich: born in St. Petersburg in 1967. Highly intelligent. Served in the Red Army for two years and quickly made officer. Then was sent to study at Moscow Engineering Physics Institute. Major area was nuclear weaponry. Finished first in his class. Went to work with the Ministry of Nuclear Engineering and Industry, which, since the fall of the Soviet Union, is now known as the Ministry of Atomic Energy. He was in line for a promotion last year. In fact, his name was bandied about as the next head of the Ministry. But the position was given to the Russian president's nephew. Qualified, but not nearly as smart as Yanovich. A pure case of nepotism. Publicly, Yanovich was gracious. Privately, he was infuriated."

"Well, lots of people get passed up for promotions. How does that translate into him taking off and joining Alfawda?"

"Yanovich has a history of instability."

"Instability?"

"Mental instability. Anger and depression. He is most likely a manic depressive. Apparently, his problems began to manifest in his childhood. He was basically an orphan. His father was killed in a construction accident not far from here when Ivan was three years old. His mother could barely care for her children after that. Apparently she had a history of depression, too. When Ivan was six, she committed suicide. He was more or less raised by the state after that. There were a series of foster parents and, fortunately, he and his sister were kept together over the years. She seems to be the only person, besides his wife, that he ever really bonded with on an emotional level. Anyway, throughout his childhood, there was a series of incidents. He was always getting into trouble, mostly for fighting. Even in the Red Army he was disciplined several times for fighting with fellow soldiers."

"Interesting," said Kori. "But he's had such an illustrious career."

"Ivan Yanovich is a true genius. In school, his coursework came easy to him. Always at the top of his class and so on. Often smarter than his instructors. But apparently he is not well-liked by his colleagues. As a professional, he has learned to control his temper somewhat, but he can be arrogant and gruff and demanding. Nevertheless, everyone has put up with him because of his intellect."

"So you think he just went off the deep end when the president's nephew got the head of the Ministry position?"

"Yes, but you see, something else happened right after that, too."

"What?"

"Yanovich's wife left him."

"Aha. That was not in my briefing notes."

"It wasn't very long ago, although the separation had, apparently, been a long time coming. She was no longer in love with him. She was, in fact, cheating on him with a colleague."

"Ouch."

"Indeed. Evidently, he found out about the affair just days after his professional setback."

"Bad timing, for sure. And so he went bonkers."

"I'm sorry?"

"He went a little insane."

"Yes, it would seem so. He quit the Ministry, left his flat in Moscow, and came back here."

"What do you know about those trips to the Middle East?"

"I do not know what to make of those. His wife, or ex-wife, has family in Tel Aviv. They traveled there often, in fact."

"Did you know that on his last trip he fell off the radar for several days?"

"Yes, Blake told me as much."

Kori smiled. "I like that our agency and your agency communicate the way we do. Let's have another shot of that vodka." She retrieved the bottle and poured. "Tell me something, Anya. Our people back in the States are under the impression you're an old, male, ex-KGB officer. Who are you really?"

Now it was Anya's turn to smile. "My father was KGB. I followed in his footsteps, but by the time I was old enough to enter the service, the KGB was no more. At least not officially."

"Not officially?"

"Oh, it is still out there. Make no mistake. Pieces anyway. Mostly it is used by the president and by the oligarchy that controls him. This puts it at odds with the Russian Foreign Intelligence Service. Most of the time. Sometimes, the desired ends are the same and they work together. There is ample opportunity for conflict of interest. And plenty of corruption to go around. Hence, my role. I work as you do. Under the radar, independent, unknown to even the intelligence agencies. Cheers." And then she downed her shot.

"Cheers," said Kori, downing hers. "But we work for our executive branch. The president. Who do you work for?"

"Do you not know? Surely you can guess."

"Well, no, I … unless … don't tell me you're with us."

"Of course," Anya laughed. "I am Rampart, like you."

"Cripes, how come nobody ever told me?"

"Because nobody knows. Just Blake. And now you. Not even your president knows. It was my idea to remain so hidden. If something were to ever befall me, my work could not be traced to the US. Your president has … how do you say it? … plausible deniability."

"Brilliant," said Kori. "I like you, Anya."

"I like you, too, Ms. Briggs."

"Kori."

"Kori. Thank you. So, anyway, somehow your CIA confused me with my father, built up a file on me assuming I am an old, male, ex-KGB officer, and the ruse was on."

"That's the CIA for you."

"Blake knew the truth about me and recruited me for Rampart. I get paid out of his expense account, which is not insignificant."

"Brilliant," Kori repeated. "You know, I always wondered how Blake got so much work done. It was always as if he were in two places at once."

"Now you know," Anya laughed. Then she turned serious. "But now back to Yanovich."

"Yes, indeed. Back to Yanovich. Have you talked to his sister yet?"

"Not as yet. I was waiting for you. I thought we could go talk to her together. She's not far from here. A twenty minute walk."

"That sounds just fine to me, Anya. I'll bring the bottle. For later."

CHAPTER 7

Along the way, Kori decided to check in with Eaglethorpe, letting him know she'd been through Yanovich's apartment, had met up with Kovalev, and now the two of them were on their way to interview Yanovich's sister.

"How is Kovalev?" Eaglethorpe said.

"Oh, he's fine," said Kori, stifling a laugh and glancing over at Anya. "You know. Typical ex-KGB. All business. Kind of gruff ... Physically? Um ... short, stocky, balding. Not much to look at. Seems half-intelligent, though."

They talked a little more, with Eaglethorpe telling Kori to be careful and then they hung up.

"Even though it's genuinely funny, I feel a little bad not being completely honest with my boss," Kori admitted to

Anya. "I mean, we're secretive enough. Do we really need secrets within secrets?"

"We all carry secrets within secrets," said Anya. "And we all have our reasons for keeping them. Secrets can be beneficial."

"Yes, I suppose so. But it seems like only a matter of time before he'll find out."

"Yes, Blake and I have discussed this many times. When the time is right, I suppose we will let him know."

The two continued to walk, both preferring the exercise to a sedentary cab ride. The route took them over the Trinity Bridge across the Neva River. The wind off the river was bracing, but both women found it invigorating. Kori enjoyed gazing around, seeing the steeple of the Saint Peter and Paul Cathedral behind them and the neoclassical Marble Palace in front of them. Russian history survives in its architecture, she thought.

Finally, they arrived at the apartment of Olga Ruslanova, older sister of Ivan Yanovich. Olga was close to sixty, a stern-looking woman with an outdated, gray, bouffant hairdo. Anya explained they were looking for her brother. Olga didn't ask why. She seemed glad to know that *somebody* was still looking for him. She'd reported him missing to the local police five days ago, she explained in Russian. The police had done nothing.

She ushered Kori and Anya inside and waved them toward the sofa. "Please, sit," she said. "I have just made a honey cake. My husband loves it, but he is not here just now. Please have some." Neither could resist. The cake was a Russian specialty. Thin layers of honeyed pastry separated by layers of custard. She brought out coffee, too.

Olga explained that one evening, Ivan was supposed to meet her and her husband for dinner, but he never showed up. This was not at all like him. When he didn't answer his phone, she went to his flat and saw that his suitcase and clothes were gone. The two siblings were close. Olga could not imagine that Ivan would leave town without telling her. The police had been no help. It seemed to them that Ivan had clearly left of his own accord. There were no signs of foul play, after all, and there was simply nothing they could do.

Anya thought of translating for Kori, but Olga was so forthcoming with information that she didn't want to interrupt the flow of the conversation. Would Olga turn quiet with an American present?

"Can you think of where your brother might have gone?" said Anya, pressing forward.

Olga shook her head. "*Nyet*. I have no idea."

Then Kori spoke up. "Was he acting in any way strange in the days before he left?" she said in perfect Russian. Anya could not suppress an admiring smile.

"Well, of course, he was depressed. And angry. That wife of his. That cyka," she spat out. "Cheating on him! I am angry, too. My brother deserves much better. And the way he was treated by the Ministry! Disgraceful."

"Did he talk about going anywhere?" asked Anya.

"*Nyet*. He would have told me, I am sure. He is a good brother."

"What about people around him? Did he mention any new friends or associates?" said Kori.

"No."

"Nobody at all?"

"Well, there was one visitor."

"A visitor?"

"Yes. You see, I went to see Ivan one evening. I knew he had been depressed. I thought it would do him good for his sister to come by. I was worried about him and I wanted to boost his spirits. I brought him stroganoff. His favorite. I was afraid he had not been eating well and he has never been able to turn down my stroganoff. It's all in the seasoning, you know."

"Of course."

"Anyway, someone was in his flat with him that evening."

"Do you know who?"

"I am afraid not. He was a stranger to me. But Ivan introduced him to me as a friend he had met on a recent trip to Tel Aviv."

"I see. And did he give you a name?"

"Hmm … maybe. I cannot remember. I'm afraid I'm not very good with names."

"Can you tell us anything at all about him?" asked Anya.

"Well, he was an American, he—"

"American?" Kori interrupted. "How do you know?"

"He said so. And he spoke only English."

"What else did he say?"

"Not much. Neither said much. Ivan took the stroganoff, thanked me, and wished me a good evening. Kind of pushed me toward the door, truth be told. I had the impression I had perhaps interrupted a conversation they were having. But, of course, that's Ivan. Sometimes he can be a bit brusque. And so I left and that was that. But truthfully, I was happy Ivan had some company. It was not good for him to be alone."

"Can you describe this American he was with?" said Kori.

"Well, he was tall. Thin. Maybe in his forties, but with very white hair. Oddly so. He was clean shaven. That's about it. Oh, and he had a rather crooked nose, as though it had at one time been broken."

Kori's mind raced. *It can't be*, she thought. She pulled her phone out and began rapidly scrolling through her photos. "Here," she said, stopping at one. "Take a look at this picture. Is this the man your brother was talking to?"

"Yes! That's him. I would recognize him anywhere. Do you know him?"

"Ms. Ruslanova," said Kori, turning very serious, "you must tell no one that your brother was with this man. He is exceedingly dangerous. Assuming your brother went off with this man of his own accord, and I suspect that he did, he is not in any immediate danger. However, if word leaks out that this man has been identified, the situation can become very volatile. Your life could be in danger, too. Mention this man to no one. In the meantime, we will find your brother."

"I ... I don't understand. Who is this man?"

"It's best if you know nothing more about him."

"But where do you think Ivan is, Ms. ... Ms. ... I'm sorry, I did not catch your name or who you are with."

"We work for ... an international intelligence agency. I'm afraid that's all I can tell you just now, Ms. Ruslanova. Please trust us."

"But you must be able to tell me something, no?"

"I'm sorry. We'll be in touch."

Olga Ruslanova's head was spinning as Kori and Anya excused themselves, thanking their host for the cake and coffee and making for the door. Kori turned around once more. "Remember, Ms. Ruslanova, you mustn't tell anyone you met this man. Good day."

Outside, under the gray skies, Anya said, "So? Who is he? Your face turned white when she identified him from your photo."

"Efron Carlisle," replied Kori.

Now Anya's face lost color. "*What?* Efron Carlisle? I thought he was dead."

"So did we. His private plane crashed in the Rockies last year. It was just him and his pilot. Two bodies, mostly burned beyond recognition, but enough of a hand left to confirm the fingerprints. We'd been looking for him for two years, ever since his escape. It was disturbing knowing such a man was out there. We slept easier knowing he'd been killed. But ... but apparently he hadn't been. He's been out there all along, Anya. He's alive. Very much alive."

Kori thought back to the capture of Carlisle ten years before. The plans of Efron Carlisle and his small army had been foiled just days before they would have been implemented. "One Hundred Bombs in One Hundred Cities," was Carlisle's name for his ambitious scheme. Over the course of a decade, he'd recruited three hundred of the country's most dangerous sociopaths to join his crusade for anarchy. These were society's outcasts, but all of them smart. Carlisle found them by combing through police and court and prison records. These were not everyday criminals. These were twisted, deranged minds—sadists looking for an outlet, timebombs waiting to go off. Once recruited, he paid them handsomely out of the inheritance he'd received from his father's estate. Grover Carlisle, the "Emperor of Silicon Valley," he'd been called, had made billions in digital technology.

Grover's son, Efron, trained his recruits in explosives and sent them in groups of threes to a hundred cities and towns across the United States. At a given time on one particular day, each group was to blow up a courthouse or legislative building or some other government structure. Carlisle was counting on the resulting chaos to lead to martial law, which he predicted would, in turn, lead to a complete collapse of societal norms and ultimately, fighting in the streets.

Eventually, the government would collapse from within. Cruelly, Carlisle had no interest at all in what would come next. He was not some evil scientist bent on world domination. He just wanted to see the collapse for its own sake, like a kid wielding a magnifying glass over a hill of ants. For him, it was entertainment.

But somebody talked. One person out of three hundred. One person slightly less sociopathic than the rest. Otherwise, the plan would have succeeded. Everyone was arrested, tried, and jailed. Carlisle was sentenced to death and was being held in the Federal Correctional Institute in Terre Haute, Indiana. But he escaped in the middle of the night. Three guards were missing, too, and it was believed he'd paid them off with, perhaps, hundreds of thousands of dollars each. His assets had been liquidated, but the fortune his father left him was extensive, reaching into the nooks and crannies of hundreds of financial accounts owned by dozens of shell companies, some of which were linked to private offshore concerns. Carlisle still had access to millions and bribing a few guards would have been easy. Two months after the escape, the bodies of all three guards were discovered in an abandoned warehouse, each done in by a bullet to the head. So much for gratitude.

The escape had been kept from the public to avoid a panic. A massive search secretly spearheaded by Rampart got underway. Then, a downed plane had been found by some hikers in Rocky Mountain National Park. The serial number of the Gulfstream 500 matched one that had at one time been owned by Carlisle. And the fingerprints of one of the two occupants confirmed it was him. Now, Kori knew it was not.

"The monster's out there somewhere," she said to Anya. "The bastard faked his own death. And now he's literally going nuclear."

"Then this isn't Alfawda at all," said Anya.

"Nope. We've been wasting time going down the wrong road. The road Carlisle sent us on. Think about it, Anya. This makes more sense than his One Hundred plan. A nuclear device is much more efficient. And more frightening."

"He can involve a lot less people, too," Anya said. "It's a lot less risky for him. Fewer people to give his plan away. But where will he use the bomb?"

"Who knows? Where's Carlisle, Anya? That's the question. He could be anywhere. We're back to square one. We've been thinking like Alfawda, trying to anticipate where they would go, calculating a possible base of operations in Afghanistan. But that's what Carlisle wants us to think. He'll be anywhere but Afghanistan."

"And *anywhere* is a pretty big place to look," said Anya, frowning.

The two walked in silence for several minutes.

"Oh, my …" said Kori at last.

"What is it?"

"I just thought about Hasan."

"Who?"

"A friend. A double agent. I was supposed to have met with him but he was murdered in his apartment in New York. He was going to pass along some intel to me. Now I know what that intel was: the thieves of Bayanovka were not from Alfawda. I'd assumed Alfawda had killed Hasan. But now we can safely say it was Carlisle all along." Kori thought back to the scene she had come across in Hasan's apartment and involuntarily shuddered. Was Efron Carlisle in that apartment only hours before she'd made the discovery of Hasan's body?

"So you're saying Carlisle is in New York?"

"Well …" Then Kori was quiet, thinking things through in her mind. No, it didn't make sense that Carlisle could get to New York so quickly from Bayanovka. At least not with a hundred pounds of uranium. "I don't think so, Anya," she said at last. "I'll bet he had Hasan killed by someone. It's not like he doesn't still know people. Cripes, I'll bet the sicko met some real winners in prison. Fellow psychos who have friends on the outside. It would have been easy for him to contact someone and have Hasan professionally done away with. Wherever the uranium is, that's where Carlisle is going to be. He's not going to allow himself to be separated from it. He's probably left Russia by now, but my guess is that he's still somewhere in Europe."

"So we're still back to the same problem of where he could be."

"Yep."

"Well, my American friend, we know one thing for sure."

"What's that?"

"You still have that bottle of vodka."

"Indeed," Kori said, forcing a smile and pulling the bottle out of her purse.

CHAPTER 8

The president looked ill. It was Eaglethorpe who broke the news. As chief of Rampart, the responsibility fell to him. In the Oval Office with Eaglethorpe were Cooper and Foster. Kori was there, too. She'd flown back shortly after leaving Olga Ruslanova's flat on an overnight flight. Anya had seen her off at the St. Petersburg airport. The pair had warmly embraced and promised each other to stay in touch. It had been another fourteen-hour odyssey to return to DC. Kori could never sleep well on a plane and planned on going directly home to bed. Instead, Eaglethorpe was waiting for her at the airport when she arrived the next morning to whisk her off to the White House. She was wearing the same clothes and desperately wished she at least would have had time to take a shower.

"How could such a mistake be made?" said the president. The tone was equal parts incredulity and accusation.

"The fingerprints, sir," said Eaglethorpe.

"And the serial number of the plane," added Cooper helpfully.

The president grunted and stared down at his desk.

"We know that a person can obviously recreate his fingerprints in a material like putty," said Eaglethorpe, "but this—the ability to recreate fingerprints on an actual finger—well, this is something completely new, Mr. President. Frankly, as far as we know, it's a first."

"We should never have stopped looking for him," said the president. "We should have assumed the body in the plane was planted and we should have kept searching. This is Efron Carlisle we're talking about!"

"Well, yes, sir. I suppose in retrospect … " said Eaglethorpe, his voice trailing off.

"And now that evil son of a bitch is out there!" said the president, banging his fist on the desk. Eaglethorpe winced. "Armed with uranium! *Uranium!*"

"Yes, sir," said Eaglethorpe. Kori felt awful for Eaglethorpe. She knew that based on the circumstances, it would have been an unreasonable use of resources to have continued searching for Carlisle. Unreasonable? It would have been crazy. It would have made no more sense than searching for Lee Harvey Oswald after he'd been gunned down in Dallas by Jack Ruby. This is what she wanted to say to the president. But she knew the smart thing was to stay quiet, let the president vent, and then move forward.

"And now he's enlisted the services of one of the world's foremost nuclear experts," the president continued. "Good God!" Nobody said a word for several seconds that seemed to Kori like hours, until the president finally repeated, "How could such a mistake be made?"

Everyone in the room knew the question was rhetorical and the silence continued. Finally, the president seemed to gather himself and said, "So what do we do now? Surely you people have a plan."

"Well, sir," said Eaglethorpe. "As a matter of fact, we've been tracing the last known movements of Ivan Yanovich. There was that trip to Tel Aviv prior to Carlisle's visit in St. Petersburg, as you'll recall."

"What of it?"

"Well, we believe he must have met with Carlisle then. That may, in fact, have been their first meeting. We think Yanovich went there on an innocent vacation. He had traveled there often, after all."

"Yes, but only with his wife," interrupted Kori. "Or I should say ex-wife. To visit her family."

"True," said Eaglethorpe, "but it's not unreasonable to imagine that in all of their trips there, he made some friends of his own. Or maybe he just liked the city. It's in the Mediterranean, after all, and beautiful; a prime vacation spot. After being passed over for head of the Ministry of Atomic Energy, Yanovich probably just needed a getaway."

71

Kori looked skeptical.

"Anyway," continued Eaglethorpe, looking back toward the president, "we think that Carlisle sent someone to cross paths with him and, perhaps, invite him to meet with Carlisle, who subsequently recruited him."

The president glanced over at Kori. "Briggs, you're not buying this. Why not?"

Kori suddenly felt uneasy and shifted in her chair. It was not proper protocol to disagree with her immediate superior, especially in front of *his* immediate superior. She shouldn't have interrupted and she knew if she hadn't been so tired, she probably wouldn't have. She looked over at Eaglethorpe, but his expression was inscrutable. If he was mad at her, he wasn't showing it. Then again, Kori knew that there would be plenty of time later to display his anger at her for having the audacity to question him in—of all places—the Oval Office. At that moment, she wished she were back in her condo soaking in a hot tub.

"Well?" said the president.

"Well, sir, it just seems … well, it seems strange that of all the places to take a vacation, Yanovich would go to a spot he was only familiar with because of his wife. There had to have been a difficult emotional connection. I mean, she had just left him. From what we've gathered, he was probably as upset about that as he was about not getting his promotion. A real getaway would have been to somewhere completely different, with no reminders of his job or his wife. Someplace absent the emotional baggage that Tel Aviv surely represented for him."

"So you're saying he went there with more than a vacation on his mind?"

"It's possible, sir."

"Yes, that makes more sense. Eaglethorpe?"

"Well, yes, sir," said Eaglethorpe. "Of course, we're keeping all possibilities open. Agent Briggs's point is a valid one, I'm sure." He gave a quick sideways glance over at Kori who averted her eyes and decided that even soaking in a cold tub would be better than this.

Foster piped in. "Well, either way, Mr. President, we have reason to believe that Carlisle has a center of operations in Israel somewhere. For all we know, he's been there for months."

"And *that's* where we think the uranium is headed," declared Eaglethorpe, hoping his conclusion would help salvage whatever credibility might have been chipped away.

"Then again," said the president, "you thought that Carlisle was dead."

So much for that *hope*, thought Eaglethorpe.

"Look," said the president, "enough of this guesswork. Go back to your offices and find a way to fix this problem. I don't even want to see you guys until you have some solid answers. Not theory, not speculation. I want to see a bona-fide plan for how we're going to thwart that son of a bitch wacko Carlisle. *Go!*"

Outside the Oval Office, Eaglethorpe glared at Kori.

"Cripes, Chief, I'm sorry. I should have kept my reservations to myself. I felt so bad for you, taking the heat for Carlisle from the president. And then I made it worse. Can you forgive me?"

Eaglethorpe softened. "It's okay, Briggs. Truthfully, I think you might have made a decent point. It would be a strange place for a vacation. But we just need to present a unified front to POTUS. We need to look like we're all on the same page. We can disagree, but not in there."

"I know, I know. It was stupid. I owe you one."

"No worries, Briggs."

"The bigger point," said Cooper, "is this: why *did* Yanovich go to Tel Aviv?"

"Well," said Foster, "if Kori is right about it not being a vacation, then he went there with the express purpose of meeting Carlisle. And if that's the case, it means Carlisle must have recruited him earlier."

"So he goes to Tel Aviv to meet with Carlisle," said Kori, "then a week or so later, Carlisle comes to St. Petersburg, and then they both go off together."

"To Bayanovka, we can assume," said Eaglethorpe. "To break into the storage facility there."

"Of course," said Kori. "Yanovich's work with the Ministry of Atomic Energy would have made him familiar with it. In a sense, it was an inside job after all."

"But none of this explains the Tel Aviv connection," said Foster. "Carlisle could have met with Yanovich anywhere. If he was recruited prior to that trip, why did Carlisle meet him in Tel Aviv?"

"Yanovich must have felt comfortable there," said Cooper. "Let's face it. Hooking up with a nutjob bent on destruction can be a little unnerving. He must have felt safe there."

"Because he knew people," said Foster.

"Yes, but only his ex-wife's relatives," Kori reminded them.

"Then maybe there's our answer," said Eaglethorpe. "His ex-wife's relatives. What do we know about them?"

"Not enough, apparently," said Cooper.

"Then that's our next rock to turn over. Come on. Let's get back to HQ. Not you, Briggs. Go get some sleep. I'm sure you're exhausted. Let us do some homework on Yanovich's in-laws. We'll see you first thing in the morning."

"Right, Chief."

"Oh, and you said you owe me one."

"Yes, Chief?"

"When you come in tomorrow, bring the donuts."

"Right, Chief."

Kori finally took that shower she'd wanted, bypassing the hot bath idea for fear of falling asleep in the tub. Then she crashed in her bed and slept for eight straight hours, waking up in time for dinner. She called the Chinese restaurant on the corner, and within fifteen minutes she was enjoying fried rice, shrimp with lobster sauce, and a bowl of egg drop soup. She poured herself a Scotch and settled into her sofa, a snug and cozy design with a hand-carved, solid wood frame. Kori knew that she didn't spend enough time in her condo to warrant the expensive furniture she'd acquired, but she couldn't resist luxury when she saw it. Maybe it was true that she wasn't home that much, but when she was home, she wanted to escape into a world of rich comfort.

She called her mother to let her know she'd made it safely home "from Montreal."

"Wonderful, dear. And how was it?"

"Good. I think I managed to square away most of the problems."

"Did you get to see the city?"

"Not too much, I'm afraid."

"Aw, that's too bad. It's supposed to be beautiful. Well, I certainly hope that company appreciates all that you do for them."

"I think they do."

Before hanging up, the two agreed to meet for dinner the next day. Then Kori flicked on the television and flipped through the channels stopping every now and again on various news stations. There was talk about the president's recent poll numbers. There had been a gang shooting in Chicago. A report from the Philippines talked of a small earthquake. A storm in the Gulf of Mexico was drenching parts of Florida. The world was operating as if it was business as usual. If only they all knew of the danger, Kori thought. A madman with a hundred pounds of uranium, enough to irradiate Washington DC or any major city in the world. Eventually, she settled on an old movie, *Roman Holiday* with Audrey Hepburn and Gregory Peck, a film she'd seen a million times before. It was comforting. It was safe.

Kori knew her internal clock was off and that she wouldn't be able to fall asleep for a while. Might as well just make it a late one, she thought. She made some popcorn and watched two other old movies before finally falling asleep on the sofa around 2 a.m. At 6, she awoke, dressed, and headed to HQ, stopping along the way for a dozen donuts—maple, Boston cream, chocolate-frosted, cinnamon, jelly-filled, and more. A promise is a promise.

She didn't notice the tan vehicle in the parking lot. Nor did she notice it pulling out behind her. It followed her, staying several car lengths behind her at all times. When she turned into the parking garage of her office building, the tan vehicle slowed down for several seconds and then sped off down the street.

"Jael Roth," said Cooper, pointing to the large screen in the front of the room. "Yanovich's brother-in-law." In the conference room of Rampart was Cooper, Foster, Eaglethorpe, Gibson, Vasquez, and Kori—the entirety of Rampart's US-based contingent, save for two agents that worked on the West Coast. On the screen was the photograph of a young man with a narrow face and dark, unruly hair. "This is the youngest brother of Yanovich's wife. He's twenty-five and something of the family black sheep. Here's the interesting thing: he's missing. The family has alerted the Tel Aviv police, but they're not taking it seriously. Jael Roth has been known to disappear for days on end. It's believed he has a drug problem."

"Here's another interesting thing," added Foster, "politically, he's something of an anarchist. He's written essays for certain online groups. And are you ready for this? One of those essays extolled the virtues of Efron Carlisle's 'One Hundred Bombs Plan.'"

"Then that's the Tel Aviv connection," said Kori. "Carlisle recruited Roth. Not a hard thing to do; he was a member of his fan club. Then, through Roth, Carlisle got to Yanovich."

"Okay, let's review," said Eaglethorpe, putting down his half-eaten, chocolate-frosted donut. "Efron Carlisle, a psychopath bent on creating worldwide anarchy, escapes from prison and subsequently fakes his own death. To better pursue his agenda, he decides he'd like to have access to a nuclear bomb. But nuclear bombs are hard to come by, so he decides he'll build one instead. For that, he needs uranium. Looking around at the world's available supply, he figures

Bayanovka is an easy target. He also knows he'd be the last person in the world anybody would suspect of the crime because, well, the world thinks he's dead. He knows the finger would be pointed at a terrorist group like Alfawda. But to pull off the heist, he needs an inside man. Somehow, he gets wind of the prototypical disgruntled employee. Ivan Yanovich, with the Russian Ministry of Atomic Energy, has just been passed over for a promotion he surely deserved. Carlisle does a little homework and discovers that Yanovich has an in-law in Tel Aviv who is an avowed anarchist. *And* a fan of his. What a find. He knows if he can get to Yanovich, he'll not only have an inside man for the burglary, he'll have someone who can build the bomb for him. Probably he went to work on Roth first, promising him who knows what if he could bring Yanovich to the party."

"And bring him to the party he did," said Kori. "We just have to figure out where that party is being held. Would they have returned to Israel?"

"Who knows?" said Eaglethorpe. "But that's probably the best place to start looking. The Israeli police haven't taken an interest in Roth and so maybe his family would welcome our involvement in his search. Let's talk to them. What do you say, Briggs? It's been more than twenty-four hours since you've been on a trip. You probably feel like a slacker. Not to worry. We'll get you on the next plane to Tel Aviv."

"Thanks, Chief," said Kori, with a wry smile. "I've been getting bored. But, say, do you mind if we involve another agent?"

"Who?"

"It would be great if Kovalev could meet me there."

"That old Russian spy? Think he could help?"

"He was surprisingly effective in St. Petersburg."

"Okay. I'll contact Blake and have him contact Kovalev. Hopefully, the Russians will let us borrow him. It's their uranium, after all. I would think they'd welcome the opportunity. And if you think Kovalev is a good man, that's good enough for me."

"Better than a good man," smiled Kori, reaching for the last jelly-filled donut.

CHAPTER 9

"Well, at least we know where her office is." Ralph Moore, with a ruddy complexion and droopy eyes, was stirring his coffee and sitting across from Earl Watson in a booth in Denny's.

"Yeah," sighed Watson. "Now all we need to figure out is who *she* is." Watson, balding and with a receding chin looked a lot older than his thirty-eight years. Moore had him in seniority, both in age—Moore was forty-three— and in years of service. Moore had been with the CIA for twenty years; Watson for ten.

"Well, she's obviously somebody," said Moore. "She seems to have a standing invitation to the Oval Office. She's there all the time."

"Same with those other guys," said Watson. "What were they all doing in the president's office yesterday morning?" As direct reports to the director, Moore and Watson had access to the West Wing. It wasn't necessarily their business to note who came and went from the Oval Office, but it was their nature.

"Cooper and Foster. They're the common denominator. Everyone assumes they're secret service. But they're always bringing the same people in to see the president. Like the girl. And they're all very mysterious. They never talk to anyone else, and nobody really knows anything about them. I've never been more sure that there's some other agency at work in the White House."

"But that's only ever been a rumor," said Watson. "Like Bigfoot. Or the Loch Ness Monster. Or my wife's cooking skills." They both snickered.

"Rumors are always based at least partly on fact," said Moore, suddenly serious. "Hell, most of our investigations start out as rumors."

"Yes, but the difference is that we haven't been given permission to start investigating these people."

"Yes, yes, I know. 'A waste of resources,' said the director. But I don't care. There's something going on and I think we need to know what it is. That's our job."

"But investigate private citizens without cause?"

They both snickered again.

"So what are you going to order?" Moore asked, idly flipping through the plastic menu.

"Dunno," Watson replied. "I'm not even hungry."

"Guess I'll get an omelet. Ham and cheese sounds good."

"Yeah, whatever. Maybe I'll get the same. So what do you make of her office?"

"The conveyor company? Conveyor, my ass. Why all the security for a conveyor company? Why the hidden entrance and the private elevator? And why is a mid-level rep for a conveyor company hanging out in the Oval Office? Is the president buying conveyor? I'm telling you, we need to get into their office."

"But without a warrant … " Watson looked dubious.

"I know. Well, we'll just have to figure a way. I'm sure we can come up with something. That office is where the answers are. Nobody else seems to know anything about her. Her boyfriend certainly seemed to swallow the conveyor thing."

"Yeah, but he didn't seem especially bright. Apparently, she had him snowed pretty good, telling him she was in New York City that time for some kind of trade show. What a wasted trip that was. Not that I mind a trip to the Big Apple. But we spent all afternoon and evening in that damn hotel lobby and she never showed. You sure we shouldn't talk to her mother?"

"We probably tipped our hand enough talking to the boyfriend. If her mother tells her that a couple of guys came by and were asking about her, it might scare her off. Besides, most likely, the mother doesn't know anything anyway. No, what we need is access to that conveyor office. We've got to get in there and plant a bug or two. You know what I mean? Good old-fashioned surveillance. Let's do a little eavesdropping."

"But all the security … "

"So what? We're CIA, dammit. If we can't figure a way around the security, what good are we?"

"Right. Okay. We'll work something out," Watson sighed. "We'll get in, plant a few bugs and get this whole damn thing figured out. Now, where the hell is that waitress?"

"I know, Mom, I'm sorry. It just came up. It's a very important meeting. A major company is opening up a humongous distribution center in Tampa and we have the opportunity to sell them all their conveyor. My boss wants me to make the presentation to their board. If we close the deal, it'll mean a big bonus for me." It sounded plausible and Kori's mom seemed to buy it, even though she was disappointed that dinner was put off again. "I'll make it up to you, I promise. Okay, Mom? We'll go anywhere you like. Martin's Tavern? You bet. Listen, I have to hang up now. We're about to take off … I love you, too."

Kori settled into her seat for the eleven-hour nonstop flight from Dulles to Ben Gurion airport. Once the plane was airborne, she opened up her tablet and began reading the lengthy file on Efron Carlisle. She knew all about the One Hundred Bombs plan but she knew very little about Carlisle's background. Did it matter? The guy was a nutjob. Still, she knew she needed to familiarize herself with the notes the FBI had made about him. They had done an exhaustive investigation, which Rampart was able to access. The president had requested the notes and had then, unbeknownst to the FBI, turned them over to Eaglethorpe who made sure they were loaded onto Kori's tablet.

Efron Carlisle was the only child of Grover, the "Emperor of Silicon Valley." Grover Carlisle was single-minded and ambitious, but was generally regarded as honest. His background was clean, as was his wife's, and there was nothing about either one that could explain the fact that they raised a monster. An FBI psychiatrist postulated that maybe Efron had harbored feelings of resentment from a lack of paternal attention, but so what? Lots of kids get ignored by their fathers and don't end up wanting to destroy the world. Kori knew this firsthand.

By all accounts, the family had started out lower-middle class. Grover worked in the tech industry making a decent living, but nothing extraordinary. Still, he was smart. And as a programmer, he often worked on his own time, intent on inventing some kind of software application that would make him rich, which he ultimately did. Grover's proprietary app became a part of pretty much every personal computer, tablet, and smartphone on the planet. Once he got his patent, he started the company that would continue expanding on his digital technology, growing it into one of the top tech companies in the world.

By then, Efron was grown and out of the house, living a relatively unremarkable life. By all accounts, he was completely estranged from his parents, though the reason remained a mystery. He'd frequently been in trouble in school, suspended several times, and finally expelled. Whether his parents had thrown him out of the house or he had left of his own accord nobody really seemed to know. After that, he repeatedly got in trouble with the law, but mostly minor infractions like petty theft and a few breaking and entering charges. He resisted arrest one time, which was what led to the broken nose. He'd refused medical help and the nose never did heal properly. Somewhere along the line, his hair turned ghostly white, which, besides the crooked nose, became his most defining physical characteristic. FBI psychologists speculated stress, though there was disagreement about that. Sociopaths don't feel stress the same way normal people do. Others felt that maybe he had some kind of autoimmune disorder that caused the strange coloring.

In any event, Carlisle worked a series of odd jobs, including truck driver and hospital janitor, never relying on his father's money, though, once again, nobody knew if it was withheld from him or he refused to take it. When his father and mother were both killed in a massive fire that gutted their 8,000-square-foot home, Efron had no choice but to take the money. His father, smart as he was, had failed to prepare a will, and his entire estate fell to Efron.

Kori remembered the fire. It was the only thing on the news for days. The tragic death of the "Emperor of Silicon Valley." Efron had been questioned about the fire, but the investigators determined that he was out of state at the time. After several months, the fire marshal's investigation eventually pinned the cause on a corroded gas pressure regulator, allowing a slow leak to filled the house with natural gas. A simple spark from somewhere most likely created a giant flash fire, engulfing the home in seconds. The Carlisles, asleep in their bedroom, never stood a chance. The insurance company argued the findings, bringing in an army of attorneys in expensive suits, but a court ruled against them and the company had to pay.

Efron, now worth billions, almost immediately began putting together his One Hundred Bombs plan. Kori knew the rest. The FBI report detailed seemingly every aspect of this chronology, but it seemed to Kori there was a big gap. No matter what she read of the report and no matter to what depth it took her, there was still no "why." Maybe, thought Kori, the question is too big. How does a person become evil? Does anyone really know? Hitler and Stalin were evil on a massive scale. Jeffrey Dahmer and Ted Bundy on a smaller one. Psychiatrists have studied them all. And still there were no definitive explanations. Just a lot of theory.

Kori had studied psychology as part of her training and she recalled something referred to as the "dark triad."

This is a dangerous personality combination of narcissism, Machiavellianism, and psychopathy. Narcissism includes grandiosity and lack of empathy. Named after Niccolò Machiavelli, a sixteenth-century philosopher and politician, Machiavellianism includes such characteristics as manipulation and absence of morality. Psychopathy includes anti-social behavior and lack of remorse. Roll all these traits together into one person, and you've got an atrocity in the making.

Efron Carlisle went a step beyond even this. Although it didn't say so in the FBI psychology report, Kori knew that Efron Carlisle fit into yet another category, making him a member of the rare "dark tetrad" club. For clearly, Carlisle was also a sadist, reveling in cruelty for its own sake.

In the back of the taxi from the airport, Kori glanced out at the strange landscape of Tel Aviv. It was dusk and the sky was an odd color, a kind of dark purplish hue that bathed the countryside. The taxi meandered around curvy roads and up and down long, flowing hills in a barren setting that looked nothing like what Kori had imagined. There were no buildings, really. Just a few primitive, ramshackle dwellings hidden among tall, weirdly shaped trees that somehow looked vaguely threatening.

In time, the taxi took a turn onto a long, straight dirt path.

"Where are we going?" asked Kori. "Are you sure this is the way to the hotel?"

The driver looked straight ahead and said nothing. Something was definitely wrong. A trap? Kori reached for her purse to grab her Glock but realized with a start that the purse was missing. Where was it? Could she have left it on the plane?

Meanwhile, the car sped up. It was practically flying down the dirt road now, the eerie, purplish landscape zipping past. Kori considered jumping but the car was moving far too fast. Then she noticed there were no door handles in the backseat. She was trapped in an automobile that must have been doing at least a hundred miles an hour. She looked out of the front windshield but it was murky, as if they were now speeding through a dense fog. But the driver only speeded up.

"Stop the car!" cried Kori. *"Stop!"*

The driver laughed. It was a long, throaty, menacing, evil laugh. Then he turned around and Kori noticed the crooked nose and the white hair. The driver was glaring at Kori with ugly, ominous eyes and Kori knew that those eyes belonged to none other than Efron Carlisle.

"Miss? Sorry to wake you," said the flight attendant. "We're getting ready to land. I need you to put your tray table up."

"Yes … yes, of course," said Kori, shaking herself awake. She shuddered and sat up and looked out of the window as the plane began its descent over the blue waters of Tel Aviv, the tall buildings along the shoreline glimmering in the sun.

CHAPTER 10

There is archeological evidence that people have lived in the ancient port city of Jaffa for more than 9,000 years. The city is repeatedly mentioned in the Bible. Some believe it to be named after Noah's son Japhet, who built the city after the flood. Jonah sailed out of Jaffa before being swallowed by the whale, and, much later, Saint Peter preached the gospel there. The history of the city is alive today in its winding, stone-paved streets and ancient stone buildings.

A couple miles north is the Tel Aviv InterContinental hotel, where Kori took in the view of the sparkling Mediterranean Sea from her twelfth-floor window. She had gotten a couple hours of restless sleep after arrival and was now dressed and ready to venture out. Anya was staying at the InterContinental as well, but had arrived earlier. She was now a ten-minute walk away, at a crowded lunch spot on HaCarmel street. That's where the agents met.

"It is good to see you, my friend."

"It's good to see you, too, Anya. I'm really happy the chief could work it out so that you could join me here. By the way, he still thinks you're a man, you know." Anya laughed.

The two sat at an outdoor table and ordered beef and chicken kabobs with grilled veggies, along with a couple of Goldstar beers. Kori was tired but the Goldstar was reviving her.

"Have you been to Tel Aviv before?" Anya asked.

"Never," replied Kori. "I've been to Jerusalem a couple of times and I once took a side trip to Bethlehem, but never Tel Aviv. I've heard good things. You?"

"Many times. As a little girl I used to travel here with my father. He had important contacts here. Of course, I knew nothing of his work at the time. But when he was done with his meetings, he used to take me to the Carmel Market. It's a wonderfully busy place just a couple of blocks from here. Vendors sell everything you can imagine. My father used to buy me hamantaschen cookies—triangular-shaped cookies filled with jam. And south of here, of course, is Jaffa, with such rich history."

"I've heard. I wish we had more time."

"There is never enough. And speaking of which, we should get moving."

"Indeed we should. Do you think Yanovich's in-laws will talk to us?"

"I don't see why not. Their son is missing and even if he has a history of disappearing, I'm sure they are still worried. But I wonder how much they know about his anarchist views."

"I guess we'll find out. But what I wonder about is how much they know about their ex-son-in-law, Ivan Yanovich. I wonder if they were close with him."

"Let's go find out. Finish your beer. You Americans drink so slowly."

Kori noticed Anya's beer was gone while hers was still half full. "Okay, okay," smiled Kori. Then she lifted her glass and chugged the rest of her beer. "Let's go. I'll get the check. This one's courtesy of the US Government."

Fifteen minutes later, they entered the small grocery shop on Trumpeldor Street that was owned by the Roths. Simon Roth and his wife Miryam had operated the small store for more than twenty years, living upstairs in a three-bedroom apartment. Their only two children were Yanovich's ex-wife Rebecca, and their son Jael.

"He can rot in hell for all I care!" said Mr. Roth when Kori and Anya had introduced themselves and mentioned they were looking for Jael. Roth was a short, portly man with a long comb-over. His wife was shorter still, but with a handsome face accented by graying hair.

"Simon, stop!" said Mrs. Roth. "He's still our son."

"Our son? On drugs? Passed out in a gutter again probably? That's our son? And with all of that anarchy baloney! Your son, maybe. *I* have no son." Then Mr. Roth went back about his business, stacking cans of soup into a pyramid shape by the front counter.

"You'll have to forgive my husband. He allows himself to be ruled by emotion. But his heart is in a good place, believe me."

Mr. Roth rolled his eyes.

"Who did you say you were with?" asked Mrs. Roth.

"We're with an international security agency, Mrs. Roth," Kori replied. "We have reason to believe that Jael might be mixed up in something pretty big."

"And dangerous," added Anya.

Mr. Roth glanced up for just a moment, but still maintained the scowl on his face.

"What do you mean something big?" said Mrs. Roth.

"Well, we're not exactly sure. That's what we're trying to determine. We think it might have to do with your son-in-law. Or, ex-son-in-law, I should say. Ivan Yanovich."

"I'm not surprised," said Mr. Roth. "I never trusted that one. He was an oddball. Smart, sure. But strange. I'm on record as being against the marriage from the start. I tried to talk Rebecca out of it. But you know kids. They always think they know more than you do."

"Well, what happened to Ivan?" Mrs. Roth asked. "We have heard nothing from him."

"Not that we expected to," said Mr. Roth. "Rebecca made it pretty clear, through her, let us say, *indiscretions*, that she no longer wanted him. I can't say I'm proud of my daughter for how she behaved, but I do have to say that I'm glad she's away from Ivan."

"Well, Ivan is why we are here," said Anya. "He is missing, you see. And we believe he might be with Jael."

"Jael?" said Mrs. Roth. "Why, the two barely knew each other. I mean, they would see each other whenever Ivan was in Tel Aviv, but it's not like they were what you would call friends."

"Nevertheless," continued Anya, "we think Jael possibly recruited Ivan into a very dangerous organization."

"Led by this man," said Kori, showing the Roths a photograph of Efron Carlisle. "Have you ever seen him?"

"Oh, yes," said Mrs. Roth. "Jael spent a lot of time with him. Jael lived at home, you know. Right upstairs with us."

"Because my wife knows nothing about tough love!" said Mr. Roth. "I wanted to throw his *tuchus* out on the street, but my wife insisted we enable the boy by allowing him to continue to sponge off of us."

"Simon!"

"It's true! You've always babied him. This is why he hooked up with these organizations of his." Then he turned to Kori and Anya and said, "That boy would have had this store one day. I tried to get him interested in the business, but he just refused to do any work."

"Yes, Mr. Roth," said Kori, nodding in understanding, "but be that as it may, what can you tell me about your son's interactions with this man?"

"Well," replied Mrs. Roth, "he came around to visit Jael often. He said his name was Barker. He never talked to us, however. He would come and get Jael and the two would go out. God only knows where."

"We think Barker was probably the guy selling Jael his drugs," said Mr. Roth. "But I never actually saw him do it. Otherwise, I'd have taught that guy a lesson, believe you me."

"I'm sure," said Kori, trying hard not to imagine Mr. Roth being taken apart limb by limb by Carlisle. "But he's not a drug dealer and his name is not Barker. It's Carlisle. And we have reason to believe he's planning a terrorist attack."

"A terrorist attack?" cried Mrs. Roth. "With Jael? But where?"

"We don't know, Mrs. Roth," Kori answered. "That's what we're trying to find out." She noticed Mr. Roth biting his lower lip just then. He looked pained and he stopped stacking cans and stood silently.

"Listen, Mr. and Mrs. Roth," said Kori, "you said Jael lived at home. I wonder if you might be kind enough to show us his room. Perhaps we can find a clue there as to his whereabouts."

Mrs. Roth glanced over at Mr. Roth who nodded to her and then snapped himself back to his gruff self, turning to

Kori and saying, "Why not? Good luck combing through that pigsty."

"I'm afraid Simon isn't kidding," said Mrs. Roth. "Our son is something of a hoarder. Last month, I tried to get him to clean up his room and throw some things out, but he yelled at me to mind my own business."

"And yet you continue to enable!" said Mr. Roth.

"Come on," said Mrs. Roth, "I'll take you upstairs."

The three began walking toward the back of the store.

"Miss," Mr. Roth called after them from behind his stack of cans.

"Yes?" said Kori, turning back to Mr. Roth.

"Do you think you can help us find our boy?"

"We're going to try, Mr. Roth. We're going to try."

At the back of the store was a private door that opened into a stairwell. The stairs went up one floor to a small landing where the door of the apartment was. Mrs. Roth unlocked the door and waved Kori and Anya inside.

"His room is through the living room and down the far hallway," she said.

They walked through the living room of the apartment and then down a hall that bordered the opposite wall of the building. There was an exterior door halfway down the hall that led out to a fire escape. Anya noticed it was slightly ajar.

"Mrs. Roth, do you typically leave this door open?"

"Why, no," said Mrs. Roth. "That door is always closed. And locked. My husband, I guess. We keep plants out on the landing of the fire escape. He must have gone out to water them. Normally, he remembers to close and lock the door when he comes back in. Well, as you can imagine, we're both rather distracted these days. It's been hard. Simon speaks badly about Jael, but I know that it's because he loves him so. He's so disappointed. And hurt. He's very worried. We both are, as you can imagine. And now to think he's mixed up with something."

"Of course," said Kori. "I know it must be difficult."

"Well, here's Jael's room."

Mrs. Roth opened the door and the three entered the bedroom. Mrs. Roth's eyes went wide and her mouth hung open.

The room was completely empty.

"The fire escape," said Kori.

"I'm on it," said Anya as she flew out of the room toward the exterior door down the hall. She swung it open but nobody was on the landing or the stairs. She ran down the stairs to the street and looked as far as she could in every direction, but saw nobody carrying anything away. It was just another busy street in Tel Aviv. If someone had broken in to take Jael's stuff, they were gone.

Anya went back up the fire escape and into the apartment and down the hall to Jael's room. "Nobody," she said.

Kori was standing in the room holding a piece of paper. "I found this taped to the wall over by the window," she said. "I think we know who the burglar is."

Anya took the slip of paper and read it out loud:

Hello, Ms. Briggs. So sorry to have missed you! Maybe next time.
Until then, please give my regards to everyone at Rampart.

All good wishes,
E.C.

CHAPTER 11

"What did you say this is?" asked Kori.

"It's called arak," said Anya. "It's made of grapes and aniseed."

The two were sitting in the atrium lobby bar at the InterContinental.

"Tastes like ouzo," said Kori.

"Yes, it has that same licorice flavor. But it's more potent."

"Potent is good. I could use potent after seeing this note." She laid it down on their table. "We must have just missed him. Or he missed us. Talk about timing."

"He had the same thought we did," said Anya. "He knew there must have been a clue or two in Jael's bedroom as to their whereabouts and the whereabouts of the uranium."

"And to be certain, rather than take out anything he thought might have been questionable, he decided to simply take everything."

"Yes. But you heard the Roths talk about the room. Carlisle could not have emptied out the room alone. You think Jael helped him?"

"I fear for Jael," said Kori. "Jael had a key. The lock on the fire escape door was picked. Why do that if Jael is with you? Let's face it, Anya. Jael had problems with drugs. He could be unpredictable. Once Jael led Carlisle to Yanovich, what would Carlisle need with Jael? Why take a chance on keeping him around?"

"The poor Roths," said Anya, taking another drink of her arak.

"Yes," said Kori, and she took another drink of hers.

"But why would Carlisle not take Jael's keys after killing him?" Anya asked. "Why did he have to pick the lock?"

"Good question. Probably because he did away with him in such a way as to leave nothing of him—even his keys."

"Like how?"

"Incinerated? Run through a woodchipper? Who knows. Efron Carlisle likes to be gruesome. The bloodier, the better. Probably only afterward did he think about the potential clues left behind in Jael's room. Maybe a journal. Maybe a map of wherever the uranium is headed. So he probably came by with some of his goons, which he always likes to surround himself with, and broke into the apartment knowing the Roths probably never leave the store during working hours. Then they threw everything into a pickup truck and took off."

"But not before writing that note. Why would he write that?"

"To toy with me, Anya. That's just like Carlisle. He wants me to know that he knows who I am and that I'm after him. Until today, I had no idea he knew anything about me. That he knew anything about Rampart. How could he know? How?"

"It's a little, how would you say … disconcerting?"

"To put it mildly. The most dangerous psychopath to probably ever live on the planet knows my name and that I'm looking for him on behalf of a super-secret US spy operation. And then to flaunt that in my face? He must be loving this. He's sitting somewhere laughing about it right now, I'm sure. Cripes, I need to call Eaglethorpe. He's not going to be very happy about this. First, let's get the waitress back over here and get us a couple more of these anzaks."

"Araks."

"Whatever."

"Good God!" cried Eaglethorpe. "How could we have been compromised?" He held the phone to his ear, scarcely believing what Kori was telling him. "It simply can't be possible!"

"I wish it wasn't, Chief." Kori was in her hotel room absently gazing out of her window at the water. It was early evening in Tel Aviv and the setting sun was producing a beautiful array of colors against the sky.

"Okay, Agent Briggs," said Eaglethorpe and then, as much for his own benefit as for Kori's, "let's calm down and try to think this through."

"Right, Chief."

"How could Carlisle have possibly learned about us?"

"Chief, what about those guys who were following me? You know, the guys who went to Ronald's place and asked about me when I was in New York to meet Hasan."

"Hmm … have you seen them since?"

"No, I can't say I have. It was just that one day."

"I can't see how they could be affiliated with Carlisle. We'd barely been on the case then. We were still chasing Alfawda."

"Yes, but Chief, remember, Carlisle knew even then we were chasing Alfawda."

"And how do we know that?"

"Because he killed Hasan. It must have been him, right? He didn't want Hasan telling anybody that Alfawda was uninvolved. So he knew we were on Alfawda's trail."

"Correction, Agent Briggs. He knew *somebody* was on Alfawda's trail. He probably assumed it was the CIA. There's no reason to believe he knew of our existence back then."

"Yes, I suppose that's true."

"So how did he learn of us? And of you in particular? I mean, if you're Carlisle and you're recruiting people in Israel and stealing uranium in Russia and murdering double agents in New York, how do you even get wind of a secret agent working out of Washington, DC?"

Kori thought for a moment. "He must have double backed."

"Huh?"

"He went back over his tracks. I'll bet he spoke to Yanovich's sister in St. Petersburg after we were there. That's when he must have learned of us. He probably had spies keeping an eye on her flat. They saw Agent Kovalev and me visiting her. Probably followed us from there. A guy like Carlisle, assuming he still has access to his money, which is a good assumption, has probably already put together a pretty decent team of fellow psychos. Carlisle can't be everywhere at once. I assume he delegated the job of taking Hasan out. I'll bet you that I've been trailed by somebody ever since."

"Then they must be good, Briggs, because you've always been observant."

"Maybe I'm slipping, Chief," sighed Kori.

"I don't believe that for a second. You're the best I have, Agent Briggs."

"Thanks, Chief."

"Besides, that still doesn't explain how he knows your name and how he knows of Rampart. Following you around for a few days isn't going to reveal any of that information. It's not like you walk around wearing a name tag."

"It's a mystery, Chief."

"And you say that nobody in the neighborhood noticed a truck pulled up to the rear of the Roths' building?"

"Nobody. We canvassed the whole area. It's a busy section with busy streets. Trucks making deliveries come and go all day. I'm sure nothing looked out of the ordinary. Nobody remembered anything helpful."

"And so we have a madman out there who knows about our agency."

"I'm afraid so. But we have something out there worse than that, Chief."

"What's that?"

"The uranium."

"True. But at least we know Carlisle is in Tel Aviv. And if that's the case, then the uranium must be there, too. But why Tel Aviv of all places?"

"Carlisle had met Jael Roth here. He probably approached Ivan Yanovich here. Both of them know people here. Roth has lived in this city his entire life. Maybe Carlisle started feeling comfortable here. Tel Aviv probably became his center of operations. Maybe he felt it was a safe place to bring the uranium and build the bomb."

"That makes sense."

"Yes, but, Chief, that's no guarantee that he's still here. Now that he knows we're on his tail, he might very well scram."

"Then we need to confirm—rather quickly—whether he's still there."

"Agreed."

"So, what's your plan, Agent Briggs?"

"Well, Carlisle probably used a rental truck to clean out Jael's room. Agent Kovalev and I can hit all the local rental truck companies. It's not much, but maybe we can luck into a clue somewhere."

"Good idea, Kori. I'll have Cooper do the research and secure a list of all the rental truck companies around the city and shoot it to you. You and Agent Kovalev will need to hurry, though. If Carlisle's not in Tel Aviv, we'll have to go back to square one. And each day lost is a day closer to him arming a nuclear bomb."

"I understand, Chief."

"Keep me posted, Briggs. Meanwhile, I have a meeting with POTUS in the morning to brief him on the situation. I didn't expect that I'd have to tell him that Carlisle is familiar with Rampart. Can't say I'm looking forward to it."

"Yeah, good luck with that, Chief."

"Thanks Briggs. I'm going to need it."

CHAPTER 12

"We'll crack this code, I'm sure of it." Ralph Moore was flipping through the lengthy transcripts that he and Earl Watson had been poring over for the last hour.

"Can't we just feed it all into the agency's computers?" Watson asked.

"I told you—no. Nobody at the agency knows we're working on this." Which is why they were working in Watson's garage, the transcripts laid out on a seldom-used workbench, the air a mix of motor oil and stale grass clippings.

"I know, I know. But I think it would actually be easier to get permission than to crack this stupid code. I mean, we might be here for days."

"The director would never give us permission to work on this. You heard her yourself. She thinks it's a waste of time. There's no amount of convincing that's going to make her believe there's a shadow agency that's reporting directly to the president of the United States. Now, come on. We can do this. We're top intelligence officers. Don't you remember the code-breaking classes from your CIA training?"

"That was a long time ago. And I guess I better confess to you that I never did very well in those classes. Reminded me of those stupid scrabble and cryptogram puzzles in the daily paper. When I was a kid, my older sister finished them in no time. Took me forever, if I finished them at all. My sister always made fun of me." Watson's voice trailed off and he suddenly looked morose.

Moore shook his head in disgust. "Well, forget about all that. It's really not that hard. All we have to do is figure out a couple of key words and the rest will fall into line. That's the secret to code-breaking, you know. That's how the Brits broke the Nazi codes in World War II."

"Yes, yes, so I've heard. But they had teams of people involved and, as I recall, a computer of sorts. Geez, why do these guys have to talk in code anyway?"

"I guess they're afraid of being bugged."

"Well," Watson said, brightening up, "I must say that their fears certainly seem justified."

"Yes, you did a fine job," said Moore. "Breaking in would have been better, but bribing the landlord wasn't bad."

"There was no way to break into that place, believe me. Tighter security than Fort Knox. And it wasn't exactly a bribe."

"You said he asked for money."

"Yes, but after telling him I was CIA and that we had reason to believe that Gladstone Conveyor represented a security threat to the country, he was glad to give me access. It's good to meet a patriot for a change, let me tell you. Everyone's so damn cynical these days. Sure, he said he needed a little something for the trouble, but I didn't think that was unreasonable. Besides, what's a hundred bucks to the agency?"

"Don't forget to put it on your expense sheet."

"Oh, don't worry about that. I'm putting it under meals and entertainment. I'll say it covered a lunch with a foreign ambassador or something."

"So you just walked in?"

"Yep. Donned my 'Ace Pest Control' suit, grabbed my sprayer, and went in along with the landlord. He told them I was there to take care of a roach problem he had noticed in the building, then started a conversation with them while I walked around the place, spraying here and there. When they weren't looking, I planted two devices. And I put them in places I'm quite sure they'll never look. Those bugs will be there forever, believe me."

"Well done. And they certainly worked. Everything was clear as a bell. And now the answers are all here on these pages, I can feel it. All we have to do is figure out what the hell they're talking about. Now, look, it seems as if the most-used words are either *flower* or *rose*. Obviously, these are key. If we can figure out what those stand for, I think we can figure out the rest."

"Their whole code seems to be flower-based. They ask for carnations and lilies and mums. I mean, what gives?"

"Yes, but Watson, it's not just the words. It's the context. That's what you have to think about. They talk about *buying* and *selling*. They talk about *gross quantities* and *shipping*. The context matters. What do they mean when they say they need to ship a certain quantity of snap dragons, for instance? Look at this page. There's an entire conversation about something referred to as a purple iris. Now, something tells me color is important. That conversation is followed by someone asking whether a certain quantity of tulips is yellow or orange. Do you see what I mean?"

"Not really."

"Well, why not just say tulips? Why specify? There's a key there somewhere, I'm sure of it."

"You know, if we hadn't witnessed these guys reporting directly to the president of the United States, I'd think these were code words for drugs. Roses could mean marijuana. Lilies could mean heroin. Etcetera. Maybe the colors indicate a particular type."

"Agreed. Same kind of thing we've heard in illegal drug operations." Moore was thoughtful for a moment and then continued. "So let's assume it's some sort of product they're dealing in, but not drugs. Something our executive branch would be involved in. Something they'd want to keep secret from the public."

"Like what?"

"I don't know. Maybe, say, weapons?"

"Yeah," Watson nodded. "Didn't the Reagan administration's guys use code words during Iran–Contra? I'm pretty sure they did."

"I think you're right," grinned Moore. "So maybe that's it. The president is making a clandestine deal with another government for weapons. Good God, maybe nuclear weapons for all we know. This is why he put together this little secret group of his. This is why nobody knows who they are."

"Well, that certainly explains the need for a code. Holy crap, Ralph. Do you realize what you're saying? This is big."

"You said it. Really big. Maybe the president is selling nukes to the Middle East. Or Russia. Heck, he could be selling them to China, for all we know."

"Skirting around Congress."

"It's impeachable."

"Borderline treasonous."

Both men stayed silent for a while, contemplating the ramifications. Both also thought about their futures. The promotions. The accolades. The respect. The director would be angry initially that they undertook an unsanctioned assignment, but once she understood the stakes involved, she'd be giving them medals.

"Okay, look Watson," said Moore at last, "we need to be very sure of ourselves. Let's go back through these transcripts very carefully. We need to put an airtight case together before we approach the director. Our careers may be at stake."

"Agreed. We need to be very sure."

"And I'll tell you what else. We need to keep up our surveillance. The code-breaking is damning, sure. But it's not as good as actual, physical proof."

"What do you have in mind?"

"Well, doesn't it sound like they're running this thing out of some warehouse somewhere? There's got to be a place where they're storing all of these weapons. You've been to the conveyor company offices. They can't store them there, right?"

"Right. The place is much too small."

"So there's a repository somewhere. And it's got to be here in DC. That's why they're all here. What if we could find this repository? Take some video of them coming and going. Sneak in. See what's there."

"Then the director would have no choice but to believe us, code or no code."

"That's what I'm saying."

"So, should we keep following the girl?" Watson asked. "She might lead us there, right? Or should we follow one of the others?"

"No, it's got to be the girl. She's the one most likely not to notice us. Everyone knows that women aren't very good at this kind of thing. She'll lead us there for sure."

"And then we'll have all the proof we'll need."

"Exactly. But, look, we still need to break this code. Finding where the weapons are stockpiled is one thing. But the code tells us where the weapons are going and to whom. That's the key."

"Right."

"So let's get back to work. We're close. Really close. Why don't you go in and tell your wife to make us some more coffee. I say we don't stop working until we've cracked this flower code. Even if it takes all night."

"Sure, no problem," Watson said. Then, shaking his head in wonder, he added, "Illegal weapons trading. Originating from the White House!"

"Unreal," agreed Moore. Then both men smiled broadly and unabashedly at each other. This was big. This was very, very big.

In the outer office of Rampart's headquarters, Darren Cooper and James Foster were drinking coffee and waiting for Eaglethorpe to arrive. From there, they'd all pile into Eaglethorpe's Escalade for the trip to the White House for the morning briefing with the president.

"The prez is gonna blow a gasket," said Cooper. "It's not going to be pretty."

Foster nodded. "What's worse is that we don't even have a decent explanation as to how Carlisle made us. Hell, we don't even have a decent guess."

"Well, we'll just have to take our medicine. He'll unload on us, but then he'll just tell us to go back to work, as always. I mean, what else can he do?"

"I suppose you're right. But it really is a puzzle, isn't it? Our own intelligence agencies can't find us. How the hell did Carlisle discover who we were?"

"One mystery at a time, my friend. Let's find Carlisle first."

"Roger that. Oh, by the way, I meant to ask about that pest control guy the other day."

"Oh, him. Yeah, CIA, for sure. Cripes, he might as well have been wearing a sign around his neck. I did a sweep the moment he left and found two bugs."

"Well, I guess that shouldn't be surprising. What did you do with them?"

"I took them down the street, snuck into that wholesale flower business, and planted them there. That ought to keep them off the trail for a while. More coffee?"

CHAPTER 13

Kori sat on the edge of the bed with her laptop looking at the list of rental truck companies Cooper had just emailed, wondering at what a long shot it was to hope someone had some information. Of course, the offices were all closed for the night. She and Anya wouldn't even be able to get started until the morning. How was she possibly going to get any sleep?

Kori went over the chain of events in her head, trying to figure out Carlisle's next step. When he'd stolen the uranium, he apparently had been happy to know that the intelligence community had implicated Alfawda. Carlisle had wanted to keep it that way, going so far as to kill Hasan el-Sadek who was about to tell Kori that Alfawda hadn't been involved at all. But how did he know about Hasan? Hasan was a double agent and even Alfawda hadn't known that. Of course, the CIA had known about Hasan. Was there a leak at the CIA? Maybe.

In the meantime, Carlisle had kept surveillance on the home of Yanovich's sister. That's how he learned about Kori and Anya. But somehow, he traced them back to Rampart. At least Kori. In fact, the note at the Roth's apartment was addressed only to Kori. Strange. Anya, of course, had been operating more in the shadows than Kori. She'd been in Russia. Everyone at Rampart, besides Kori and Blake, had assumed she was a man. So whatever information Carlisle had about Rampart, he'd apparently only gotten it from the States. But how? Good God, thought Kori. Was there a leak at Rampart?

One by one, Kori thought about each member of Rampart. By design, there weren't many. Most worked out of the DC office. Eaglethorpe, Cooper, Foster, Gibson, and Vasquez. There were a couple of agents on the West Coast. There was Blake in Russia, and Anya, of course. And a few other agents posted at various hot spots around the world. Kori knew firsthand what it took to become one of these super-elite agents. She knew what she'd had to go through and she knew that every agent had to go through a similar process. All were vetted, their backgrounds scrutinized. It was inconceivable to her that one of them could have somehow compromised the agency. And, yet, how else to explain it?

And now that Carlisle knew about Rampart, and about Kori in particular, it seemed as if he wanted to have a little fun. It would have been easy enough to clear out Jael Roth's bedroom and simply be on his way. He didn't need to give himself away with a note. But that was just like Carlisle. This had become a game to him. No doubt he was enjoying it immensely.

Meanwhile, now that Carlisle had covered all his potential tracks, including doing away with Jael, he was God only knows where. He and Yanovich, turning the stolen uranium into a weapon of mass destruction. Kori was optimistic by nature. Determined. Confident. But sitting on her bed, thinking about how big the world was and knowing there was a madman hiding somewhere with a nuclear bomb, she was hit with a thought she could not shake. Nobody was going to able to stop Carlisle from using that bomb. Hundreds of thousands, perhaps millions, were going to die, and it seemed to Kori that the only questions left were where and when.

She shuddered. Then she texted Anya. Want to meet in the bar for a drink? Seconds later came Anya's reply: I could use one. See you in the bar.

Eaglethorpe and Cooper and Foster somberly entered the Oval Office. After Eaglethorpe had gotten off the phone with Kori, he had called his two agents and briefed them on the situation. He was scheduled for a morning meeting to bring the president up to date on the latest developments, but he certainly hadn't planned on having to brief him on the exposure of Rampart.

Eaglethorpe dove in, thinking to himself that revealing the news would be best done quickly, like pulling off a band-aid.

"The news is bad, Mr. President," he said, immediately after taking his seat along with Cooper and Foster across the desk from the president. "Very bad, I'm afraid."

The president arched his eyebrows. "Oh? How so?"

"Well, sir, Carlisle knows he's being followed. Worse, he knows by whom. He knows of Agent Briggs and, further, he knows that she's an employee of our agency. He knows, that is to say, about Rampart."

Eaglethorpe drew a breath and held a steady gaze, knowing that the president respected strength. All he could do was hope that on some level, the president would appreciate his honesty, candidness, and the fact that he didn't beat around the bush. He had come right out with it. He was obviously willing to face the music and take responsibility. That wouldn't matter initially, of course, but hopefully, later, as the president came to view the situation, he would think about how Eaglethorpe had handled himself. *Just maybe*, thought Eaglethorpe, *I can save my job.*

"How did he find out?" said the president evenly.

"Frankly, we don't know, sir." Eaglethorpe wanted to say something about how the important thing now was to move forward and determine the next steps, but he knew it was too soon. The president had to process what he'd just heard and react to it. That reaction was no doubt going to be ugly, but eventually, they'd all move past it. Nonetheless, Eaglethorpe wanted to block immediately one possible thought the president might have been having. "I don't believe it was a leak, sir," he added. "I know my people. I would stake my life on their integrity and competence. Wherever Carlisle got his information, it did not come from inside Rampart."

Slowly, the president stood. Then he turned and walked over to the window, gazing out with his hands clasped behind his back. Eaglethorpe glanced over at Cooper and Foster who both looked as uneasy as Eaglethorpe felt. The president's reaction was one they'd never seen from him before. Where was the fist-pounding and the yelling?

The president stood looking out of the window for a long enough time that the Rampart agents began to think he'd actually forgotten they were sitting there.

Finally, he spoke. "You're wrong, Richard," he said quietly, using Eaglethorpe's first name, something Eaglethorpe could never remember him ever doing. "It *was* a leak. And I know from whom."

"You ... do?" said Eaglethorpe.

"Yes. I do." Then the president turned toward the agents, the color drained from his face. "It came from this very office. I'm afraid, gentlemen, that it was me. I'm the leak. I'm the reason Efron Carlisle knows about Rampart."

CHAPTER 14

The president sat back down at his desk and leaned back in his chair.

"Grover Carlisle," he said.

"Sir?"

"He was a close personal friend of mine," said the president.

"I was not aware of that," said Eaglethorpe.

"He was a major contributor to my campaign. The fact is, I probably wouldn't have gotten elected to my first term without his help. He was a major contributor to something else, too, gentlemen. He was a major contributor to Rampart."

"I didn't know that we had outside contributors, Mr. President," said Eaglethorpe. "I assumed everything was funded by … " Eaglethorpe paused for a moment, thinking. "Well, by … by … "

"Yes, exactly," said the president. "Who could fund a spy organization as secret as Rampart? Did you assume it was the executive branch? The Department of Defense? Homeland Security? The CIA? Your organization, Agent Eaglethorpe, is unknown to all of them. We're able to siphon off some cash from each in small increments without raising flags, but not nearly enough to keep Rampart running. We have had benefactors since the beginning, since the Kennedy days. Back then, it was J. Paul Getty, the oil tycoon. Other benefactors have come and gone. For the past decade, Rampart has been surviving on a grant from Grover Carlisle. You see, every president, once briefed on the existence of Rampart, has had to basically go, hat in hand, to the wealthiest Americans, imploring them as patriots to do a service for the country, the country that has enabled them to make their fortunes. Most consider it an honor."

"But, sir, doesn't involving a member of the public risk exposing Rampart's identity?" Eaglethorpe asked. "What if the benefactor revealed us?"

"Rampart has built-in deniability. As you know, there are no records of you anywhere. We can shut your office down in a flash. That's why Rampart has been kept so small. It's not because growth involves more people and therefore more risk of exposure; it's so that Rampart can be easily wiped clean. As if the organization never existed."

"But, sir," said Cooper thoughtfully, "doesn't financially involving someone risk compromising our mission?"

"The piper calls the tune," nodded Eaglethorpe. "Isn't it possible, sir, that a person with a financial stake is going to want to know what he's getting for his money? And, perhaps, make requests toward that end? At the least, it seems like a conflict of interest, does it not?"

"The understanding," said the president, "has always been that the benefactor stays out of things. It is made clear that he will have no influence whatsoever. He is asked to donate only under those conditions."

"So ... the motive for the benefactor is pure patriotism?" Foster asked, looking skeptical.

"I didn't say that exactly," replied the president. "That's the basis upon which we solicit the benefactor's funding. To be honest, however, the funding sometimes comes with a condition or two, mostly having to do with things like tax breaks, relief on tariffs, a quicker path to patent approvals, and things of that nature. Nothing egregious or completely out of hand, I assure you."

Eaglethorpe and Cooper and Foster were silent, each turning over in their minds the implications of what they'd been hearing. Suddenly, the purity of their organization was in doubt. The one thing they had all appreciated about Rampart, its independence from the political and bureaucratic machinations of the other intelligence agencies, had apparently been a falsehood. They were smaller, but they were still beholden to economic and political forces beyond their control. There were others who were pulling the strings, or at least exerting outside influence. And at the taxpayer's unknowing expense. Eaglethorpe felt like he needed a shower.

"Look," said the president, "I know what you're all thinking, but it's not like that. For most of Rampart's history, you've been able to operate as a distinctly separate organization with your own mission. Just as designed. But … well, Grover Carlisle was different. He wanted to remain informed. He insisted on knowing all of the details of what we were up to. I don't know; it became kind of a hobby for him. It was like he was living vicariously through you guys. I briefed him weekly, I am sorry and embarrassed to now have to report to you. I thought he'd keep it all secret. But somehow, and I don't know how, his son obviously found out. I assume Grover probably kept notes somewhere, maybe in his study in his mansion. Or in the library. Who knows?"

The president paused and reached for the bottled water on his desk and took a long sip. Then he continued. "The thing is, Grover had names and everything. He never wanted to get involved, mind you. He just liked following along, the way a baseball fan might follow his team, keeping track of batting averages and so on. Whatever notes he had, Efron must have stumbled upon them. I knew as soon as you said that Efron Carlisle had learned of Rampart just how he had learned. It was something I've been fearing from the moment you told me he was still alive. I had hoped the notes had burned up in the house fire, but I should have known that would have been too good to be true. Looking back, of course I should have made it clear to Grover right from the start that his need for information could not be a part of the deal. But, as I said, he was a friend. And … " the president cast his eyes downward, "a campaign contributor. I needed his help, gentlemen."

There were several moments of awkward silence before Eaglethorpe finally said, "Well, sir, the question now is what Efron is going to do with the information. If what you say is true, he knows our names and I think we can safely assume he knows where we work out of, and where we live."

"Most likely," said the president, solemnly.

"He also knows enough to know that we're the one agency in the world that can thwart his plans. Right now, we're his number one enemy."

"Yes. As painful as it is to think about, it's probably a good bet that all of your lives are in real and imminent danger. Of course it goes without saying that you have the full support of the executive branch at your disposal. Just let me know what you need. You will be protected. You have my word."

No thanks, Eaglethorpe wanted to tell him. *I think you've done enough already.* Instead he forced a half-smile and said, "Thank you, Mr. President."

Kori's badge was silver and was embossed with "Agent Kori Briggs." Her official-looking identification card read, "International Criminal Police Investigations." She had one for the States that read, "National Bureau of Criminal Investigations." Nowhere on any of her identification did it say "Rampart." Anya had similar badges and cards. The agents used them to question people who expressed skepticism. The IDs always worked.

At Sharif Truck Rental, the questioning yielded no answers. It was the same result at Yunis Trucks. Kori and Anya had risen early, gotten a quick breakfast at the hotel restaurant, and had begun hitting the truck rental agencies one by one. It was a sunny morning, but warm and muggy. Cooper's list had a dozen entries and it was shaping up to be a long day. Kori and Anya had shown the managers at Sharif and Yunis pictures of Carlisle, Roth, and Yanovich, and asked them to check their records for the names. They'd found nothing. But at the third place, Dizengoff Truck Rentals, the manager perked up at the picture of Carlisle.

"Oh, yes, I remember him well," he said. "Odd looking guy. How could I forget? Plus, he owes us money. Let me see ... " he began tapping at his computer for the rental record. "Yes, here it is. His name is Jael Roth."

"Are you sure?" said Kori.

"Yes, it's right here."

"Take a look at this man." Then Kori showed him a picture of Roth.

"Hmm … no, I can't say I've ever seen him. But Roth was the name of that other guy you showed me. With the white hair."

Kori and Anya glanced at each other, each knowing the other's thoughts. This did not bode well for Jael. Carlisle had Jael's ID and it could only be assumed that Jael was now dead, his body probably never to be found.

"Anyway," said the manager, "the man paid us with cash up front, but we had to search for the truck. He never returned it."

"Oh?" said Kori.

"Yes, it turned out he'd abandoned it."

"Where?" asked Anya.

"We found it yesterday at the airport. We only found out about it because it had been parked in a tow-away zone. Near where the cargo planes fly out of. Anyway, we got a call from the tow company. We had to pay an impound fee. I tried to charge Roth's credit card but it didn't go through. Bastard owes us 600 shekels. Do you know where he is?"

"No," said Kori, "you see, we're looking for him."

"Aha. What is he, some kind of con man or something?"

"Yes, something like that."

"Well, I hope you find him."

"We hope so, too," said Kori. "You say you found the truck where the cargo planes fly out of?"

"Yes. Just abandoned there."

"Well, thank you. You've been very helpful."

The two left the company's office and walked out to the street to hail a cab. "Well, the good news," Kori said, "is that we can stop investigating truck rental companies."

"And the bad news," said Anya, "is that Carlisle is no doubt gone."

"I'm afraid so. He and his uranium jumped on a cargo plane. That helps explain his desire to come back here to Tel Aviv. I told the chief that this was probably the center of his operations. He'd met people here. He probably got to someone at the airport. Maybe even planted someone there. Paid them off to look the other way while his uranium was being loaded for shipment."

"Or else he bribed an inspector."

"Correct. Ben Gurion is extremely secure. You absolutely have to have someone on the inside. With Carlisle's money, he could pay whatever he needed to pay. From Bayanovka, Carlisle probably traveled by truck or small plane to get back here, moving small, inefficient distances at a time. But now, with contacts at the airport, he can take things up a notch."

"He can have the uranium flown to anywhere in the world."

"Yep. Including the United States," said Kori. "And Ben Gurion is one of the busiest airports in the Middle East. Do you know how many cargo planes fly out of Tel Aviv every day?"

"Too many to track?"

"Way too many."

Kori flagged down a taxi and the two slid into the backseat.

"InterContinental, please," said Kori, figuring they might as well go back to the hotel. And from there? Neither Kori nor Anya had a clue.

CHAPTER 15

In the rear of a nondescript, empty warehouse in the northeast part of the city, the Washington, DC members of Rampart sat in a circle on the concrete floor.

"Not exactly luxury, Chief," said Kori. After calling Eaglethorpe from Tel Aviv, Kori had headed for the airport to take the next flight back to Washington. Eaglethorpe had decided that the best thing would be to get Kori back to Rampart HQ, to regroup, and try to determine what the next move should be. She had briefed Eaglethorpe on Carlisle's exit from Tel Aviv and Eaglethorpe had briefed her on the president's inadvertent exposure of Rampart. Kori had said her goodbyes to Anya for the time being and then boarded a plane bound for DC, landing in the middle of the night and catching a few winks of sleep at the airport Hyatt before meeting with the group. She knew she could not go back to her apartment.

"No, it's not exactly luxury," said Eaglethorpe, "but it's where we're meeting today. We'll meet somewhere else tomorrow. And we'll remain on the move. The office is shut down, and nobody is to go back to their homes for the foreseeable future. Not until we find Carlisle. And no interaction with friends or family. It's safe to assume that, by now, Carlisle knows everything about us. We'll all be operating underground from this point forward. Each of you has your secure place to stay. You know where it is; we've all prepared for something like this. Your secondary vehicles are ready and waiting for you in their secure locations."

I'm going to miss my Tesla, thought Kori.

Eaglethorpe continued, pulling phones out of a box and handing one to each member. "Shut down your old phones. Communication will be by these cell phones only. And only to one another. From this point forward, you are all ghosts."

Kori knew the importance of remaining untraceable, to the mission and to the organization. Enough had been compromised. Still, she knew it would be hard on her mother. On the way to the warehouse, she'd called Joan and told her a tale about her boss pulling her away to a company team-building exercise in the Rocky Mountains. "Yep, no rest for the weary," she'd said. "I'm taking a flight directly from Tampa to Denver." Then she had let her mother know that for a week, she'd be out of cell phone range. The participants were all going to rough it as part of some grand motivational training program. Her mother had said she understood, but Kori could sense the disappointment in her voice. With some skepticism mixed in? Kori couldn't tell.

"Rampart being compromised," said Eaglethorpe, "is unfortunate, but it happened. We need to move forward and the question now is this: what's our next step? Thoughts?"

"Well," said Cooper, "I think we can assume that the most efficient course of action for Carlisle would be to have the bomb built as close to where he wants to detonate it as possible. That way, he doesn't have to worry about traveling around the world with a nuclear bomb in his suitcase. Traveling with the uranium is bad enough. But once it's rigged as a bomb, that's a different ballgame."

"And so by that same logic," added Foster, "we can assume, by way of the fact that he took off in a cargo plane, that the bomb, as yet, remains unbuilt."

"Well, that's a little bit of a relief," said Eaglethorpe. "But it doesn't help us determine where he plans to set it off."

"I think we can pretty easily narrow that down," Kori piped in.

"How so, Agent Briggs?"

"He's going to set it off here, in the United States."

"What makes you so sure?"

"Because he has a vendetta against this country. He resents America, for some reason. Maybe because his father made a zillion dollars here and he always hated his father, or something, who knows? But think about it. The One Hundred Bombs plan was here, right? Since then, he's spent time in an American prison, probably fueling his resentment. He's toying with us, an *American* intelligence agency. We're the enemy and we represent the United States. Chief, I've never been more sure of anything in my life. If he's not here yet, he's soon going to be. This is going to be his battlefield."

"But, wait a minute," said Gibson. "That means that he's somehow found a way to smuggle the uranium into the country. But how? On the cargo plane from Tel Aviv?"

"We always figured it would be by boat," said Cooper.

"Yep," agreed Foster. "That was the way we had always modeled it. He'd sail it into a port somewhere."

"Well, if he got it into the country by plane, then he managed to get it past Homeland and customs inspectors," said Eaglethorpe. "Pretty lucky. I know there are some holes here and there, but that's still not exactly a slam dunk proposition."

"Exactly," said Kori. "Which is why he wouldn't have done it that way."

"What do you mean?"

"It's too risky, Chief. He wouldn't have gone to all this trouble and then left it up to chance, hoping he could sneak the uranium past the inspectors. He's too smart. Look, you guys based the model on the normal terrorist. There's nothing normal about Efron Carlisle. He's devious and calculating. He's diabolical. He found a way to fly the uranium in and he found a way to do it with the odds stacked in his favor. He used his money to put his own people on the inside, just like in Tel Aviv. Homeland, customs, baggage handlers, freight inspectors—whoever he needed. You have to remember, we only learned about this a few days ago with the burglary in Bayanovka. But Carlisle has probably been planning this for years. Probably ever since the fake plane accident. There's not a trick he's going to miss."

"She's right," said Eaglethorpe to the others. "He's been stacking the deck for quite a while. And you can bet his tracks into this country are untraceable. The fact is, he's here now. Somewhere. But where? Where in the United States of America is this bomb going to go off?"

"I think we need to assume he'd want the biggest impact, the largest amount of damage and death," said Foster.

"Agreed," said Cooper. "It's got to be a major metropolitan area. Like New York. Or maybe here in DC."

"Or Los Angeles or San Francisco," said Foster.

"Could be Chicago," added Gibson. "Or Seattle or Miami."

"Boston or Philadelphia, perhaps," said Vasquez, "or maybe—"

"Okay, okay," interrupted Eaglethorpe, "this is getting us nowhere. Let's face it. The best we can do is guess."

"Not necessarily," said Kori. "I think we can do better than guess."

"Explain."

"Look, we can't find Carlisle, right? So instead of us trying to find him, why don't we let him try to find us?"

"Meaning what, Briggs?"

"He knows we're on to him. But it's a game to him. He could have killed me and Any—uh … Agent Kovalev the other day at the Roth's place, but he didn't. It was enough for him to let us know he knows about us. He left that note just to have a little twisted fun with us. It's cat and mouse to him. All we need to do is keep being the mouse. You see? He'll show himself eventually."

"You mean we present ourselves as some kind of … bait?"

"No, not all of us. He knows most specifically about me. I suggest everyone continue with their ghosting. Everyone but me."

"But Briggs—"

"Chief, it might be the only way. We'll never be able to track him down and, even if we could, we'd probably be too late. Every day that goes by is another day closer to Yanovich putting the finishing touches on the bomb. Now, look, I'll continue as though everything is normal. I'll go about in broad daylight. I'll go back to my apartment. I'll drive my car. I'll use my cell phone. I'll even go into the office. I'll let him come get me."

"He'll kill you."

"Not if you are all watching me, too. From the shadows. He'll come for me and you'll be there."

"You're willing to do this, Agent Briggs?"

"What choice have we got, Chief?"

Eaglethorpe looked around the room at the other faces, hoping someone would jump in with an alternative, one that wouldn't put his top agent's life in jeopardy, but his gaze was met with silence. "It's … Kori, it's going to be dangerous."

"Nature of the job, Chief," Kori smiled. "That's why I get the big bucks, remember? Besides, I'm not worried at all. With you guys watching over me? What could go wrong?" Inside, she wanted to believe her confidence was justified. And in any other situation, it would have been. These were the best agents in the world. But this wasn't any other situation. This was Efron Carlisle, the most dangerous man on the face of the planet.

CHAPTER 16

The following morning, Kori drove her Tesla to the office just like normal. She spent close to two hours there, mostly drinking coffee and playing solitaire on the computer. Then she left, got into her Tesla, and drove up and down various DC streets, checking her rearview mirror, certain that Efron Carlisle would be following her. She couldn't say she was exactly *hoping* he'd be following. Of course, that was the goal. But allowing Efron Carlisle to follow her was probably the most perilous thing she'd ever done as a Rampart agent. And Kori Briggs had done some perilous things.

It helped that she knew the other agents were out there, too. Gibson and Vasquez positioned themselves outside the office. As she drove, she knew that Cooper was perpetually three cars behind her. The route had been predetermined and Foster and Eaglethorpe positioned themselves at various checkpoints along the way, leapfrogging each other along the course. Eaglethorpe would drive a few miles ahead, park at a certain spot, get out of his car, and take a position somewhere where he could get a higher view of the roadway, maybe on a hillside or out of the upper floor window of an office building. When Kori's car passed, he'd move on to a spot farther along the route, with Foster taking a position in between. They'd note the cars following Kori's.

Kori spent a full afternoon on the road. None of the agents spotted anything. Nobody was following. Finally, she went back to her apartment. Vasquez had gotten there first, driving slowly along the street in front, checking out the parked cars, and then, finally, walking around the grounds and the lobby dressed as a maintenance worker. Everything was clear when Kori entered.

Gibson, meanwhile, also dressed as a maintenance worker, had positioned himself on her floor, pretending to be working on the hallway lights. He'd seen nobody come or go. Kori passed him after getting off the elevator, nodded at him quickly, then entered her apartment.

Once inside, there was nothing to do but pour a glass of Scotch and start thinking about dinner. She called a gourmet pizza place a few blocks away and ordered their specialty, a thin crust number topped with spicy tandoori sauce, red onions, and green peppers. By the time she made the call, Foster had been sitting in the restaurant's parking lot for twenty minutes, watching customers come and go. Cooper was inside, finishing off a calzone. It was not a stretch to believe that Kori's phone calls were being hacked. Consequently, they'd all agreed on the pizza place beforehand. For the time being, there wasn't going to be much of Kori's life that was going to be spontaneous.

Both Cooper and Foster could attest that nobody suspicious had come or gone from the restaurant. Eaglethorpe, meanwhile, showed up in time to follow the delivery person from the restaurant to Kori's building. Vasquez and Gibson kept their eyes on him from there.

Kori finished half the pizza and put the rest into the fridge for later. She turned on the TV and tried to get interested in the news, but it seemed to her as if they were the same stories as the day before and the day before that. Finally, she turned on an old Katherine Hepburn–Spencer Tracy movie and fell asleep on the sofa, waking around midnight and forcing herself to get up and make the trek into the bedroom, where she disrobed and climbed into bed, feeling safe knowing that the other agents were taking shifts in both the hallway and out in front of the building.

For three days, this was more or less Kori's life. Driving to the office, driving around the city, visiting various restaurants, and hanging out in her apartment, giving the impression of normalcy. And for three days, nobody had attempted to follow her. She started thinking she had a greater chance of running into her mother somewhere than in having Carlisle attempt to get to her. She rehearsed possible excuses as to why she was home and not in Colorado at a team-building exercise, but she could never settle on something that didn't sound completely lame. Just got home? Was ill and had to cut her trip short? Would have called, but her phone wasn't working? Finally, she just went ahead with her daily movements, leaving it to fate and hoping that if her mother accidentally bumped into her, she'd be able to come up with something believable in the heat of the moment. She always thought best under pressure anyhow.

Meanwhile, she knew that those three days were three more days that Ivan Yanovich had to turn the stolen uranium into a bomb for Efron Carlisle's use. *Maybe this is a waste of time*, thought Kori. Maybe Carlisle was so certain of the untraceability of his whereabouts that he figured Rampart wasn't even a factor. Why spend resources on stopping a pursuer that isn't even close to you?

But on the morning of the fourth day, driving along the Southwest Freeway, with Cooper once again following, Kori noticed a tan Crown Victoria two cars behind her that seemed to be copying her every move, changing lanes when she did and speeding up or slowing down to maintain the same distance. Could this be what they'd been waiting for? Was Carlisle finally making a move? The morning rush hour had mostly abated; the traffic was heavy, but moving. "Coop," Kori said into the radio clipped onto her steering wheel, "do you see the Crown Vic?"

"I got him," replied Cooper from behind her. "Right in front of me. Two males. But neither looks like Carlisle."

"Probably delegated the job of killing me," Kori said. "Finally. I was getting bored. Okay, so where do we want to take these guys?"

Eaglethorpe was up ahead two exits. "Take 'em to South Capitol Street," he chimed in. "A couple miles south is a convenience store on the northwest corner of M Street. Pull in there. I'll be waiting."

"Roger that, Chief."

"Foster, Vasquez, Gibson," said Eaglethorpe, "you guys copy that? Everyone meets there. Let's go. Let's give these losers a most cordial welcome."

The agents all replied affirmatively and Kori began looking for the exit that would put her on Capitol Street. She moved into the right lane and noticed the Crown Victoria doing the same. Now there were no cars between hers and the Crown Vic. Nearing the exit, she put her right turn blinker on and, sure enough, the Crown Victoria followed suit.

Then, within fifty yards of the exit, she noticed a different car approaching rapidly from the rear, a white BMW X3 sports utility vehicle. It swerved around the right side of the Crown Victoria onto the shoulder and then came up alongside Kori's Tesla, blocking the exit ramp. With no choice, she stayed on the freeway, bypassing the exit. In her rearview mirror, she could see the Crown Victoria following her, bypassing the exit as well, his turning signal now dark. The BMW settled back behind the Crown Vic and soon started fading even farther back. Cooper, meanwhile, had been too far back to see what had happened and got off the exit, assuming Kori was still in front of him.

"Kori," he said into his radio, "where are you? I've lost visual."

"I missed it!" she radioed back. "I missed the exit. Damn it!"

"What happened?" said Eaglethorpe.

"Some idiot in a Beemer almost got me killed," she said. "That's what happened. Came up alongside me on the shoulder. He blocked the exit. Can you believe that? All of this concern about Carlisle and I'm going to meet my demise in an everyday freeway accident by some knuckle-head who doesn't know how to drive. What the hell is the matter with people?"

"Keep going," said Eaglethorpe. "We'll rendezvous at the next exit."

Kori moved to the center lane, but through her rear-view mirror, she could see that the Crown Vic was falling back. It was now several cars behind her and slowing down. "I'm losing them," Kori reported. "They must have gotten spooked. They know they've been spotted. Damn!"

Kori slowed down and soon saw two semi-trucks coming up behind her in the right lane. She let the first pass her on the right and then slid into the lane between them, hopeful that the Crown Vic hadn't seen the move. The lane was moving much slower than the other lanes and it was the perfect spot to hide out. Sure enough, about a minute later, she spotted the Crown Vic in her side mirror, still in the middle lane, moving up fast. It wasn't until it was almost even with her that the car's occupants noticed her Tesla. She tried to get a look at them but all she could see were two middle-aged men.

Kori wondered for a moment if they might take the opportunity to run her off the road, but instead, they kept their heads down and passed her by. *Enough of this stupid game*, she thought. Once the Crown Vic was past her, she swerved back into the middle lane, right on its tail.

"I'm now in pursuit," she said into the radio.

"Agent Briggs," said Eaglethorpe, "wait for backup."

"No time, Chief. These chumps are mine."

The driver of the Crown Vic, realizing they were now being pursued, sped up, shifting into the far left lane and hammering the gas pedal. Kori followed, knowing the Crown Vic was no match for her Tesla.

"Agent Briggs!" Eaglethorpe said, "don't mess with these guys alone! Wait for us to rendezvous with you."

"Too late, Chief. I've got 'em on the run. You're more than welcome to join the chase, but I think you're too far back and we can't afford to let 'em go. This might be our only chance."

"Well … what's your plan?"

"I'll run 'em off the road, pull 'em out of the car, and then beat Carlisle's whereabouts out of them. Unless you've got a better idea, Chief."

Knowing he had nothing really constructive to offer, all Eaglethorpe could muster was, "Be careful, Kori."

"Roger that, Chief."

As the next exit quickly approached, the driver of the Crown Vic made a desperate move, veering right and crossing all three lanes of traffic to make the exit. But Kori did the same, following them off the ramp and onto an access road. From there, the Crown Vic made a hard right turn onto a street that cut through an abandoned industrial park. There was no traffic now, just the two cars flying down a long straightaway.

Kori inched closer to the Crown Victoria until she was finally able to nudge the rear of the car, causing it to spin out into a grassy field, mud flying everywhere. The car kept spinning until finally it hit sideways against a light pole. Kori pulled up close and jumped out of the Tesla with her Glock pointed at the windshield of the crashed vehicle.

"Out of the car!" she screamed. "Get your asses out of the car!"

Slowly the front doors opened and the two shell-shocked occupants of the car stepped out, hands in the air. Neither was Carlisle. *Two of his henchmen,* thought Kori. *How many rules will I have to break to get them to tell me where Carlisle is?*

"Don't shoot," the driver said. "You don't know who you're messing with."

"I have a pretty good idea," said Kori. "But why don't you tell me anyway?"

The driver hesitated, looked over at his accomplice, and then said, "I'm Agent Ralph Moore. This is my partner Earl Watson. We're with the CIA."

CHAPTER 17

On the floor of another warehouse in another part of the city, the members of Rampart once again sat in a semicircle around Eaglethorpe.

Two hours before, Kori had made Moore and Watson lie down flat on their stomachs. "Please don't shoot us," Watson had blubbered. "Then please don't follow me," Kori had answered with a mocking smile. "That's the best way you can prevent yourselves from being shot." She was certain their car, in the state it was in, wouldn't function, but, taking no chances, she had taken their keys. Then she'd gotten back in her Tesla and had driven off, leaving the two CIA agents in the unenviable position of having to explain how their government-issued car, the keys of which they had lost, had become involved in an accident with a light pole in the middle of an abandoned industrial park.

Back together, the group was going over the chain of events.

"I don't think the appearance of the white BMW was an accident," said Eaglethorpe.

"I think I have to agree with you, Chief," said Kori. "At first, I thought it was just some aggressive driver looking for a way around me to hit the exit. But he stayed behind me, even as I missed it. He never intended to get off the freeway. His purpose was to make sure I didn't, either."

"But why?" said Vasquez. "Let's suppose the Beemer was Carlisle. Why not just follow you off the exit?"

"Who knows?" said Eaglethorpe. "Maybe he wanted to take Agent Briggs to somewhere specific. Maybe they had an ambush set up somewhere."

"Or," said Kori, thoughtfully, "maybe he knew you were all waiting for me if I got off at that exit."

"Meaning our communications were compromised," said Cooper.

"Looks that way," said Kori.

"But it's not like we were on a standard radio frequency. We had those transmissions routed through our own secure servers."

"Well, they hacked in somehow," said Eaglethorpe. "Agent Cooper, upgrade our system immediately. Tear it down and rebuild it. That's what we pay you guys for. Whatever you think is the most secure you can make our communications system, I want it ten times more secure than that. Understood?"

"Yes, sir," said Cooper.

Foster spoke up. "Okay, so Carlisle effectively kept Kori from hooking up with all of us, which otherwise would have presented him with some difficulties. But why stop the chase? Once he made her miss the exit, he had her alone. Why did he fall back?"

"Not quite alone," said Eaglethorpe. "There was still the Crown Vic. I think he probably started out with the intention of intercepting Kori, but then he must have suspected that the other guys were CIA or some kind of law enforcement agency. Smart man. Why expose himself any further? It's bad enough for him that *we're* chasing him. So he gave up, probably figuring he'd try another time. The real question is, what do we do now? Carlisle's not going to let himself be lured into a trap a second time. He now knows we're using Agent Briggs as bait."

"So we need another strategy," said Cooper.

"We need more than that," said Kori.

"Explain, Agent Briggs," said Eaglethorpe.

"Well, we're assuming that Carlisle is going to expend all his energy in trying to find me, or us. To get rid of us. But he's got bigger fish to fry. He's got Yanovich building him a nuclear bomb. He knows now that we know he's here. In this city. If I'm Carlisle, I'm not spinning my wheels trying to get to us. I'm hightailing it out of here. When he gave up the chase, he probably drove directly to wherever Yanovich was, loaded him and his uranium into the Beemer, and took off. He's already wasted precious time and effort trying to stop us, and, as much as I'm sure he enjoyed his little cat and mouse game, he's intelligent enough to know where his focus needs to be at this point. I'm telling you, he's gone."

Cooper nodded. "Yep. And that was over two hours ago. Probably took some time to get everything packed up, but he's still got a big jump on us."

"I could make a call and have roadblocks set up everywhere," said Eaglethorpe. "Stop and search every white BMW X3 leaving the area. But he's too smart not to use another vehicle. We'd never find him or stop him."

"So now we're back to the original problem," said Vasquez. "How to narrow down the search for where he's going to set off the bomb."

The agents sat quietly. For the longest time, no one said a word. Finally, Kori spoke up. "We'll find him," she said, "the way that we find ninety percent of the bad guys."

"How's that?" said Eaglethorpe.

"He'll make a mistake. He'll trip himself up. He'll show himself. Someone will say something. Mark my words."

"I hope you're right, Agent Briggs. The stakes are high. If you're wrong, we'll eventually find him in the worst possible way."

"What's that, Chief?"

"We'll find him by spotting the inevitable mushroom cloud."

Back in her apartment, Kori shed her clothes and slipped into her whirlpool tub, made foamy by the Laura Mercier bubble bath. The hot jets felt wonderful on her aching body. It had been a long, frustrating, depressing day. Eaglethorpe had eventually sent everyone home. Continued discussion was getting them nowhere. He ordered everyone to reconvene at yet another off-site location early the next morning. Still taking no chances, the other agents retired to their secure, alternate locations, with the exception of Vasquez and Gibson. Eaglethorpe decided Kori should remain in the open on the off chance that Carlisle might make another attempt to get to her, long shot though that might be. Vasquez and Gibson followed Kori home and were guarding the entrance to the building.

Kori slid completely underwater and then brought her head up to notice in the candlelight of her bathroom the flashing of her agency phone. *Now what?* she thought.

"Briggs," she said into the phone.

"Hello, my American friend," said a warm Russian voice.

"Anya! How nice to hear from you. Where are you calling from?"

"I am still in Israel. I stuck around and decided to follow a hunch. And I have news, Kori. Big news."

"What, Anya?"

"Jael Roth. He is still alive. Moreover, I have spoken to him."

"No way!"

"Yes. As we suspected, Carlisle tried to have him killed. As far as Carlisle knows, he succeeded. Jael is in a Tel Aviv hospital in critical condition. He was shot four times and left for dead in a ditch by the side of a road outside the city. Somehow, he crawled up onto the road and was spotted by a passing motorist. He's been in intensive care for several days, close to death. He's not expected to make it."

"Hmm … a simple gunshot killing? That doesn't sound like Carlisle. I remember thinking woodchipper."

"It wasn't Carlisle. It was somebody working for Carlisle."

"That makes sense, Anya. Carlisle is here. In Washington. Or at least he was."

"No, Kori, he is not there. He never was. That is my news. I went back to see the Roths today and that's when I learned that Jael was in the hospital. I was able to see him tonight. He was fading in and out of consciousness, but he was able to speak to me. I just left the hospital. Carlisle is in France, Kori. So is Yanovich and the uranium. That is where he is planning on detonating the bomb. He means to destroy the city of Paris."

"Are you sure, Anya? Can we trust Jael?"

"He is dying and he knows it. He has no reason to lie. He was sincere; I could tell. Besides, he might be an anarchist, but we can assume he is no longer a fan of Carlisle."

"True. But why Paris? We've assumed the US. I was followed today, Anya. If Carlisle's not here, somebody working for him sure is."

"He probably knew you would assume the US. If someone followed you, it was to throw you off the track."

"Well, it worked. I would have bet my life savings on him wanting to make his statement on American soil."

"Apparently not. As to why Paris, I do not know."

"Did Jael say where, specifically?"

"No. But there is a man there. He is an anarchist whom Carlisle had mentioned. That is all I know. It's not much to follow up on, but it's something."

"Anya, how does an all-expenses-paid trip to the City of Lights sound?"

"I can be on the next plane."

"See you there, *mon amie*."

It was decided that Kori go on to Paris alone to meet up with Agent Kovalev. Once Eaglethorpe heard the news, he put a plan in place. The rest of the Rampart agents would come out of hiding and go back to their routines, signaling to any of Carlisle's people that Rampart was none the wiser and that they all still believed the target would be Washington, DC. A plane full of agents on the way to Paris would have the opposite effect. Once Kori could confirm the presence of Carlisle in Paris, only then would the other agents follow. But Eaglethorpe wasn't convinced. "How do we know Carlisle told Jael Roth the truth?" he had asked Kori when she'd called him after hanging up with Anya. "Maybe he was using Roth as a way to disseminate inaccurate information." Kori had to admit that she didn't have a good answer. Having it heard it straight from Anya, Kori sensed it in her bones that Carlisle was in Paris, but she knew that that was not enough to convince the chief of Rampart.

At 2 a.m., Vasquez took Kori to the airport and put her on a private jet. Then he went back to her place, setting up timers for lights and the TV to give the impression to anyone watching her apartment that she was still there.

On the jet, Kori called her mother, telling her the team-building exercises in the Rocky Mountains were going well. "I managed to slip away to a spot with cell service," she said. "I can't talk long, though."

"Well, when will you be home, dear?"

"Oh, probably in a few days. Yes, I promise we'll get together for dinner. Give Baxter a scratch for me. Love you, Mom."

At around 5 p.m. Paris time, Kori's plane touched down at Charles de Gaulle airport. Twenty minutes later, she was in the city. She perked up like a tourist as her taxi wound around the Arc de Triomphe and then proceeded down brick-paved Avenue Marceau. She loved the French architecture, the five- and six-story, cream-colored, limestone apartment buildings—the so-called Haussmann buildings, named after Georges Eugène Haussmann, whom Napoleon III had appointed in the 1860s to oversee the redevelopment of Paris. Kori loved the lack of tall buildings. Nothing in the city was allowed to be higher than eleven stories. The taxi went by crowded outdoor cafés and bistros, then toward her hotel, finally arriving at the Four Seasons on Avenue George V.

Kori checked in and found Anya in the lobby bar working on a plate of various cheeses and a vodka martini. The bartender came over to where they were both seated and Kori pointed at Anya's drink. "*J'aurai ce qu'elle a,*" she said.

"*Bien sur, madame,*" the bartender replied, going off to mix the drink.

"So you speak French, as well as Russian?" said Anya.

"*Un peu,*" said Kori. "A little. Truthfully, I speak seven languages."

"I feel so incompetent," said Anya, smiling. "I speak only six. I will have to take up another one, Agent Briggs."

"Indeed, Agent Kovalev," Kori smiled back.

"All in good time, I suppose. First, we should probably concern ourselves with saving this beautiful city."

"Well, someone has to," said Kori. "Who better than us?" The bartender place Kori's martini in front of her. "*Merci.*" She waited for him to retreat behind the bar and said, "So what have you got so far, Anya?"

Anya pulled out her tablet and opened it to reveal a picture of a man with a square face, pockmarked skin, unruly eyebrows, and long sideburns.

"Who's this beauty?" said Kori, picking a piece of Laguiole off the cheese plate.

"This is Gustave Trémaux. The man Jael Roth told me Carlisle had mentioned. Until recently, Trémaux was a member of *Le Désordre*, a French anarchist group."

"Until recently?"

"I had Blake do some digging. Trémaux was ousted from the group."

"How come?"

"Apparently he was too much of a … how do you say? … loose cannon."

Kori chuckled. "I thought that was the point. He's an anarchist. They're all loose cannons."

"Yes, but I suppose even amid disorder, there must be some order. The other members of the group deemed him too dangerous. He wanted violence. He preached a complete teardown of existing political structures and he argued that there was no price too high to pay, even if it included the death of innocents. He had, that is to say, become a terrorist."

"Perfect guy to hook up with our favorite psychopath," mused Kori.

"Yes. If Carlisle is here, Trémaux is probably giving him safe refuge."

"So where do we find him?"

"I have arranged for us to meet with the head of the Paris directorate of intelligence and security of defense. He is a contact Blake made after the Alfawda attack here a few years ago. He thinks we are CIA. Blake has told him only that we are interested in Trémaux. He knows nothing of Carlisle. I think it wise for now to keep Carlisle a secret, yes?"

"Agreed, Anya. Director Eaglethorpe and I have discussed this. We can't risk Carlisle's plans getting out. First, we don't even know if we're right about his being here. Second, imagine the panic that would ensue. Maybe in time, we can come to trust this French agent. *If* we decide that reinforcements are necessary. For now, I think we have to proceed alone. The quieter this operation can be, the better."

"Yes," said Anya. "Then again, if Paris is in danger, then should not the French be informed? Think about it, Kori. What if the French had intelligence that a terrorist was targeting New York City? I think we would want to know this, yes?"

"I don't necessarily disagree, Anya," said Kori. "But all in good time. Yes, the target is in France, but the terrorist is an American. When it gets right down to it, we're the ones who let him loose. We assumed he was dead. This is a mess we made and we have to clean it up ourselves. If we can. If we can't, we'll ask for help. In the meantime, this contact of Blake's can help us find Trémaux. Trémaux will lead us to Carlisle. We'll take Carlisle out, grab the uranium, arrest Yanovich, and go home. Goodbye, mess. Easy-peasy."

"What could go wrong?" smiled Anya.

"Exactly," grinned Kori. "Okay, let's finish our drinks and go see this guy of Blake's. *Le plus tôt sera le mieux.*"

"Yes," Anya agreed. "The sooner the better."

CHAPTER 18

Kori had always been especially fond of the concept of hiding in plain sight. Anya apparently felt the same way. If Carlisle somehow suspected that Rampart had tracked him to Paris, the last place he would think to look for an agent would be in a crowded tourist spot. Hence, Anya had arranged for the meeting with the head of the Paris directorate of intelligence to take place on the observation deck of the Eiffel Tower.

The sun was setting by the time Kori and Anya made their way to the deck. They walked to where they had the best view of the Seine and watched as the sun began to drop behind the city's horizon. The view was magnificent and there was a gentle warm breeze and Kori knew that if she allowed herself, she could easily get swept up in the magic of an evening in Paris. But there was work to be done.

"He will meet us right here," said Anya. And then, as if reading Kori's thoughts, "It is beautiful, no?"

"Indeed," said Kori. "I have always loved Paris."

"You've been here often?"

"Not often enough, I'm afraid. And always on business. There is never time to relax."

"Yes," sighed Anya wistfully. "But this is the life we have chosen."

"Do you ever regret it, Anya?" asked Kori. "Do you ever regret not getting a regular civilian job and settling down somewhere and leaving the problems of the world for others to solve? Get a home in the country somewhere? Take vacations to the shore?"

Anya was thoughtful for a moment. "Sometimes. Yes, of course. You?"

"Sometimes," replied Kori.

"And would you have anybody to settle down with?"

"Presently, no, I'm afraid. There have been men, but I'm a bit of a loner, I suppose. Independence makes men nervous. And you?"

Anya nodded. "My boyfriend back in Moscow. Nikolai. Perhaps one day we will settle down. It is hard, though. I understand what you mean. We are similar, you and I. Nikolai understands my need for space. But he does not know what I do. He thinks I am with the Russian

Commerce Agency. My presumed job is to bring industry to Russia from other countries."

"Good cover. Explains the traveling."

"Yes, but it is not good to be unable to confide in the man you love."

Now, Kori was thoughtful for a moment. "We all carry secrets," she said at last.

From behind them came a voice. "*Excusez moi, madames.* Can you tell me … is that the Pont de Bir-Hakeim bridge?"

The man pointing toward the bridge below them was handsome, with neatly combed dark hair, a chiseled face, and broad shoulders.

"*Oui,*" said Anya. "Do you like bridges, *monsieur?*"

"Well, they are good for getting … "

"From one place to another," Anya said, finishing the code phrase.

"*Bonsoir,*" said the man, lowering his voice. "I am Marc Chardin from the directorate of intelligence. At your service, *madames.*" Chardin reached out and shook Anya's hand and then Kori's, holding Kori's hand for a long moment and looking into her eyes and smiling.

"Monsieur Chardin," said Kori

"*S'il vous plaît,* call me Marc." The smile remained and Kori noticed his light dimples. She was a sucker for dimples.

"Marc. Thank you. Marc, as I'm sure Blake explained to you, we have been sent here to find Gustave Trémaux."

158

"May I know the reason, uh … "

"You can call me Kori."

"Kori. *Merci.* May I know the reason, Kori?"

Kori kept to the agreed-upon script. There would be no mention of Carlisle or anything even remotely related to him. "Strictly an American matter," she said. "We're not here to interfere at all, please understand. It seems that he has been in contact with a US citizen who has a bit of a bone to pick with our Internal Revenue Service. This citizen is here. He has made some threats. Nothing too serious, but we feel that Trémaux may shed some light on his exact motives and movements. He may give us the evidence we need to proceed with an arrest and have this citizen brought back to the States. At the very least, we think he can lead us to our suspect. We anticipate being out of your hair within twenty-four hours."

"Hmm … pity," smiled Chardin. Kori smiled back. Chardin continued, "Well, of course, we have been keeping an eye on Trémaux. There are rumblings that he has been contemplating terrorist activity."

"So I understand."

"There has been nothing so far. Nevertheless, we keep him under routine surveillance. Frankly, notwithstanding what our sources tell us, he seems fairly harmless to me. His bark, as they say, is bigger than his bite. Word on the street is that he was bounced out of *Le Désordre* not so much for his violent tendencies as because, well, he was simply too obnoxious to be around."

"So where can we find him?" Anya asked.

"There is a café in Montmartre in which Trémaux hangs out," Chardin replied. "He rents a flat not far from there, but he is in the café more than he is in his flat. It's practically a second home to him. He will be there at this time of the evening. If you *mademoiselles* would like, I would be happy to take you to this café. It's a bit on the rustic side, but it is not without its charms. If you're hungry, it has a menu that is not altogether unappealing. And at night, they play live jazz."

"*Oui*," said Anya.

"*Oui*," agreed Kori. "Sounds delightful." The three began walking toward the elevator. Kori turned back around and scanned the horizon once more, not so much for a final glimpse of the view, but for a thought that popped into her head: *He's out there … somewhere.* Then the three left the deck and descended to the ground. They walked a few blocks to Chardin's car and drove off into the Paris night.

Twenty minutes later, the three were in the café, sitting at a small table. It was a dimly lit place with red brick walls and a low, black ceiling. Chardin bought a round of drinks—a gin and tonic for himself, a vodka martini for Anya, and a Scotch for Kori—while a jazz trio played on a small stage in the corner of the café. Most of the tables were full and a group of young men and women were standing at the bar, immersed in some kind of conversation that was creating much laughter among them.

"I don't see him in here," said Chardin, looking around. "Strange. I would have bet a hundred euros that he would be here."

Anya and Kori exchanged glances, both knowing what the other was thinking: If Trémaux wasn't there, it was probably because he was with Carlisle. But where? Paris was a big city and Trémaux was their only lead. They needed to find him.

"Maybe we should check out his flat," said Kori. "Where is it?"

"Seven Rue Girardon. Not too far from here. Ah, but, wait, there he is." Chardin nodded almost imperceptibly toward the door where a tall, lanky man made his way in. He glanced about the café, but the lighting was such that Kori couldn't get a good look at his face.

"Are you sure that's him?" she said. "That's Trémaux?"

"Oh, I'm sure. That's Gustave Trémaux all right."

The man jostled past the group of young people to get to the bar and by the time he got there, the bartender had already poured him a bourbon. The two exchanged a few words and then Trémaux must have said something amusing because the bartender laughed. It was clear these two were not unacquainted with each other.

"So now what?" Anya asked.

"Now we wait," replied Kori. "We have to see where he goes from here."

"How do we know he won't simply go back to his flat at the end of the night?"

Kori thought for a moment. "Marc," she said, "tell us about Trémaux's apartment. Is it big enough to hold two more people and some ... laboratory equipment?"

"No, it's quite small, actually," Chardin answered. "A first-floor studio. One room, plus a bathroom. There's barely enough room for one person. But why do you ask about the laboratory equipment?"

"Oh, nothing. Just curious."

Chardin furrowed his brow.

Anya stepped in. "It's possible this man we are after might be manufacturing drugs."

"I see," said Chardin. "You know, this sounds as if it might be a matter for the police. If you'd like, I could make a call to the local constabulary."

"Oh, no, that won't be necessary," said Kori.

"It would be a very simple matter."

"I'm sure. But, as I said, our major interest is the IRS charges. Tax evasion. Strictly an American affair."

"Yes, but you see the drug manufacturing is—how do you say?—a different ballgame. This would now concern the Paris police. Perhaps we should be involved."

Kori regretted bringing up the laboratory equipment just as Anya was regretting using the drug manufacturing story. Chardin had suddenly turned serious. Too serious. Both knew that it was too soon to involve the French authorities in Carlisle's master plan. If anything,

Chardin's involvement at this point would only complicate matters.

Kori did some quick thinking. "I'm afraid we might have misspoken," she said. "You see, the drug thing is merely a wild theory that my colleague here has been floating, mostly, it seems to me, to amuse herself. There is no evidence of it at all, and yet she continues to flog this ludicrous idea. It actually has become something of an annoyance, if I may speak frankly."

Anya picked up on the ruse. "Ludicrous?!" she shouted. "An annoyance?! How so? He is a known tax evader, a scofflaw. He obviously cares nothing about the normal rules of society. Why would it be so surprising that he would turn to making drugs? It's a perfectly natural assumption."

"I keep telling you, Anya, we need proof. *Evidence.* You know? Something that can actually be admitted into a court of law? We have nothing on him. Oh, and don't bring up your senseless *gut feel* to me. How is that helping?"

"Instinct is a big part of the police process, Briggs. Isn't it, Director Chardin?"

The last thing Chardin apparently wanted was to get in the middle of the argument. "Well, I, uh—"

"You might know something about instinct, Briggs," Anya continued, "if you had any of your own."

"Oh, really?" said Kori, now pretending to seethe. "I have no instinct for police work? Is that what you're saying?"

"Ladies, ladies," chuckled Chardin, deciding to break in after all. "Please. This seems like nothing to fight about. You apparently have him on the tax charges, correct? Whether there are drug charges as well is something you will learn, no doubt, in time. I will say only that if you need our help, we will gladly step in. Until then, I trust you know how best to proceed."

"Thank you, Director," Kori said.

"Of course. Now, if you'll excuse me, I find myself needing to use the men's room. Why don't I send our server back over, and let us have another round of drinks."

Chardin rose and walked toward the restroom. When he disappeared, Anya and Kori broke into laughter.

"That was a close one," said Kori.

"Too close," Anya agreed. "We need to lose Director Chardin, I believe."

"Too bad," said Kori. "He's not too hard to look at, I must say. And charming, in that distinctive French way."

"Nevertheless. He cannot know why we are here. He has brought us to Trémaux and we do not need him anymore. At least not yet."

"You're right, of course. At this point, all he'd do is slow us down."

"In the meantime, we now know that Carlisle and Yanovich cannot be staying with Trémaux. It seems as if there is hardly room for three to sleep in his place, let alone set up the equipment necessary to turn a hundred pounds of uranium into a bomb."

"They're probably hiding out in a warehouse some-where," said Kori. "Maybe on the outskirts of the city. Or even in the French countryside, for all we know. At this point, we have no choice but to follow Trémaux. We have to hope he leads us there. It's our only play."

"But I wonder why he is here tonight," said Anya. "Why is he not with them, helping?"

"Carlisle's smart. If he thought we had somehow picked up on the Trémaux connection, he might have told Trémaux to keep to his regular routine. It would look suspicious if he *didn't* come here tonight. Besides, what could he help with? The nuclear stuff is Yanovich's domain. He's probably not letting anybody else anywhere near the uranium."

"Yes, that's probably true," said Anya. Then, looking suddenly uneasy, she said, "Kori, if you're right that Carlisle wanted Trémaux to stick to his routine because he thought we might be onto him, then Carlisle would also be smart enough to have Trémaux tailed, to see if we are following him."

The thought made Kori's blood run cold. "Cripes, Anya, you're right. Some of Carlisle's people could be here right now," she said. "Or even Carlisle himself."

The two turned and slowly looked around at the other patrons of the café. Nobody seemed to be looking their way. Most were engaged in conversation, sharing laughter and bottles of wine. Some were focused on the jazz trio, tapping their feet and keeping the rhythm. *Parisiennes, all out for a good time*, thought Kori. *Nobody with any idea of what might befall their beautiful city.*

"I do not see anyone suspicious," said Anya.

"Neither do I. Just the same, when we follow Trémaux out of here, we'll need to make sure we're not being followed ourselves. We need to keep our eyes open."

"Yes. In the meantime, how do we lose Chardin, handsome though he is? Here, he is coming back."

"I've got an idea. Just play along, Anya." Kori pulled out her phone and put it to her ear. As Chardin approached the table, she began speaking loudly into it. "Are you sure, Chief? Are you sure it's him? Excellent! Well, then I guess our work is done. Tell the guys congratulations from us. Great job all around. Right. Okay, see you back at the hotel."

Chardin took his seat.

"Well, Marc," said Kori, "I'm afraid we have brought you out for no reason. It seems the other members of our team have nabbed our guy. We are to rendezvous with them back at the hotel and then we are on the first flight back to the States. Everything is all wrapped up very neatly. We are, of course, sorry for any inconvenience."

"Nonsense," said Chardin. "It has been my pleasure to share a cocktail and some fine music with two such beautiful ladies."

"*Merci*. I only wish we had more time to spend here. This has been a very fine evening. Perhaps we'll cross paths again someday."

"I hope so. And I am glad that you have found what you came here for. Please allow me to give you a lift back to your hotel."

"I'm afraid we've burdened you enough already, Marc. Besides, our chief has sent a car. It should be here very soon."

"Well, then, at least let me wait outside with you until the car shows up. It's the gentlemanly thing to do."

"Oh, that is really unnecessary," said Anya. "We will be fine."

"Sorry," smiled Chardin, "but I cannot allow you to wait by yourselves. I will not take no for an answer. Here, let me settle the bill and then we will be on our way."

Kori and Anya could see that there was no arguing with Chardin. They would simply have to leave the café with him and wait out front for a nonexistent car. They glanced at each other, each with a look that said, *Now what do we do?*

The three left the café and stood outside on the sidewalk for a minute or so watching the traffic go by before Kori tried once more. "Really, Marc, this is not necessary. It was gracious enough for you to have paid for the drinks. We're holding you up. The car will be here any moment."

"I assure you, it is no problem. It is such a beautiful night and it is good to be out here with you both."

The traffic light in front of the café turned red just then. Anya elbowed Kori and pointed to the first car stopped at the light and said, "Isn't that our ride there?"

"Yes," said Kori, "I believe that's Roger at the wheel. Hi, Roger!" She waved at the solitary male driver who, taken aback, involuntarily waved back. "Well, Marc, again, this has been fun. If you're ever in the States."

"Yes," added Anya. "Delightful. Thank you for your help."

Before Chardin could reply, the two women stepped off the sidewalk and darted toward the stopped car, opening the backdoor and piling in just as the light turned green.

"*Aller*," said Kori, with a flirtatious smile. "Go, *mon belle homme*."

The driver, who was not a handsome man as Kori said, but instead a chubby man with a round face and oval glasses, smiled back and proceeded through the light.

"*Bonjour, mademoiselles*," he beamed, scarcely believing his luck. And then he asked what two beautiful women were doing out by themselves on such a night and would they, perhaps, like to go somewhere for a drink or maybe even back to his place, which wasn't far, and was clean, even quite stylish, he assured them, as he was certain he had a nice bottle of wine or two in the house that they could share together, and wouldn't that be marvelous, the three of them together, drinking wine in his stylish place?

Anya and Kori nodded and then glanced at each other, neither one needing to say what they both had in mind. About a half mile from the café, the round-faced man stopped at a red light and without any further ado, Kori and Anya bolted from the car.

"*Au revoir*," Kori said behind her.

"Wait!" the man yelled after them. "Where are you going?" And then the light turned green and the cars behind him began honking, forcing him to move onward, wondering why the two beautiful women had entered his car only to leave so abruptly, and thinking how cruel life could be.

"Kori," said Anya, after the two had ducked down a side street, "let's go around the block. If Chardin took the same route we did, he might see us doubling back to the café."

"Agreed," said Kori. They chose an alleyway that ran perpendicular to the main avenue that the café was located on then came upon it from the other side. Out front, they looked all around but saw no sign of Chardin. The agents entered the café and moved toward an empty table near the wall. Chardin was gone, but so, it seemed, was Trémaux.

"Where could he be?" said Kori after they sat down.

"We were not gone that long," said Anya.

"Fifteen minutes, tops."

"Perhaps he is in the men's room."

"Let's hope. I don't see him anywhere else."

The two waited, ordering drinks from the server while looking around for Trémaux and keeping an eye on the restrooms. Five minutes went by. Then ten. Then fifteen.

"We're wasting time," said Kori finally. "I'm going in." She rose from the table and headed toward the men's room. Without any hesitation, she pushed the door open and walked in. An older man with a stunned expression was standing at one of the small bathroom's two urinals. "*Je suis désolé*," she said. "So sorry." Then she pushed open the door to the lone stall, only to find it empty.

Returning to the table, she said, "He's gone, Anya. We lost him. We lost the only man in Paris who could lead us to Carlisle."

CHAPTER 19

"This is the address," said Kori. "Seven Rue Girardon. This is where Chardin said that Trémaux lived. But if he's not here, then it's back to square one." The two stood in front of a three-story rowhouse, a ten-minute walk from the café.

Anya peered inside the window. "It's dark. I don't think he is home, but perhaps there are clues."

"Right. Let's go in," said Kori. "Let's see what we can find." She pulled her lock pick out of her purse and with a quick jiggle the door was opened.

Anya found a light switch on the wall and flicked it on to reveal a cramped and cluttered room, books and magazines stacked on the floor, clothes carelessly strewn over a sagging sofa, empty wine bottles here and there. "Not exactly luxury," she said.

"Apparently, anarchists don't live very well," said Kori.

"There, his laptop," said Anya, pointing toward a small wooden table in the corner. She walked over and opened the laptop and powered it on. "It's password-protected."

"Nothing's ever easy, is it?" said Kori. "Can you get in?"

"Of course." Anya dug into her purse and pulled out what looked to Kori like a thumb drive. She inserted it into the computer and in less than ten seconds, announced, "I'm in."

"Slick. What do you have there?"

"A de-encryption device. Do you not have one of these?"

"No, but it's certainly going on my Christmas list."

The two hovered over the screen as Anya browsed around documents, pictures, and videos. She searched the name "Carlisle," and words like "uranium" and "bomb" but found nothing. She opened his browser and scrolled through his history.

"Cripes," said Kori, "this guy seems like he's way more interested in porn than politics."

"Yes, some pretty strange stuff, too," said Anya. "He seems to like Russian women. I suppose I should be flattered."

"Or grossed out."

"Yes, that."

172

"Strange that there are no links to any anarchist sites. No links to anything political, in fact. And, Anya, check out the books around here." Kori meandered around the room, picking up various books and leafing through them. "Baudelaire, Flaubert, Proust, Voltaire. And American authors, too. And look, books on literary theory. They look like textbooks. What the heck kind of anarchist is this guy, anyway?"

"Nothing incriminating in his emails, either," said Anya, still scrutinizing the laptop. She was about to say something about the name that Trémaux was apparently using in his emails when the door burst open.

"Hey!" said a male voice, "what are you doing in my flat?!"

Anya and Kori swung toward the door. A man stepped in, tall and lanky, the same man from the café, but now the light was on him and both agents could tell it was not the face Anya had on her tablet, the pock-marked skin and long sideburns. This man had a long, thin face with a clear complexion, and short blondish hair. Kori figured he was in his early twenties. Trémaux was closing in on forty.

Kori was taking no chances. She pulled out her Glock and leveled it at the man. "Gustave Trémaux?"

The man's hands instinctively went up in the air. "Eh?"

"Are you Gustave Trémaux?"

"Who? Gustave? What? *Non.*"

"Then who are you and why are you here?"

"My name is Geoffroy Clair. I live here. Please do not shoot me. Take anything you like. I don't have much, but you are welcome to it."

Kori could see the young man beginning to shake. She lowered the gun. "Let me see some identification, Geoffroy."

With trembling hands, the young man pulled out his wallet and handed Kori his national identification card. "He's who he says he is," said Kori, turning to Anya.

"That explains his email address," said Anya. "Geoffroyclair08."

"What are you doing on my computer?" said Clair. "Who are you two? What do you want?"

"Geoffroy," said Kori, smiling reassuringly and putting the Glock away, "what do you do?"

"I'm a graduate student. I'm studying literature at Université de Paris. Next year I hope to be an assistant professor."

"You can put your hands down, Geoffroy."

"*Merci.*"

"Do you know a man named Gustave Trémaux?"

"No. I have never heard of this man."

"How long have you lived here?" asked Anya.

"About two years. Why? Why are you asking me these questions?"

"Have you ever seen this man?" Anya pulled her tablet out of her purse and showed Clair the picture of Trémaux.

"No. I've never seen him in my life."

"Think, Geoffroy," said Kori. "Around the neighborhood? In a shop? At that little jazz café you frequent?"

"How do you know … no, I've never seen him. I swear. Now, what's this all about, *s'il vous plaît*?

Kori looked over at Anya, who could offer nothing but a shrug.

"Nothing," said Kori. "Wrong apartment, apparently. *Pardonnez-nous.*"

The two moved toward the door. Kori smiled on the way out and gestured back toward the open laptop. "By the way, you ought to get yourself a girlfriend, Geoff."

The young man blushed. "*Oui*," was all he could say.

"Is it possible that Chardin mistook this poor graduate student for Trémaux?" said Anya. The two were back at the bar at the Four Seasons, Anya with a vodka martini and Kori back to her Scotch.

"I think we both know that's hardly likely," said Kori. "The two look nothing alike. Chardin did his homework. He found some sap, found out where he lived, found out where he hung out, and then purposely put us on his trail to mislead us."

"For what reason? It makes no sense. Why would the Paris directorate of intelligence want to mislead two agents he assumes are American CIA?"

"Maybe he didn't buy the fact that we're CIA."

"It was Blake who told him we are with the CIA. Certainly he trusts Blake. The two worked closely together during the Paris Alfawda attack."

"Maybe he didn't buy the IRS story. Or … or maybe he didn't want us coming into contact with Trémaux."

"But why?"

"Maybe he's got intelligence that Trémaux is up to something. Heck, he might even have some kind of inkling about Carlisle. Maybe he's surveilling Trémaux. Perhaps he thought our following Trémaux would interfere with his own agency's work. He could have been afraid that we would have unwittingly tipped Trémaux off."

"But then why would he not tell us that?" Anya asked. "Why would he not want to enlist the help of the CIA if he fears Trémaux to be a threat?"

"Well, sometimes, especially early in an investigation, it's wise to keep your cards close to your vest. Think about it. Why are we not enlisting the help of French intelligence?"

"Yes, I see what you are saying. Still, there had to have been a better way than to lead us on, how do you say it? a chase for a wild goose."

Kori sighed. "Agreed. And such a good-looking guy, too. Did you notice the dimples?" Just then her phone rang. "It's Blake," she said, looking at the screen. "Returning my call. Let's see what he can tell us. Blake?"

"Hi, Briggs," came Agent Blake's voice. "Did you make contact with Chardin?"

"We sure did. That's what we want to talk to you about. Your man gave us a red herring, purposely misidentifying our suspect and having us break into some schmuck student's flat in the middle of the night for no reason at all."

"What? Briggs, what are you talking about? That doesn't sound like Marc. Are you sure?"

"We're sure all right. He took us to a little jazz club where he pointed out a guy as Trémaux and even gave us his address. Only problem was, it wasn't Trémaux. We had a couple drinks, gave Chardin the slip, then went to the address—"

"Wait, you all had drinks?"

"Yes."

"Chardin, too?"

"Sure. I think he had a gin and tonic."

"Kori, Chardin doesn't drink."

"No?"

"No. What did this guy look like?"

"Tall, good-looking, dark hair, dimples, broad shoulders."

"Kori," said Blake in a sudden serious tone. "I think we have a problem. Chardin is short, pudgy, balding. I don't know who you met with, but I can assure you that it wasn't the Paris directorate of intelligence."

"I see," said Kori. For several long seconds, both were quiet, each coming to grips with the new reality of the situation. Finally, Kori said it out loud. "Then our operation has been compromised."

"Yes," said Blake. "Our operation has been compromised."

CHAPTER 20

Blake gave Kori Chardin's home address and Kori and Anya wasted no time getting there. For the imposter to have known to meet the agents at the Eiffel Tower and, further, to know the code phrase, he must have gotten to the real Chardin. Did he hack into his phone? Computer? Blake was certain it was Chardin he had talked to the day before to arrange the meeting. Of that, there was no doubt. Chardin knew where to meet and what code phrase to use. How did the imposter get the information and, more ominously, what did he do with Chardin? After Kori had hung up with Blake, Blake tried reaching Chardin but got no answer.

Now, Kori and Anya stood outside of Chardin's home, a twenty-minute taxi ride from the Four Seasons across the

Seine and into the neighborhood of Chatou. The house was a modest, two-story stone home, but modest as it was, Kori knew it was still close enough to the city to be worth well over two million in American dollars.

The house was dark and so was the street, the moon and a single lamppost fifty yards down the lane the only sources of any light. Kori knocked loudly on the front door and then, hearing nothing, knocked even louder.

"I don't like this," she said. "I've got a bad feeling."

"Let's go in," said Anya.

Kori picked the lock and the two stepped inside. Anya turned on a table lamp near the door to reveal a living room in a state of disarray. A chair was turned over and a glass coffee table lay in shards. A lamp was resting on the floor and so was the small porcelain sculpture of a horse, broken in two, the carpet underneath soaked in dark red, the distinctive color of blood.

"Director!" Kori called out, looking around, the sound echoing off the dark walls. "Are you here?" No reply. She pulled out her weapon and Anya did the same. They walked stealthily around the first floor of the house, from the living room into the dining room, then the kitchen and a bathroom. Kori poked her head out of the back door which led into a small, fenced yard but nothing looked amiss.

"Let's go up," Kori said, and the two ascended the stairs to the second floor. Three bedrooms, none of them disturbed.

"I saw steps through the kitchen leading down to a cellar," said Anya.

"Me, too," said Kori. "I guess that's where we're headed next."

This time through the kitchen, Kori found a switch that operated two sections of track lighting and now, in the brightness of the kitchen, they could see the tracks of blood leading to the cellar staircase. They both paused at the top.

"*Après vous*," said Kori, managing a grim smile.

"No, no," said Anya. "I insist. After you."

Kori nodded and reluctantly made her way down the creaky wooden steps, Anya following right behind. In the dim light coming down from the kitchen, Kori spied a string hanging from the pull chain of a single lightbulb fixture on the ceiling. She yanked it and the small cellar lit up. Heaped in the far corner, looking as though it had been tossed there like a rag doll, was the bloody body of a short, pudgy, balding man. "I think we found the director," said Kori.

The murder of the Paris directorate of intelligence was all over the news the next day. Kori had called it into the Paris police using her best French accent, telling them she was a passerby who noticed some suspicious activity at the directorate's home. The police discovered the body and immediately kicked the case up to France's intelligence agency. But there was no keeping it secret. Crime scene investigators and forensics teams were all over the place. So were media vans and TV reporters.

On a call with Eaglethorpe from the hotel around daybreak, Kori wondered aloud if they shouldn't engage French intelligence in the hunt for Efron Carlisle and his hundred pounds of stolen uranium.

"I mean, Chief, they're kind of involved now, anyway, right? They're going to be digging into the director's murder, spinning their wheels and wasting a lot of time. We can help. Together, we can find the imposter that Agent Kovalev and I had drinks with, and we can all work together to track down Carlisle from there."

"Yes, but Briggs, right now nobody knows Carlisle is alive but us," said Eaglethorpe. "More to the point, nobody besides us knows what he's planning on doing. I'd prefer to keep it that way. We've talked about this. If what we know were to leak out to the media, think about the consequences, the sheer panic. Look at the media circus that's going on there right now. Image a city the size of Paris with its entire population trying to evacuate at once. And we have to be honest; we still don't know for certain that Carlisle is even there."

"Well, how do you explain last night's ruse and the murder of the director? Obviously, someone is trying very hard to keep us from finding Trémaux, our only real lead, our only potential Paris link to Carlisle."

"I hear you, Kori. But there's no guarantee that French intelligence could even help us. They may even make things worse."

"How so?"

"Cooper and Foster ran some models. Well, here, I'll let Cooper explain it."

Eaglethorpe placed the call on speaker and Kori heard Cooper clear his throat and jump in. "Well, the fact is, we anticipate a greater than fifty percent chance that Carlisle would detonate his bomb sooner, rather than later, if he knew that others besides Rampart were closing in on him. Fifty-nine percent, to be exact. Meanwhile, since the French authorities would be starting from scratch and have to be brought up to speed, thus costing valuable time, we anticipate only a thirty-two percent chance of the French providing any meaningful help at this point. Moreover, the inclusion of another law enforcement agency would result in a greater than sixty percent chance of the potential attack being leaked to the public, thus creating a full-blown panic, the consequences of which, well, let's just say the numbers don't look good."

"Math," said Eaglethorpe. "Can't argue with it."

"I suppose you're right," said Kori. "But something Agent Kovalev said is nagging at me, Chief."

"What's that?"

"What if the roles were reversed and French intelligence had reason to believe a US city was the target of a potential nuclear explosion? What if a couple of French agents were nosing around Washington, trying to find a nuclear bomb? We'd sure as hell like to know about that, wouldn't we? Wouldn't we claim that we have the right to know?"

"I understand what you're saying, Kori. And I don't necessarily disagree that, notwithstanding the numbers, perhaps the French should be informed. But for now, keeping this to ourselves comes strictly from the top. I briefed POTUS yesterday. He wants us to solve this. Between you and me and the lamppost, I think he's worried about how we'll look on the world stage if it got out that we bungled Carlisle's presumed death so badly. We let a madman loose. Nevertheless, the president does have his limits on this. He's giving us twenty-four hours, after which, he's going to place a call personally to the French president."

"I understand, Chief."

"But remember those numbers that Cooper and Foster calculated. Our best bet is for you and Kovalev to find Carlisle first. That's the ideal scenario and the one we need to shoot for."

"Right, Chief. And believe me, finding Carlisle is quickly becoming my number one goal in life. But to do so, we still need to find Trémaux. He's still our only decent lead."

"Yes, I'm going to get on top of that myself. We haven't been able to find anything useful about Trémaux here. No residence, no family information, no employment record. The guy must live pretty much off the grid. But, if the director knew his whereabouts, so do other members of the French intelligence. And if French intelligence knows, then our own CIA knows. At least that's what they're getting paid for. I'm going to make a call to the president. He can worm the information out of the CIA. Probably, we should have done that from the start, but Blake making contact with the Paris director meant far fewer people involved and a much straighter line to Trémaux. The CIA is going to ask questions. They can be a nosey bunch, as I think we all know. But I don't see that we have much of a choice at this point, do you?"

Kori thought for a moment. "There might be another way, Chief," she said.

"What's that?"

"Well, we know that Trémaux used to be a member of *Le Désordre.*"

"The French anarchist group."

"Right. We must know from our own files who the head of the group is, right? And where they operate from?"

"I'm sure I could have Foster text you a name and address, of course. But how could they help?"

"They had a falling out, right? Trémaux got booted out of the group. From what I understand, it was not a decision reached mutually. That might make Trémaux dangerous to *Le Désordre*. He's supposedly on the violent side, right? Nobody would have a better reason to keep an eye on him than *Le Désordre.*"

"Well, yes, that makes sense, but what makes you think they'll talk to us? We're government. We're law and order. We're everything a good anarchist stands against."

"Chief, think about it. You could be the most anti-government person in the world, wishing every day for a complete breakdown of the current order, but if someone were to tell you that millions of people were about to be killed and an iconic, beloved city destroyed, wouldn't you help?"

"You know whom you just described, Briggs? Anti-government, wishing for a complete breakdown of society? Efron Carlisle."

"Yes, but Efron Carlisle is something else, as well, Chief. He's a psychopath, a sadist, a member of the dark tetrad. The head of *Le Désordre* is still a human being. Heck, maybe even a family man. Remember, *Le Désordre* wanted Trémaux out because they didn't agree with his violent methods."

"You really want to confide in the head of *Le Désordre* about Carlisle? About the uranium?"

"Well, we don't necessarily need to get into the details. And besides, we know he's not likely to go to the police with the information."

"He could go to the media."

"They'd never believe him. An anarchist spouting about a dead man come back to life to irradiate the city? Chief, he might be the one guy we *can* confide in."

Eaglethorpe was quiet for a moment, turning the idea over in his head. "Okay, Briggs," he said at last. "I'll get with Foster and have the information to you pronto."

Kori hung up and turned to Anya who had been listening in on the conversation. "So, wanna interview an anarchist?"

"Sure. As long as we can stop along the way for coffee."

"We have twenty-four hours to find Carlisle, Agent Kovalev," replied Kori sternly. Then she smiled. "There's plenty of time for coffee."

CHAPTER 21

Ten minutes later, a cab dropped Kori and Anya off at Rue Saint-Laurent, no more than an alleyway that ran between two major boulevards. The sun was now higher in the sky and the city had come to life again. It was shaping up to be another beautiful summer day in Paris. Both agents had ducked into a bakery and grabbed espressos. As they walked down the street, they were also chowing down on brasillés—flaky, sweet, puff pastries. Both Kori and Anya were in need of sustenance and sleep. The brasillés would take care of the former and the espressos would have to substitute for the latter.

They stopped in front of an unremarkable storefront.

"This is the address," said Kori. "This is where *Le*

Désordre works out of. They publish a weekly paper and originate their online content here, according to Foster."

"Doesn't look like much," said Anya.

"No, but Foster says this group has quite a large following. Lots of angry, frustrated people out there, I guess. Anyway, the guy we want to talk to is Léon Millet."

"Well, what are we waiting for?"

The two entered a small foyer beyond which they could see a conventional-looking office with several desks, three of them with people sitting behind computers, tapping away on keyboards. Anti-government posters were plastered on the walls and the smell of burnt coffee drifted in the air. Upon Kori and Anya's entrance, one of the workers looked up.

"*Puis-je vous aider?*" he asked.

"Yes, you might be able to help us," replied Kori. "We're looking for Léon Millet. We'd like to speak with him. It's a matter of some urgency."

"Indeed. And what is your business with Monsieur Millet?"

"We're hoping he knows the whereabouts of someone who used to be affiliated with your organization. Gustave Trémaux."

At that, the others looked up from their work. Without saying a word, the first worker rose from his desk and walked toward the back of the office, knocking on the door of a room marked *Privé*: "Private."

"*Entrez,*" came a voice within. The worker stepped inside and closed the door behind him. Moments later, a tall, slim man with close-cropped hair, a stubbled face, and a serious expression came out. Kori and Anya stepped into the general office area without waiting to be asked.

"I am Millet," said the tall, slim man. "And who are you?"

"My name is Briggs and this is Kovalev. May we speak privately?"

Millet said nothing for a moment and then waved them back toward his private office. Inside, he gestured for them to sit in the chairs that were facing his large, wooden desk, stacks of papers and worn, dog-eared books resting on top of it as though they'd been there forever. Millet sat down and said, "So. Who are you with?"

"We're with the United States government," said Kori.

"I see. Why are you looking for Trémaux?"

"We have reason to believe he's planning a massive terrorist attack." *No reason yet,* thought Kori, *to invoke the words "Efron Carlisle" or "nuclear."*

"I must say, this is hardly surprising to me," said Millet. "The man has been going off the rails for some time now. You realize he is no longer working with us, *oui*? In fact, he has been unaffiliated with us for some time."

"Yes, we know," said Anya. "But we believe you might know where he is."

"It is possible," Millet shrugged, noncommittedly.

"Monsieur Millet," said Kori, "what do you mean by going off the rails?"

189

"Gustave Trémaux was beginning to suggest violence as a means by which to get the people's attention to our cause. He had become quite … adamant about it, in fact."

Kori couldn't resist. "And? Is this unusual for an anarchist?"

Millet winced as if in pain. "We stand for freedom, Mademoiselle Briggs, not violence," he said loudly, and then his voice became progressively louder as he spoke. "We stand for equality, and emancipation of all individuals from the bondage of tyrannical, capitalistic societies ruled by the elite and structured into unnatural hierarchies held in place by corrupt governments. We most assuredly do not stand for violence. You would know this if you were not so blinded by your foolish allegiance to your own corrupt government and beholden to its bogus propaganda!"

"Thanks," smiled Kori. "I'll keep that in mind. Maybe I'll subscribe to your newsletter."

"Monsieur Millet," said Anya, sensing that the conversation itself was going off the rails, "can you help us?"

Millet collected himself. "What is Trémaux up to exactly?" he said.

"That is what we would like to know," said Anya. "We have some intelligence that says he may be involved with a terrorist group planning an attack on the city. An attack that could come very soon."

"What terrorist group?"

"We're not at liberty to say," said Kori. "But we were hoping you might know where we can find Trémaux."

Millet was silent for several seconds, struggling, the agents knew, with the idea of cooperating with a governmental law enforcement agency, especially one that represented the United States, the ultimate bastion of capitalism and all that *Le Désordre* stood against. "How big an attack?" he asked at last.

"Does it matter?" Kori replied. "How many lives would need to be lost before you'd consider helping us?"

"How many lives lost has your own government been responsible for?" Millet retorted. "How much genocide and murder and oppression from your imperialistic invasions and occupations, not to mention the subjugation of your own people at the hands of—"

"Big," said Anya. "It is going to be a big attack, Monsieur Millet. The lives of thousands are at stake, perhaps hundreds of thousands."

"Is this true?"

"It's true, Monsieur Millet," said Kori. "Someday, perhaps we can sit down, you and I, over a bottle of your favorite French wine and we can discuss history and governments and geopolitics. You can throw Proudhon and Déjacque at me, and I can toss back Locke and Jefferson. I would like nothing better. But I'm afraid we're up against the clock right now and every second counts."

"You seem very well read, Ms. Briggs."

"Yes, well, a girl needs her distractions. But today, lives are at stake, Monsieur Millet."

"Okay," said Millet quietly. "I understand. Of course. Nobody wants to see that kind of harm. Well, let's see—Trémaux has a chateau in the countryside, about an hour from here on the road to Chartres. That might be a good place to start. It's a huge, nineteenth century monstrosity. The perfect example of conspicuous consumption, made manifest on the backs of common laborers for someone's luxurious amusement, no doubt."

"No doubt," said Kori.

"Yes, well, anyway, Trémaux inherited it. It has been in his family for five generations. Trémaux comes from money, which he more less has rejected, but for some reason he never divested himself of the family manor. He hangs out there when he is not here in Paris, although God knows why. It is a cold, lonely place. Not to mention its historical connections with wealth."

"Are you sure about this chateau?" said Kori. "We would have been able to easily search for a piece of property tied to Trémaux, but our people have found nothing."

"It is not in his name, you see. Years ago, he put it in the name of *Le Désordre*. We used to meet there quite often. It was a place where we could get out of the city. To plan, to strategize, to keep a lower profile when the situation warranted it. He more or less donated it to us for our use. I couldn't say whose name the chateau is in now. We wanted nothing to do with Trémaux after we expelled him from the group and so I signed away any rights that *Le Désordre* might have had in the property. But we have kept an eye on Trémaux, driving out there from time. He has been living there. I can say this for certain."

"So you know this chateau?" asked Kori.

"*Oui.*"

"Do you know it well?"

"As I said, we spent quite a bit of time there."

"Monsieur Millet, could you please sketch out a general plan of the property—a floor plan, a sketch of the grounds?"

"If you think it would help."

"It might help a great deal."

Millet pulled out a sheet of paper and drew a rough plan of the first two floors of the chateau, jotting down the property address along the top of the page. "There is an upper third floor, but I have never been up there. I believe it's mostly bedrooms. There are bedrooms on the second floor, too, along with a storage room and a music room. There is a cellar, too. Gustave used to retrieve wine from there, but I have not been in the cellar, either." As he was sketching, he called out to the outer office. "Henri!" he said. The worker who had met Kori and Anya when they'd first come in appeared in the doorway.

"*Oui?*"

"Go to the map application on your computer and print out a satellite picture of the Gustave's chateau for these mademoiselles." The worker retreated to his desk and came back a minute later with a printout, handing it to Millet, who passed it to Kori, along with his floor sketches. "Here you are ladies," said Millet. "Floor plan and image of the grounds."

"Thank you, Monsieur Millet," said Kori.

"You are welcome," said Millet. "Good luck to you." Then he became thoughtful and added, "You know, there was a time Gustave and I wanted the same thing. He was a good friend of mine. In fact, probably my best friend. But no matter what you think of us, Mademoiselle Briggs, we wish nobody harm, certainly not the innocent. I cannot explain Gustave's actions. Perhaps he has his reasons, though certainly they escape my grasp. In any event, I am sorry that it has come to this. I am sorry that I must be the one to give him up, as it were."

"You're doing the right thing, Monsieur Millet," said Kori. "Oh, and I was serious about that bottle of wine."

Millet managed a smile, the first of his that the agents had seen. "I will look forward to our discussion."

Outside on the street, Anya pulled out her phone and entered Trémaux's address into her GPS. "Millet is correct. One hour from here. But that assumes a car."

"I don't feel like taking the time to rent one, do you?" said Kori. "Nor do I want to call for a driver."

"Then how will we get there?"

"Well, there are plenty of cars around," Kori said, waving her hand at the street in front of them, lined with parked vehicles. "Which one do you fancy?"

"Steal one, Agent Briggs?" smiled Anya.

"Borrow, Agent Kovalev. We'll find a way to give it back."

"Of course, Agent Briggs." Anya looked around. "Well, there are certainly plenty of good candidates. I do not like inconveniencing a civilian on a police matter, however. But up there just around the corner—is that a police car I see?"

"Indeed it is. That would be more appropriate, wouldn't it? And a siren would get us there much faster, wouldn't you agree? The advantages seem to favor the idea, and it doesn't appear as though it's occupied. I would bet the car's authorized occupants are in that bistro across the street having breakfast."

"I think you're right," said Anya, as the two walked toward the police car. "They'll see us from the driver's side. We'll both have to enter from the passenger side."

Kori and Anya ducked down as they approached the vehicle. Coming up to the passenger side, Kori tried the door, which opened. "Cops never think their own cars are going to get stolen," she said over her shoulder as she slid across to the driver's seat with Anya right behind her. Then she punched hard at the panel below the ignition, breaking it apart and revealing the ignition wires underneath. She dug into her pocketbook and pulled out a small wire stripper, a tool that had come in handy for her in the past on several occasions. In short order, she identified and stripped off the ends of the ignition wire and the battery wire. Touching the bare metal ends together, she heard the engine turn over and a moment later, she and Anya were on the road. Kori waited until they were out of earshot of the bistro and then she flipped on the siren.

"It's no Tesla and I've never really warmed up to the sound of the French siren," she said, as she weaved in and out of the Paris traffic, "but the price was right. I guess it'll have to do."

CHAPTER 22

Kori and Anya ditched the car about two miles short of the address of the chateau, electing to walk the remaining distance. It wasn't as if they could very well drive a police car up to the front entrance of the chateau. After a mile or so of walking, Kori called the police department and reported the location of the car, saying she was a passerby and that she'd noticed it looked suspicious. It was the second time she'd used that line in twelve hours. Fortunately, the dispatcher was a different person each time or they might have put two and two together.

"I'm always surprised by how quickly the urban turns to the rural here," remarked Kori as the pair walked down the country road in the general direction of the chateau.

"No matter where you are an hour outside of a city like New York, it still looks like a city. Office buildings, industrial areas, row houses. An hour outside of Paris and you think you're in another country."

"It's beautiful," said Anya. "Peaceful. Look there, beyond the wheat field. That old stone farmhouse. Probably a hundred years old, at least."

"Charming," Kori agreed. "I feel like I'm walking in a Monet painting."

"So where is the chateau?"

"According to the GPS, it's around the bend up ahead. There, is that it? Beyond that grove of trees?" Kori pointed to a large manor in the distance that sat upon a rise.

Anya pulled a small pair of binoculars out of her pocketbook and focused in on the estate. "Wow," she said. "Renaissance-style with a touch of late gothic."

"Oh yeah?"

"I studied architecture in school. Among other things. Yes, heavy masonry construction clad with stone. Check out the steep pitch of the roof and the parapet dormers on the ends. Huge chimneys and spires. Tall, arched windows on the first floor. It's a classic. It must have been some place in its day. Probably the envy of all the neighbors. Looks a bit rundown, though, at least from here. Too bad. So what is our plan?"

"Great question, Anya. Well, what do you think about knocking on the front door and asking if Efron Carlisle is home?"

"Hmm … maybe I can suggest a better plan," smiled Anya.

"I'm all ears."

"Let's work our way around the trees, toward the rear of the house. There must be at least several entrances to a place so big. They can't guard them all."

"I don't know about that, Anya. For all we know, Carlisle's amassed a small army by now. According to this satellite photo of the grounds, the land right around the chateau is pretty clear. Once you get past the trees, there are not many places to hide. If there's someone standing guard at each entrance, or maybe standing at one of those parapets on the roof, they'll see us coming for sure."

"What do you suggest?"

"The way I see it, we've got two choices. First, we can call it in. Get reinforcements. We can call Eaglethorpe, he can call the proper French authorities, and they can storm the place. Most likely, they'll send the *Groupe d'intervention de la Gendarmerie nationale*—the GIGN. Their elite tactical unit, their version of a SWAT team. But there's a downside."

"What's that?"

"Carlisle's people are going to be heavily armed. There's no way to storm a place that big without giving the occupants enough time to respond. And when they respond, it's going to get ugly. Could be a real bloodbath."

"Yes, I see what you mean. What is the other choice?"

"You and I go in. Quietly, stealthily, unseen."

199

"But what you said about the grounds around the house … they'll see us coming."

"Sure, at this time of day. But not at night. Not in the dark."

"We wait until night?"

"Yes. Normally, the advantage of darkness goes to the one who's most familiar with the terrain. That will be them, but it won't be that much of an advantage because we have an accurate floor plan we can study and memorize. If we can sneak up to the house unseen and find a way in, we can take them by surprise."

"Just the two of us? What it you're right about Carlisle having put together a small army? Whether we have the element of surprise or not, your Glock and my Sig Sauer aren't going to help us very much."

"Sure, but armies have to sleep. I'm not suggesting right after sunset. I'm thinking around 2 a.m. And besides, if they've got somebody on guard duty, they'll probably be looking for someone approaching in a vehicle. From the front. They'll be watching for police cars. We'll be sneaking through the trees and coming in the back. And the people inside are probably scattered all about the house. It's not like they're all going to be just standing at the door when we come in. We can do this, Anya. We can sneak in, grab the uranium, find Carlisle and Yanovich, and take them away at gunpoint before the rest of the household will know what's happened."

"You know, my friend, I think I like your idea of knocking on the door better."

"You think I'm being too bold?"

"I do."

"Dangerous?"

"Perhaps. A little."

"Well, my Russian friend, do you have an alternative?"

"Reconnaissance. That is why we are here, no? Not to save the day, although that would be nice, but to determine the lay of the land. We will have to call this in eventually, Kori. It is the only way. The stakes are too high to gamble. You are right that storming the chateau could end in a—how did you say?— bloodbath. But we can lessen the risk if we can report to the GIGN where in the chateau the uranium is, where Carlisle is, where Yanovich is, how many others there are, where they are stationed, how they are armed, where the best entrances are, etcetera. So we split the difference, you see. We break in at 2 a.m., not to make arrests, but to scope the place out. We slip in, we slip out. And we give the GIGN the information and the edge they need."

"My way seems like a lot more fun," smiled Kori. "But you make a lot of sense, Anya. Okay, okay. Let's do it your way." She glanced down at her watch. "We have some time to kill. About twelve hours, in fact."

"The GPS says there is a small village where the road splits off up ahead, in the opposite direction of the chateau, about a half a mile. There is a bed and breakfast there with a small restaurant. '*L'Auberge.*'"

"Some food and rest sounds like a great idea to me. Shall we?"

L'Auberge was a French Tudor-style inn that happened to have a couple of rooms available on its second floor. There was a fine restaurant on the first floor, but small, with only eight tables; four of them currently occupied, including the one at which Kori and Anya sat. There was a stone fireplace in the restaurant and a wood-beamed ceiling. Old oil paintings adorned the walls. The agents were working on a bottle of sauvignon blanc from a winery not too far away, and eating duck—"our specialty" the proprietor had assured them.

"I didn't realize how hungry I was," said Kori between mouthfuls. "And she wasn't kidding about the duck."

"Indeed," said Anya. "And I didn't realize how thirsty I was. I love this wine."

"It really hits the spot, doesn't it? We'll have time for a nap, too. I'm glad we found this place."

Before their late lunch, the agents had checked in with the proprietor, an older, portly woman with charcoal gray hair who had smiled warmly at them and introduced herself as Madame Duchamp. The rooms were rustic but charming. They had beds in them and, besides lunch, that was all Kori and Anya really cared about. They knew they wouldn't be staying for long.

Dessert was *poire belle Hélène*—pears poached in sugar syrup with ice cream and melted chocolate. Neither agent could turn it down.

"We'll eat a light dinner," laughed Kori.

"Yes, after this, I suppose we will have to," said Anya.

"I'll call the chief after we're done here and let him know our plan. It'll be his decision as to what to do after that. I imagine he'll call the president who will call the French president who will call the GIGN. That'll be it then. The secret of Efron Carlisle's being alive will be out there. So will the knowledge that he has a nuclear bomb on the outskirts of Paris. Let's hope to God the information doesn't leak to the public. But the French need to know. And our reconnaissance might save the day."

"Unless Carlisle is not there," said Anya.

"What do you mean?"

"I have been thinking, Kori. Let us be honest, we have been making a lot of assumptions, starting with the assumption that Carlisle is in France with Gustave Trémaux."

"That's what Jael Roth said. To you, Anya. On his deathbed."

"True, but that is not evidence. That is a lead and we are wise to follow to see where it goes, but it is not more than that at this point. Jael mentioned Trémaux as a possibility. It was a name Carlisle had spoken of, an anarchist and presumably a dangerous one. But as sincere as Jael seemed, he himself did not know if there was any more to the connection."

"Well, someone was certainly disturbed that we were getting close to Trémaux," said Kori. "It cost the Paris directorate of intelligence his life."

"Again, a solid lead, but no more. Besides, we are assuming that Carlisle would be manufacturing his bomb at Trémaux's chateau. In truth, he could be anywhere. You yourself had mentioned that they could be in a warehouse somewhere for all we know. In which case, we have a lot of looking to do and very little to go on."

"I see what you're getting at, Anya, and I don't necessarily disagree. We both concur that the French have a right to know, but we don't want to make an international case out of a hunch, even if it's a good one. The less chance of a leak to the public, the better. I'm with you. But we've at least got to tell the chief where we're going tonight. In case … well, you know."

"In case we do not make it out of there."

"Yes. He'll at least know where to start looking for Carlisle. I mean, we have to hope the chateau has at least some kind of clue, even if Carlisle isn't there. Maybe just by digging through Trémaux's personal stuff we can find something. Anything. And no matter what, we'll still be within the twenty-four-hour window POTUS has given us. So we'll go to the chateau and check it out. If Carlisle and the uranium aren't there, then there will be no reason to send for the GIGN unit. Then again, if Carlisle is not there, we have bigger problems."

"Yes," said Anya. "If Carlisle is not there, and we can determine nothing from a search of the premises, then we'll have no idea where he is."

CHAPTER 23

The agents agreed to meet back downstairs at the restaurant at 8 p.m. Kori went back to her room and called Eaglethorpe, who agreed with their assessment. "But call me as soon as you've scoped the place out," Eaglethorpe had told her. "We're on pins and needles here." Then Kori lay down on the bed and slept, but only for a couple of hours. Once she awoke, she struggled with getting back to sleep, visions of Efron Carlisle coursing through her mind. She still hoped she and Anya could take him out themselves. Perhaps it was just him and Trémaux and Yanovich at the chateau, sleeping deeply in their beds. But she knew that was unlikely.

She thought about all the people who Carlisle had to have involved by now. The logistics of moving the uranium from Bayanovka were staggering. All along the way, there were customs officials who needed to be in on the plan, inspectors Carlisle had to have been paid off. Then again, none of that would have been a problem for Carlisle and his billions. How much would it cost to bribe an inspector to look the other way, an inspector who probably thought that the owner of the private jet in question was most likely just bringing cocaine into the country? None of them would have guessed Carlisle was smuggling uranium around the world. Cocaine? What's another few kilos against a payoff of 10,000 euros, or 50,000, or even 100,000? Carlisle could pay whatever it took.

And it was this modus operandi that assured Carlisle that he could have a veritable standing army at his disposal. The sociopathic anarchists like Trémaux that he surrounded himself with were probably only too willing to help. Carlisle probably hadn't even apprised the lower echelon soldiers of the uranium. Why take the chance? They were being well paid to guard Carlisle and Yanovich while most likely believing that the two were concocting some kind of explosive to blow up a building or a train depot, not a nuclear device to destroy an entire city. There are only so many people you can possibly enlist to help with something like that. Best to keep the true nature of the bomb a secret. Even still, the more people involved, the more risk to any operation. This was the only thing that gave Kori hope that the numbers at the chateau might be small.

This thought gave her an idea, something she knew she should have thought of before. She splashed some water on her face, ran a brush through her hair, and went downstairs to find the proprietor who was hovering around the dining room in apparent anticipation of anyone wandering in for an early dinner.

"Madame Duchamp," said Kori.

"Yes, my dear," Madame Duchamp replied. "Are you back already? I'm so glad you like our little dining establishment. How is your room? Feel free to take any table you like."

"Oh, no, thank you. As of this moment, I'm still quite satisfied with lunch. And the room is fine. I just wanted to ask you if you've ever seen this man in here." Kori showed Madame Duchamp a photo of Carlisle on her phone.

Madame Duchamp hesitated for a moment and then said, "Why, no, I'm afraid not."

"No? Are you sure?"

"Yes, quite sure. Who is he, might I ask?"

"Oh, nobody important. We were … supposed to meet him here." She scrolled to another photo, this one of Yanovich. "How about this man?"

Madame Duchamp shook her head.

"And this one?"

"Oh, well, yes, I've seen him. He owns that big chateau down the road. Gustave something. I knew the family."

"Have you seen him lately?"

"No. Not for a long time, I'm afraid."

"Are there a lot of other cafés or bistros around here?"

"There are just a couple. None so nice as ours," Madame Duchamp smiled proudly. "Everybody comes here. How did you like your duck?"

"Oh, very nice, *merci*. But you are sure you have not seen these men? And Gustave not for a while?"

"I am quite sure."

"And have you noticed any other strangers coming in here?"

"Well, of course, we get a lot of tourists in this area, my dear. It is wine country, you know. A wide variety of people pass through here all the time."

"Yes, of course, but I'm referring to people who might have been coming in here somewhat regularly over the past few days, but people who are not from around here. Not locals, but tourists who have remained for a time."

"Hmm … no, I can't say that I have."

"Thank you, Madame Duchamp. You've been very helpful."

A quizzical look passed over Madame Duchamp's face, but she nevertheless smiled politely. "You're welcome, my dear."

Kori walked out of the rear of the inn and sat on a bench that was part of a colorful patio. There were large flowerpots and string lights and a small, gurgling fountain at the center.

"I see you couldn't sleep much, either," came a voice behind her.

"Anya, hi. No, I'm afraid not."

"I have been thinking about the fact that Carlisle is here in France," said Anya sitting down beside Kori on the bench.

"And?"

"The initial thinking was that the uranium was being taken by boat somewhere. Now we know it has been flown here."

"Yes, I was thinking about that, too."

"Well, a boat would have taken much longer. Obviously. Maybe a week, maybe more. This means we have much less time to work with than we had originally thought. The theft of the uranium was almost two weeks ago. Yes, Carlisle took it through Tel Aviv where he had helpful contacts, and that most certainly slowed him down. Nevertheless, Yanovich has still had plenty of time to work on making the uranium into a workable bomb. He might have finished some of the work in Tel Aviv. Maybe he has only to put the finishing touches on it here. That is what I have been thinking. This is why I could not sleep."

"Yes, but on the other hand, we are closer to the uranium now. We know where it is."

"We think."

"Yes," said Kori. "We think. But, listen, Anya, I have some news. Maybe good, maybe bad. I talked to Madame Duchamp. Showed her pictures of Carlisle and Yanovich and Trémaux. She recognized only Trémaux, but said he hasn't been here for a long time. She's never seen the others and she also said that there haven't been any strangers coming in here on a routine basis lately."

"Meaning what exactly?"

"Meaning that if someone were staying in the chateau, isn't it likely they'd come into the village here for at least an occasional meal? I mean, would they stay cooped up in the chateau? No matter how secretive your work, you're going to want to at least get out of the house sometime, right? Madame Duchamp says there are a couple of other places, but I get the sense this is the place most people come to for a decent lunch or dinner and a bottle of wine."

"Yes. And if Carlisle had a full gang of people involved, she would have seen at least a few strangers coming and going in the past few days. This inn seems like something of a focal point around here."

"Which means that they're either keeping an extraordinarily low profile, or they're not here at all."

"Or they could be here, but maybe it is just Carlisle and Yanovich and Trémaux. A low profile is workable only with small numbers."

"Right. So if Carlisle is here, perhaps he's not surrounded by a slew of psychos. I feel better about sneaking into the chateau now."

"But the other possibility … that he's not here … "

"Yes, I'm starting to think we're running out of time, Anya. If he's not in the chateau, then we need to start looking elsewhere immediately. Suddenly, I don't want to wait until the wee hours to explore the chateau."

"Me neither."

"Right after sunset work for you?"

Kori and Anya had their light dinner topped off with a couple of espressos and started for the chateau just as the sun sunk behind the flat landscape of the French countryside. By then, both had memorized the floor plans that Millet had drawn up. They approached the chateau through the grove of trees that ringed the property, working their way around toward the rear of the building. The house was about forty yards from the trees. There were no exterior lights and the only illumination on the property was cast by the night's half-moon.

They paused and knelt down at the edge of the woods once they had a good view of the house. "There's not a single light on," remarked Kori. "It looks deserted. Damn."

"There are some interior rooms without windows," said Anya. "And don't forget the wine cellar."

"Right," said Kori. Then she pointed toward some shrubbery up against the building. "There. Let's hit that corner. We can take cover there. Then we can jump the balustrade onto the rear veranda and that will give us access to any one of those tall windows. A good a place as any to gain entrance, I would think. Hopefully, there are no motion sensors. The place is run down. If there's a burglar alarm system, it wouldn't surprise me that it's inoperable."

"Let us hope so," said Anya.

"Okay, ready? Let's go."

The two sprinted across the grounds toward the near corner of the building and crouched down behind the shrubs. The veranda was accessible from the formal steps that led up to it, but if anyone would be looking out of the windows, they'd easily spot the agents coming up the steps. The better idea was to climb the balustrade along the side of the veranda. The veranda was a good five feet above the ground and the balustrade was three feet above that.

"Here, give me a leg up," whispered Kori. Anya clasped her hands together under Kori's foot and boosted her to where she could reach the top of the balustrade. She pulled herself over it and then dropped to the deck of the veranda, remaining still for a moment before looking around carefully and seeing no movement. Then she rose and leaned back over the balustrade, grabbing hold of Anya's hands and pulling her up and over. The two sat on their heels and scoped out the back entrance.

"I suppose we could try those huge double doors," whispered Kori. "Probably a very old lock. But I'm inclined to try a window. If Carlisle did take the time to wire this place, he probably focused on the doors. I mean, there must be a hundred windows."

"Agreed," said Anya. "But they're all heavily draped. It would be nice to get a glimpse inside first, just to give us a little idea of the place. The floor plans are good, but they don't take into account furniture and so forth."

"Right," said Kori, looking around. "There. The drapes aren't quite closed all the way on that one. Let's take a look."

Both agents moved to one of the tall, arched windows, crouching underneath it. Kori poked her head up and took a glance between the drapes, a space of about eight inches. Then she crouched back down. "It looks clear. It's a large, deep hallway that runs parallel to the windows, just like Millet's diagram. That's all I could see. There's supposed to be a stairway to the left, but I couldn't tell from the angle. Nobody appears to be around, anyway. I still didn't see any light coming from anywhere. The place might be empty."

"Did you get a look at the windows themselves?"

"Yes. They're double-swing windows hinged to open vertically. They swing outward. There's a simple latch on the window and the glass looks to be about one-eighth inch thick."

"Got it," said Anya. "But just in case someone is around that you could not see, let's go in through the next window, where they will not see us between the closed drapes."

"Good idea."

They moved to the next window and Anya jumped up onto the block sill, taking a glass cutter out of her bag. She placed a small suction cup on the window adjacent to where the inside latch was and then traced a perfect circle around it with the cutter. She pulled on the suction cup and removed the circle of glass she'd just cut, stuck her hand in through the hole, lifted the latch, and gently swung the window open. Then she took a quick peek behind the drapes, saw nothing, and dropped inside to the floor of the hallway. Kori followed right behind.

Both stood looking warily about them. Kori shone her flashlight around the hall. It ran back twenty feet to two different doorways that the floor plans indicated opened into the formal living and dining rooms. There were a couple of old pieces of dusty furniture scattered about and an eclectic mix of paintings on the high walls. A wide stairway to the left led to the second floor. The place smelled stale and looked to Kori as if it had been empty for years.

"It's creepy in here," she whispered.

"And quiet," whispered Anya.

"Yes. Much too quiet. Well, we're not getting any younger. Let's take a little tour of Chateau Trémaux, shall we?"

CHAPTER 24

The agents decided to search the chateau systematically, starting on the third floor and then working their way down to the cellar. They slowly crept up the hardwood stairway, each with a flashlight in one hand and a pistol in the other. Though they tried to be as light on their feet as possible, they couldn't avoid the occasional creak under foot. Each creak brought them to a full stop and they'd listen intently for any noise at all that would indicate they'd been heard. Then, they'd start climbing again.

When they made it to the second-floor landing, Kori shone her light down the hallway toward the bedrooms but saw nothing. Then they continued up the stairs to the third floor, the one area of the house, beside the cellar, that Millet had never been.

"More bedrooms, it looks like," Kori whispered to Anya once they'd reached the top. "Well, one by one, I guess."

Unlike the creaking stairs, the hallway was carpeted, for which both agents were grateful. When they came to the first room, Kori moved to one side of the open door and Anya to the other. Then Kori crouched low and spun inside pointing her Glock while Anya simultaneously turned toward the room pointing the flashlight.

"Empty," said Kori. They walked around the room, but saw nothing but boxes, an old wooden chair, and cobwebs in every corner. "Okay," said Kori. "Next room."

They entered two more rooms in like manner, Kori entering with her Glock and Anya lighting up the room with her flashlight. Both rooms were as empty as the first. But the next door, at the end of the hallway, was closed, unlike the doors to the previous rooms. This time, Anya squared herself to the door and stood with her arms extended, pointing her gun at the door, ready to shoot whoever was on the other side. Kori angled herself to the side of the door, closed her hand over the knob, and very gently began turning it. There was no resistance and Kori knew it was unlocked. All that remained was for her to push the door wide open to give Anya a clear shot. She looked at Anya and Anya nodded—ready. Kori got down low, shoved the door open, and shone her flashlight into the darkness. But nobody was there.

They entered the room and walked around. This room was much larger than the others. It was cleaner, too, and fully furnished with an unmade king size bed, dresser, wardrobe, and two overstuffed chairs. The ceiling was peaked and there was a large dormer window that let in a diffused ray of moonlight.

"Look at the glass of water on the nightstand," said Anya. "Somebody's living in this one."

"*Oui!*" came a deep voice behind them. "And that somebody is me."

The agents wheeled around to see a dark figure in the doorway holding an automatic rifle. "Drop your weapons," the figure said. "Very carefully."

"Damn," said Kori under her breath. *How could this man have come in so quietly?* She tossed her pistol on the bed and Anya did the same. Then the man flipped on a light switch and in the light of the room, the agents could see the man's face, recognizing it immediately.

"Gustave Trémaux, I presume," said Kori.

"Who wants to know?" said Trémaux.

"Pleasure to meet you, Gustave. Say, what's that you got there? Looks like a Chinese Type 56."

"A poor man's Russian AK-47," added Anya.

"I'll repeat the question," said Trémaux. "Who wants to know?"

Kori moved ever so imperceptibly toward the wall to the left of the door where Trémaux stood. Anya moved ever so imperceptibly toward the wall to the right. Both were positioning themselves as far apart from each other as they could, dividing Trémaux's attention and testing the limits of his peripheral vision.

"Nice place you have here," said Kori. "But I'll bet the taxes are killer. And then, of course, there's the upkeep. Although I must say it doesn't appear as though you waste a lot of money on any kind of cleaning service."

"Perhaps Monsieur Trémaux is just frugal with his money," offered Anya. "I, for one, appreciate practicality in a man."

"Don't take another step," said Trémaux. "Neither of you."

"Oh, by the way, Léon Millet says hello," said Kori, and Trémaux raised his eyebrows. "He says they miss you around the office. The place just isn't the same without you. You know, the laughter and hijinks."

"Yes," smiled Anya. "In fact, they are thinking of closing down. Getting out of the anarchy business. They're thinking it's a dead end. They've been tossing around the idea of opening an art gallery instead."

"Yes, they sent us to get your thoughts on the matter," said Kori.

"They know you're a lover of art. Take this piece here for instance," Anya said, waving her hand toward an abstract oil painting on the wall behind her.

It was just enough to divert Trémaux's gaze for the split second that Kori needed. She took a long, smooth stride toward Trémaux, planted her left foot, leapt, and did a reverse spin with her extended right leg, catching Trémaux squarely on the jaw with her right boot. Trémaux went flying backward, loosening his grip on the rifle. Anya swooped in and grabbed it out of his hands, pointing it at him as he lay prone of the floor.

"Where's Carlisle?!" she demanded.

"I don't know what you mean," said Trémaux, pushing himself up to a sitting position against the wall.

"C'mon, you know," said Kori. "About yea high, white hair, crooked nose, likes to kill lots of people for no reason?"

"Don't make us search the rest of the house," said Anya. "We'll parade you in front of us, just in case one of your compatriots is a little trigger happy."

"Search the house, I do not care," said Trémaux, rubbing his jaw. "I do not know who this Carlisle person is you speak of. I have never heard this name."

This time, the sole of Kori's boot knocked hard against Trémaux's forehead and snapped his head back into the wall. "Are you sure you don't know him?" said Kori.

"Think real hard," said Anya, then she lowered the barrel of the rifle, pointing it right below Trémaux's belt. "You know, sometimes these Chinese knockoffs have a tendency to go off accidentally."

"Okay, okay," said Trémaux, now rubbing the back of his head. "I will tell you. Please stop pointing the gun."

Anya lowered the rifle.

"He was here," said Trémaux. "Now he's gone. To where, I do not know."

"Was he with Ivan Yanovich?" asked Kori.

"Who?"

"Don't play stupid, Gustave. The Russian mad scientist."

"I don't know who you mean."

Anya raised the gun up toward Trémaux's crotch again.

"Yes, yes," he said. "He was with Yanovich."

"Who else?"

"Just a couple of security people Carlisle hired."

"And you expect us to believe they all just left?" said Anya.

"They knew you were coming."

"That's impossible," said Kori. "No one knows where we are except my boss and we've only communicated through our just-upgraded server system. You guys might be smart, but you're no match for a 512-bit-key, triple-encrypted, reverse-algorithmed phone."

"We have eyes in the village."

"What do you mean?"

"Did you order the duck? It's their specialty you know."

"Madame Duchamp?!"

"*Oui.*"

"How could you possibly have gotten that sweet woman involved in this? I don't believe it."

"She's not *involved*. As it happens, she is an old friend of the family. She knew my parents quite well. She has no idea of my work or what we were doing here. I merely asked her to keep an eye on strangers coming through and asking questions. She was happy to do an old friend a favor. And, to be certain, we gave her a little … gratuity for keeping us informed. She runs a profitable establishment, but who couldn't use an extra 10,000 euros?"

"Anya," said Kori, "remind me to downgrade my Yelp review of L'Auberge."

Anya turned toward Trémaux. "So where did Carlisle's little gang go and why are you not with them?"

"It was thought it best to leave one of us behind. To intercept you." Trémaux looked sheepishly down at the floor. "I was supposed to capture you."

"That didn't work out so good, did it, scooter?" said Kori.

"Apparently not," said Trémaux, still looking down at the floor.

"But if Carlisle knew we were here," said Anya, "then why didn't he just come and kill us?"

"Too much commotion would not be good. Carlisle became a little concerned about all of the attention with the death of the directorate of intelligence."

"You mean the murder," said Kori. "And who was responsible for that? Carlisle himself?"

"The fake director. I believe you met him. Upon Carlisle's orders, of course. The point is, Carlisle felt things were getting too hot. Operations have been moved."

"To where?" asked Anya.

"I do not know."

Anya raised the rifle.

"It's true," said Trémaux. "I do not know. He was going to call me and let me know. I think he was undecided."

"Carlisle's never been undecided about anything in his life," said Kori. She raised her boot above Trémaux's head.

"I swear I do not know! You can kick me and beat me all you want and even shoot me, but I swear I do not know where they went. You must believe me!"

Kori lowered her foot to the ground. "Okay, Gustave. Then we just have one more question for you."

"What is that?"

"Where do you keep your duct tape?"

CHAPTER 25

After the agents had duct-taped Trémaux to his bed, they knew they needed to search the rest of the chateau. It was possible Trémaux was lying and that Carlisle and the others were still present. Flashlights and weapons in hand, Kori and Anya went quietly and methodically through the rooms on the second floor—four bedrooms, a storage room, and a large music room complete with a baby grand piano.

Kori marveled at the music room, which seemed almost out of place in a house that, in other respects, was in such disarray. Facing the back of the house, the room was probably thirty feet by twenty. In addition to the piano, there was a beautiful harp standing in the far corner of the room and a double bass leaning against the near wall. She shone her flashlight around and saw nothing else. There was nothing in the storage room, either, except a stack of folding chairs, and file boxes coated with dust as if they hadn't been touched for years. The bedrooms, on the other hand, showed signs of use. "They slept up here," said Kori. "Probably worked on the first floor. Let's go check it out."

The first floor had high ceilings and consisted of large, formal dining and living rooms, a massive kitchen, a library, a sitting room, billiard room, and a large foyer at the front of the house. The kitchen had been used, with dishes still wet in the sink. The billiard room looked as if it had seen some recent activity as well, with ashtrays full of cigarettes, an odor that still hung in the air. But after a half hour of searching, Kori and Anya found no signs of Carlisle and his men.

"This must have been impressive in its day," said Anya as they stood in the foyer underneath a tall chandelier. "Can you imagine walking into this house, through this room, back when the original owners lived here? But look at the paint peeling. And did you notice how worn the rugs are all throughout?"

"And the furniture's been out of date for decades," said Kori. "But then what would you expect from an anarchist? Look at that big bare spot on the wall, Anya. You can tell by the faded paint around it that something hung there at one time. Probably something beautiful. Well, at any rate, it doesn't look like anybody is here. Nor does it look like any work has been done here."

"How do you know?" Anya asked.

"I would expect to see machine tools. As Cooper explained it, you'd need to produce the two containers to house the uranium. Then you'd need a cannon-like device to shoot one at the other to start the nuclear reaction. And you need a detonating device. All of it would need to be housed in a larger container that you'd probably have to manufacture special for the job at hand. I don't see any welding torches or gas cylinders or metal scraps or anything of that sort."

"So you think they just lived here and worked elsewhere?"

"Well, it kind of looks that way."

"Wait," said Anya. "The cellar."

"Yes, of course! Millet said he'd never been down there. He assumed it was a wine cellar. Probably it was at one time. Shall we? I believe it's off the kitchen."

"So was the cellar at Inspector Chardin's house."

"Right. Second cellar in twenty-four hours. Anya, we've got to find better ways to spend our time."

The two walked quietly through the kitchen. "I'll bet the steps are in the pantry," said Anya. They slipped into the walk-in pantry, past shelves of canned goods, to a door that was slightly ajar, revealing a wooden staircase leading downward. They paused at the door and Kori whispered, "Um … I believe I went first last time."

"Indeed," sighed Anya. Then she muttered something under her breath, which Kori could only assume was a

Russian profanity, and gently opened the door into the pitch blackness. "If they're down there," she whispered to Kori, "then they must be operating in the dark."

Kori grabbed Anya's elbow and pulled her back into the pantry. "Right. So they're either not down there, or they know we're here and they're lying in wait for us. They'll shoot as soon as they see a flashlight. We need a better way."

"There is a light switch right inside the door. I presume it works an overhead light."

"Yes, let's light the place up first before we go down. Put things on an even playing field. Better still, we can lie in wait for them up here. They have to come up eventually."

"Unless there is another way out of the cellar."

"True, but I didn't notice any exterior cellar doors when we were outside, did you? If we hit the light and they come up here, we've got 'em. I don't care how many of them there are, they can only fit one at a time through this door. And I don't have any problem shooting them one at a time."

"Same here. Okay, let me hit the switch." Anya reached inside the door and flipped the switch on and a flood of light came from below. She stepped back out and the two listened intently for any sounds of movement. For five long minutes they stood quietly, hardly breathing.

"Anya, I don't think anybody is down there," Kori said at last. "We'd have heard something by now."

"Agreed. Shall we go down?"

"Sure. *Après vous*," grinned Kori.

Anya went first with Kori right behind, both agents crouching, guns drawn and pointing forward. At the bottom of the steps, they looked around the cellar. It was a rectangle of about thirty feet by forty. There didn't appear to be any other exits or rooms, just four flat walls.

"Nobody," said Kori, lowering her gun.

"No, but look around," said Anya. "Here is what you were looking for, no?"

Gas cylinders, welding goggles, metal scraps, a lathe, a pallet mover, and more. "It's a veritable metal shop," said Kori. "Everything they would have needed. And look at that, a short wall of heavy metal that I would guess might be lead. They probably housed the uranium behind it. Definitely looks like the kind of place where a wacko and his trusted scientist friend could produce a serious bomb."

"Kori, I have a sense they were here not too long ago. But where could they have gone? And why would they leave so much behind? All the tools and everything one would need. It's all still here."

"They had to leave in a hurry, I guess," said Kori. "They knew we were coming and only had time to grab the uranium and go. Maybe they figured they'd come back later for all this stuff."

Both agents looked around, remaining quiet for the moment. But their minds were racing. They came to the same conclusion almost simultaneously.

"Unless ... " started Anya.

"They don't need the tools anymore," said Kori, continuing Anya's thought.

"Because they're finished making the bomb," Anya concluded.

"Yep."

"Damn."

"Anya, we need to figure out where they went and I mean we need to figure it out *now*. We have to conclude that the bomb is ready to be detonated. I say we go back upstairs and beat the information out of Trémaux."

"But you saw the look in his eyes when we threatened him before. He knows nothing, I can tell. He's an agitator on the outside, threatening violent anarchy, but a coward on the inside. Besides, why would Carlisle even tell him? Carlisle is much too smart to tell the one person he left behind where he was going."

"True. But can't we beat him up anyway? I think I'd feel much better."

"Kori, my American friend, we must keep our heads about us. Let us think for a moment. To figure out where they went, it might help to know how they took the bomb out of here."

"Right. Hopefully, there'll be time to beat Trémaux up later. Well, let's see. You'd have to figure the bomb's got to be at least five feet long, right? Long enough for one of the containers of uranium to achieve sufficient velocity to smack into the other. You need room for the detonating device and, of course, the containers of uranium themselves. So it's probably about five feet wide, too, and maybe the same height. And it's going to be heavy. They'd have a hell of a job taking it up the stairs we just came down. I'm not even sure it would fit."

"But there are no other exits to this cellar," said Anya.

"Wait, what's on that wall?" said Kori, walking over to the far end of the room. "A tapestry. Why would you hang a tapestry down here in this musty old cellar?"

"Yes, odd."

The agents stood in front of it. The tapestry was probably about eight feet square and depicted a faded coat of arms on heavy wool.

"The foyer, Anya," said Kori. "The bare spot on the wall. Wouldn't you say it's about the same size as this tapestry? Somebody took it from there and hung it up here."

"Do you feel that?" said Anya, "There's a cool draft coming from behind it."

The agents looked at each other and then back at the tapestry. Each grabbed a side of it and yanked. The tapestry fell, landing heavily on the floor and coughing up a small cloud of dust. Behind it was darkness, deep darkness.

Kori shone her flashlight into the black to reveal a tunnel, the end of which they couldn't see. "Well, that answers the first question. This was their exit. Obviously, they took the bomb through here. C'mon."

The two stepped into the cold, dank tunnel, drawing their guns and shining their flashlights in front of them but the darkness ahead seemed endless.

"We have to hurry," said Kori. "If you were Efron Carlisle and you managed to get your nuclear device to the other end of this tunnel, wherever that is, what's the one thing you'd make certain to do?"

"Destroy the tunnel behind you, of course," said Anya.

"Yep."

"He may be too far ahead of us already, Kori."

"Let's just walk down a ways and see if we can at least tell where it leads. It can't be long. He didn't have that much time to build it. I mean, we didn't see any excavation tools or anything. Plus, where would he have put the dirt?"

"The tunnel must already have been in existence," said Anya.

"That explains the musty, damp, rotten-earth smell. And look at the ceiling. These old beams have been in place forever. Of course. Anya, this tunnel was most likely built during World War II after Germany had overrun the whole area. Maybe resistance fighters used it. Or maybe it was used as a bomb shelter or hiding place. After the war, they probably just walled it up. But Trémaux must have known about its existence, so they punched through the wall and had themselves an instant escape route. It's probably one of the things that convinced Carlisle to make use of Trémaux's place. It's a pretty handy amenity for a guy who's always in danger of having someone find him."

The two walked carefully and quietly forward, flashlights and guns pointed ahead. The tunnel was about six feet wide and six feet high. The agents had to duck down at points to walk under wooden support beams that were bowed by the years. Groundwater created a couple of inches of mud at their feet. "Sonofabitch Carlisle's going to pay for these boots," muttered Kori.

Anya was thinking of other things. "Do you think there are rats down here?"

"Probably."

After about forty yards, the tunnel took a ninety-degree turn. Kori angled up to the corner and put her hand up to signal for Anya to stop. "For all we know, they could be right around the corner waiting for us," she whispered. Anya nodded. "Ready? *Now.*"

Kori swung around with her Glock while Anya penetrated the darkness with her flashlight. But there was nothing but more darkness.

"Carlisle's men must have had a hell of a time bringing the bomb through here," said Kori. "There's barely enough room. I hope he paid them overtime. Want to keep going?"

"A little more." They continued walking, their flashlight beams never reaching the end of the blackness that lay in front of them.

Suddenly, Anya stopped. "Do you hear that?" Kori heard it a split second later—a low rumbling, followed by the sensation of the tunnel shaking, moving beneath them. Dirt from the ceiling began to fall in clumps to the floor.

"He's blowing the tunnel!" said Kori. "Run!"

Both agents turned around and ran, the beams from their flashlights bouncing on the walls and ceiling of the tunnel, the rumbling behind them getting louder, getting nearer. Kori looked over her shoulder to see dirt cascading toward them like a giant wave. Finally, they reached the ninety-degree turn and flung themselves around the corner just as the flood of dirt and mud and broken wooden supports came barreling past them.

Both agents lay on the floor of the one remaining branch of the tunnel, catching their breaths.

"Are you all right?" said Anya.

"Yes, but let me tell you, Efron Carlisle's going to get a big dry cleaning bill. You?"

"I'm good, but we need to get out of here. This section may go, too."

"You'll get no argument from me."

Kori and Anya ran back toward the tunnel's entrance and dove back into the cellar, but the rumbling behind them had stopped. The initial section of tunnel remained secure.

"Close one," said Anya, standing up and brushing the dirt and mud off of her clothes.

"A little too close," said Kori, flicking dirt out of her hair. "Hey, I think you got some dirt on you."

"No kidding? Well guess what … I think you got some dirt on you, too."

They both laughed, then Kori turned serious. "Anya, how do we find out now where that tunnel ended?"

"We'll have to follow it above ground. It was deep, but maybe not deep enough to where there wouldn't be a depression in the ground from the collapse, running along the tunnel's route."

"Right. Let's go. We're close to sunrise, too. Hopefully, there'll be enough light."

Outside, the agents ran to the far end of the chateau. "The tunnel came out of this side of the cellar," said Kori. "We're right on top of it. It ran straight out before it took the turn. How far do you figure we went before that?"

"Maybe thirty or forty yards?"

"Come on."

The sky was lightening ever so slightly and the agents could make out the contours of the ground underneath their feet. They walked through high grass until they came to a point where the land seemed to suddenly dip.

"Here," said Kori. Perpendicular to their position ran a long, straight depression in the ground, a six-foot-wide furrow, still covered in grass, but sunken from the sudden implosion of the tunnel underneath it. "The second half of the tunnel is right underneath. All we have to do is follow this ditch."

"Let's walk clear of it," said Anya. "It might not be done giving way."

Kori walked along one side of the depression while Anya walked along the other, both of them keeping several feet from the edge. For seventy more yards they walked, eventually through a small grove of trees and then, finally, out into an open field where the depression abruptly stopped.

"They must have come up here," said Kori.

Both agents looked around warily but saw nothing. There were no signs of anybody around and few places to hide. The field in front of them was expansive, at least an acre, flat, with short-cut grass. Morning dew was beginning to reflect the light from the rising sun.

"They must have had a vehicle waiting for them here," said Anya. "How else could they move the bomb?"

"But from where?" said Kori. "Look around the edge of the field. I see woods and adjoining farmland, but no access roads. What is this field, anyway? It didn't show up on any of the satellite photos."

"It's odd," said Anya. "It's as if they came out of the tunnel and vanished."

The two walked deep into the field, gazing around, both taking notice of how hard-packed the soil was. After ten minutes, Anya stopped and said, "Here! Tire tracks. Strange looking, though. See? Whatever it is, the tires sit about nine feet apart. And look at the track between the tires. It's like a third tire in the middle. What kind of vehicle must this be? And how could you even get it on the road? And how, from here?"

The agents followed the tracks until the tracks stopped.

"Gone," said Anya. "As though the vehicle just disappeared."

All at once, Kori realized what they were seeing. "You don't need to get it on the road, Anya. Don't you get what this is? We're walking on a landing strip. These tracks are the tracks of a small jet plane. Carlisle is airborne. So is the bomb. It's not a nuclear bomb anymore, my friend. Now, it's a nuclear missile."

CHAPTER 26

Kori called Eaglethorpe who called the president who called the French president who called the head of the European Organization for the Safety of Air Navigation, otherwise known as EUROCONTROL. Headquartered in Brussels, EUROCONTROL provided air traffic control for the continent, handling some 30,000 flights a day. Now, every plane flying anywhere over Europe needed to be taken into account—commercial aircraft, cargo planes, private jets, anything with wings. Somewhere, there was a small jet on a flight path that hadn't been approved and hadn't been tracked. Every air traffic control station throughout Europe was now feeding information to EUROCONTROL's supercomputer to ferret out, by process of elimination, the one rogue plane.

Meanwhile, American fighter jets had been scrambled from Ramstein Air Base in Germany. France had fighter jets in the air as well. The prime minister of the UK had been notified and jets from the Royal Air Force soon joined in. From the tracks in the field, Kori figured the wheelbase of the plane was roughly the same as what you'd find with a Gulfstream 500, the same kind of small jet that Carlisle had owned before; the one he had used to stage his death. Ordinarily, the luxury Gulfstream holds up to fifteen passengers in its fifty-foot-long cabin. Now it held a nuclear bomb. More problematic, Kori knew that a Gulfstream 500 had a top speed of over 500 miles per hour, could climb above 50,000 feet, and, most significantly, had a range of over 7,000 miles before it needed to refuel. All of which meant that Efron Carlisle's plane could be almost anywhere. And heading almost anywhere else.

Kori and Anya were back in Paris, sitting in the office of Assistant Directorate of Intelligence and Security of Defense Bernard Boffrand. Kori had called the authorities who had come to the chateau, arrested Trémaux, and given the Rampart agents a ride to Boffrand's office. Eaglethorpe was present via speakerphone. Now they were all just waiting for news from EUROCONTROL.

The office of the assistant was spacious, with a large desk, two facing chairs (occupied by Kori and Anya), and a large conference table. But Kori noticed nothing of a personal nature in the room. None of the requisite family pictures or framed photographs on the walls of places or people dear to the office's occupant. There wasn't even a single green plant. In fact, there seemed to be little of anything that wasn't a piece of furniture.

Bernard Boffrand, a short, compact man with a thick neck that his collar was straining against, did not embrace such frivolity. He was a serious man, but not because of his dedication to his job. He was simply not a man who understood frivolity. Joviality was not in his nature. And it certainly wasn't at this particular moment. His sudden promotion to de facto directorate was a position that came to him by default a little more than twenty-four hours before upon the discovery of Directorate Marc Chardin's body. He did not welcome it. It was, in fact, the last thing Boffrand had ever wanted. He had been more than content to be assistant. Assistant came with a little more work, but a lot less responsibility. Responsibility made Boffrand nervous and edgy. It also made him more difficult to work with, something his subordinates had long known about him. His colleagues considered him to be knowledgeable and competent, but his people skills left much to be desired. This would be forgivable if he cared. But it was clear to anyone he worked with that he did not.

Now, behind his desk, he was shaking his head. "We should have been notified that Carlisle was in our country days ago!" he huffed. "Days ago! Your secrecy is an outrage!"

"I told you, Director Boffrand, I take full responsibility," said Eaglethorpe over the speaker on Boffrand's desk, "but we could not allow what we knew to leak out. Especially since we had no tangible evidence of Carlisle's whereabouts. It would have been irresponsible on our part to take such a chance."

"You do not think we can keep a secret," Boffrand snapped. "Is that it?"

"From the public, sure. Of course. But when you consider the fact that Carlisle has gotten as far he's gotten—starting in Bayanovka, deep in Russia, mind you—then it's clear that he's got a slew of people helping him. He has spies, Director. Everywhere. And we calculated that if Carlisle knew of any extra scrutiny, he would be much more likely to detonate the bomb sooner. We had to buy time. Meanwhile, I was in contact with our president throughout and he was prepared to contact your president the moment the situation warranted it, which, of course, was this morning. Nothing anybody would have done in the meantime could have altered the set of circumstances we now face."

"He's right, Director," said Kori. "Carlisle no doubt planned an escape from that chateau the moment he learned about it. And I know Carlisle. He is not a man who leaves things to chance. If you don't think he had eyes and ears on your agency, then you're mistaken. I mean, with all due respect, sir. The fact is, he would have blown the bomb sooner had he known you'd been informed, or he would have taken off sooner and gone somewhere else and we'd be back to square one."

"Which is where we seem to be now," said Boffrand. "No?"

"Well, yes, but at least we know he's in the air. Somewhere."

"Yes, somewhere. But if only we knew where, mademoiselle. You clearly do not know. And if Carlisle is as smart and resourceful as you say, capable of spying on our agency, do you not think he would somehow have infiltrated you at the CIA?"

Kori said nothing, allowing Eaglethorpe to take the question. There was silence on the speaker for a moment before Eaglethorpe finally said, "Well, Director, we're not exactly CIA."

"No?" The director arched his eyebrows. "Then who are you?"

"I'm not at liberty to say, I'm afraid."

"You are not at liberty?" Boffrand was incredulous. "We have placed EUROCONTROL into security code six, the highest level there is. We have scrambled fighter jets. We are scouring the skies for a rogue jet. Every agency we have is on high alert status. All because of your reports to us about Efron Carlisle, who, the last I knew, was dead. And you cannot tell me who you are?!"

"Negative, sir," said Eaglethorpe. "Other than to say that we are a United States intelligence agency. Your president knows, and I'm afraid he's the only one authorized to know at this point in time."

"But we do not even know if this Carlisle, supposedly alive, has a nuclear device," said Boffrand. "Why should we listen to you people when you do not even identify yourselves?"

"Again, sir, you can take that up with your president. I assume you're under his authority, correct?"

Boffrand grimaced and began searching for something to say when a red light on his desk lit up and a voice from another speaker filled the office. "Sir, we have located an unidentified aircraft. It appears to be a Gulfstream."

Kori and Anya perked up, leaning forward in their chairs across from Boffrand.

"Where?" said Boffrand.

"Forty-seven degrees, thirteen minutes north; thirty-three degrees, ten minutes west."

Kori took out her phone and plugged in the coordinates. "Nantes," she said.

"Yes, toward the coast," said Boffrand. "A city of about 300,000."

"That can't be the target," said Kori.

"And why not?" said Boffrand.

"Because Carlisle would choose a much more populous place. No, he's on his way somewhere else; I can guarantee it."

"But where, mademoiselle?"

"Do we have a visual on the pilot?" came Eaglethorpe's voice over the first speaker.

"Did you hear that, Louis?" said Boffrand. "The chief of a completely unknown agency, whose anonymous agents are sitting in my office, wishes to know if you have a visual on the pilot. Monsieur Eaglethorpe, the other voice you hear is Louis Boudier of our air force chief of staff's office. Louis, perhaps you would be so kind as to tell these mysterious persons whether we have a visual on the pilot."

Kori couldn't help but smile at the level of sarcasm.

"The pilot and copilot are wearing ski masks," came Boudier's voice. "We have two Mirages in pursuit. Shall we shoot it down?"

"Negative!" shouted Eaglethorpe. "The fallout would be almost as destructive as if the bomb were detonated on the ground."

"Well, we cannot simply let them slam into the city," said Boffrand. "If what you say is true about this plane."

Kori and Anya exchanged glances. Both knew that at this point the options were limited. "Almost as destructive" might be the best they could hope for. Either way, a lot of people were going to pay the price for Carlisle's evilness.

"Our pilots have reported the Gulfstream has now turned due west," came the voice of Boudier over the speaker. "They are over the Bay of Biscay and heading toward the Atlantic."

"Well, what do you know?" said Boffrand. "It appears they are headed away from France. Perhaps to the US?"

Kori noticed the slightest trace of a grin. "But that doesn't make sense," she said. "He knows he'd never make it before being shot down. It's 3,600 miles. More than seven hours flying time. Why would he try for the US?"

"I cannot speculate," said Boffrand. "Nevertheless, when he reaches a distance of 22.2 kilometers from our coast, he is in international air space. And I will leave the matter to you."

"Chief," said Kori, "we need to know it's him before we shoot him down."

"What do you propose, Agent Briggs?"

"Vélizy-Villacoublay Air Base is about eight miles from where we are. I'll head there right now. Reroute an American fighter to there and let me catch a ride out to intercept the Gulfstream. Let me make a visual. Maybe I can tell. Even with a mask on his face, I might be able to see something that could tell us it's really him. Without a positive identification, we're always going to be wondering where Carlisle is."

"Agreed," said Eaglethorpe. "Director Boffrand, can you clear one of our jets to land at Vélizy-Villacoublay?"

"Would it get you out of my hair quicker? Then yes, I will clear it for you."

"On my way, Chief," said Kori. Then she and Anya rose and started out of the office. Turning back at the door, Kori said, "Oh, and Director Boffrand, might you be so kind as to get one of your people to give us a lift there?"

The director frowned and shrugged and waved to one of his assistants who escorted Kori and Anya out of the office and down the hallway. But before they could reach the elevator, Boffrand came bounding after them. "Wait just a moment, please."

"Yes, Director?" said Kori.

"There is the matter of Director Chardin's death. I have a distinct feeling that all of this is connected to it. Am I wrong to presume so?"

"No," Kori said. "No, not at all."

"I thought as much. Then I am going to need a complete statement from you. Before you leave."

"But, Director—"

"Before you leave," Boffrand repeated. "Otherwise, I have no guarantee that I will be able to find you again."

"Kori," said Anya, "you go ahead. I will stay and fill Director Boffrand in. Would that be okay, Director?"

Boffrand shrugged approval.

"Go, Kori," said Anya. "You need to get to that plane. Godspeed, my American friend."

"Thanks, my Russian friend."

By the time Kori made it to Vélizy-Villacoublay, a US Air Force fighter jet was waiting for her on the tarmac. Standing beside it was a tall, broad-shouldered man in a flight suit. He had short, wavy blond hair, sharp cheekbones, a square jaw, and the bluest eyes Kori had ever seen.

"Agent Briggs," said the man, "I'm Captain Shane Scott. Are you ready?" Kori nodded. "Here's your foam dome," he said, handing her a flight helmet. "You ever been up in one of these before?"

"An F-15E Strike Eagle? I've flown them, Captain. I'm a fan. Although, personally, I often find myself preferring the Navy's Super Hornet. No offense."

"None taken," the captain grinned, taken aback by Kori's knowledge. "This one's a bit faster, of course."

"Yes, but it's not quite as versatile. You can't land it on an aircraft carrier, for instance. Speed is fine, Blue Eyes, but I'm a girl who likes a little versatility."

"Roger that, Agent Briggs," the captain said, chuckling. "I'll try to remember that."

"Call me Kori, Blue Eyes. Now, let's get this bird in the air."

CHAPTER 27

The Gulfstream was now about three hundred miles off the coast heading west. Airborne, from the seat behind Captain Shane Scott, Kori did a quick calculation in her head figuring the Gulf Stream's top speed of 500 miles per hour and the Strike Eagle's top speed of over Mach 2.5—1,875 miles per hour.

"We should intercept them in about nineteen minutes, Blue Eyes," she said into the intra-flight communication microphone in her helmet.

"Roger that, Agent Briggs."

"What did I say? Call me *Kori*."

"Roger that, Agent Kori. Say, may I ask what this is all about?"

"I'm afraid I'm not authorized to say."

"Well, it must be important. We were scrambled from Ramstein by orders that came from the White House. All of this for one rogue private jet?"

"Well, it's not just any jet. And that's all I can say for now."

"Roger that, Agent Kori."

Kori gazed out of the cockpit window. Nothing but blue sky. It was now early afternoon and a gorgeous day for flying. *If only the fate of thousands of people weren't up for grabs,* she thought. *An afternoon buzzing around in an F-15 with Captain Shane Scott would have been a terrific time.*

Scott was soon in communication with the French Mirages that had been tailing the Gulfstream. "We're coming up on it," he said to Kori. "There. At two-o'clock."

"Get right beside it. I need to take a good look at the crew."

Scott slowed and descended, and shortly the planes were parallel to each other about fifty yards apart. The Gulfstream was not wavering from its path.

"Closer," said Kori.

Scott positioned the F-15 to within twenty yards. Kori could see two men at the controls. Both wore ski masks. She looked into the passenger windows but saw no sign of any activity, no sign of any additional people. "Damn," she muttered under her breath. "Blue Eyes, can you get me radio contact?"

"Roger. There's a channel open. Go ahead, Agent Kori."

"Gulfstream, this is the United States government," said Kori. "Identify yourselves." She listened, but nothing came back but silence. "I repeat, identify yourselves. Your plane and your lives are in danger. We *will* shoot you down."

Still nothing.

"This is your final warning," she said, and then for good measure, she added, "Carlisle if that's you, you're going to die for nothing, you freaking wacko."

More silence.

"What do you want to do?" said Scott.

"There's nothing else we can do," said Kori. "Take him down."

Scott was silent for a moment, and then said in a suddenly serious tone, "I need to confirm, Agent Briggs. I understand you have warned the target and the target has failed to respond. But, for the record, you're asking me to fire upon a civilian aircraft over international waters?"

"Yep. Your authorization came this morning from the president, Captain," said Kori, matching the seriousness. "I believe the order was clear, was it not? If necessary, force is to be used to terminate the threat."

"Understood, Agent Briggs. But I'm not seeing a threat. At least not an immediate one."

"Then I need to tell you something about that plane, Captain Scott, but it stays here. This cannot be repeated."

"Roger that, ma'am."

"There's a nuclear device aboard that Gulfstream, Captain. Unimpeded, the pilot will probably fly it into Manhattan or Washington, DC. Is that a sufficient threat?"

"Yes, ma'am, I'd have to say it is."

"We need to take him out now, over the water, where the fallout will cause minimal damage if the device detonates. And you're going to want to create some distance between us and them before you fire. A lot of distance. Use one of your AIM-7 Sparrow III's. If memory serves, those missiles have a range of fifty-three miles."

"Wow," said Scott. "Just who are you?"

"Wouldn't you like to know, Blue Eyes?" Kori said, softening.

Captain Scott peeled off from the Gulfstream and increased altitude. He took a position above and to the side of the small jet, allowing the Gulfstream to continue on its course until it was several miles distant and no more than a speck against the ocean below.

"Okay, Blue Eyes," said Kori. "This ought to work. Fire!"

"Firing!"

Kori watched the smoke trail of the missile as it raced downward, finding its target below them within seconds.

"Go up!" said Kori. "Get us clear of the explosion!"

The Strike Eagle shot upward and Kori could feel herself being pinned to her seat by the sudden upward momentum of the plane. Then Scott leveled off, reporting on his radio to Paris that the threat had been neutralized.

"Come around and let's take a look at the damage," said Kori.

"Roger. Coming around."

Kori could see that the Gulfstream was in flames as it tumbled toward the ocean, but clearly, the only explosion was the plane itself.

"Well, I guess that's that," said Scott. "Crisis averted, huh?"

"I wish," said Kori. "Unfortunately, it's not that simple. That Gulfstream going down the way it did tells me only one thing. There wasn't a nuclear device on board."

"Well, that's a good thing, right?"

"You don't understand, Blue Eyes. We know there's a rogue nuclear device out there. But now, the only other thing we know is that it wasn't on that plane. At this point, that's the only place in the world that we can safely rule out. You see? We've been following a red herring. A distraction. Right now, I can't even say with any degree of certainty that the bomb was ever in France."

"Wow. So, who has this rogue nuclear device? You mentioned the name Carlisle. Who's that?"

"Sorry. I can't say anymore."

"Well, it must be someone with a lot of hate in his heart, Agent Kori."

"Indeed it is, Blue Eyes. A despicable man."

"Well, you know what Gandhi said. Hate the sin, love the sinner."

"Nobody could love this sinner, Captain, believe me."

"I understand."

"Gandhi, huh?"

"Sure."

"You're an interesting man, Blue Eyes."

"Thanks. You're pretty interesting yourself."

"Well, I guess I'd better have you take me back to Vélizy-Villacoublay. Would you?"

"Roger that, Agent Kori."

Down on the ground, Kori handed her flight helmet back to Captain Shane Scott. "Thanks for the ride. Under better circumstances, I would have really enjoyed it. You seem pretty good with that thing."

"Thanks. I like to think so. Another time, maybe? Under better circumstances?"

"Sure. Another time." Kori turned to walk away then turned back toward the captain once more. "So. Tell me. Is there a Mrs. Blue Eyes?"

"Nope. Why do you ask?"

"Just curious."

"Uh huh. Well, you know, Curious," the captain said, taking a step toward Kori, "if you find yourself looking for a little getaway when this whole thing is over, might I suggest a side trip to Ramstein Air Base?"

"Yeah?"

"Sure. We can take a nice drive through the German countryside. It's beautiful this time of year. Ever been to Heidelberg?"

"Can't say that I have."

"I think you'd like it. It's what you think of when you think of old Germany. It's a charming town on a river with brick streets and little cafés that serve authentic sauerbraten and German beer in large steins. There's a big castle there and everything."

"Sounds nice."

"It's very romantic."

"Romantic, huh?"

"Yep. If, uh, you're into that kind of thing."

"Well, I just might be. I must say, a little German café sounds nice. And over some sauerbraten and beer, we can discuss Gandhi."

"It would be my pleasure. Then it's a date, Agent Kori?"

"Then it's a date, Blue Eyes. First, of course, there's this small matter of a psycho with a nuclear device."

"You'll find him, Kori. I know you will."

"Thanks, Shane," she smiled. "See ya later."

CHAPTER 28

"Okay, that should do it." The man with the broad shoulders and neatly combed dark hair stood up in the back of the flatbed truck and beheld the work in front of him. He pointed the long screwdriver in his hand toward the near end of the metalwork in the oversized wooden crate. "There's your firing mechanism. It's rigged with the cell number I gave you. A simple phone call will activate the mechanism. That will create the detonation which will send this cannister into the cannister at the other end at … what speed did you say, Professor?"

"Precisely 2,600 feet per second," came the confident reply. Ivan Yanovich, also in the back of the truck, didn't especially care for the nickname. He was not, in fact, a professor, nor did he care for professors. His academic career was one in which he had felt significantly smarter than those who taught him, and he believed the university life was strictly for those without the ambition to do really important things. The Russian Ministry of Atomic Energy was where all the power lay. By all rights, he should have been in charge of it. Nobody was more qualified. And perhaps then, his beloved Rebecca would not have left him for another man. It was a simple chain of events, really. The Ministry erred in bypassing Ivan, his wife left him, and he was now doing the only logical thing: making the universe pay for its mistreatment of him. The nuclear bomb in front of him was as much a product of the cosmic affronts he had endured as his own brilliant handiwork.

"Yes," said the dark-haired man. "A speed of 2,600 feet per second. And that will more than suffice."

"Well, Jean-Phillippe, you appear to be a better mechanic than an actor," smiled the third man in the back of the truck, a man with very white hair and a crooked nose.

The dark-haired man frowned. Efron Carlisle's smile belied the irritation that he had made most apparent to Jean-Phillippe the night he came back from the jazz club to report that he had lost the two Rampart agents. It wasn't as if Jean-Phillippe wasn't carrying his load. After all, who volunteered to take care of the real Director Chardin in the first place? That was well above and beyond the call of duty. And it sure hadn't been easy. For a short, portly man,

Chardin was quite a fighter. Jean-Phillippe had gone into his house with the idea of strangling him with piano wire, but the son of a bitch fought back, and he fought back hard. The two had rolled around Chardin's living room and Jean-Phillippe had ended up grabbing a porcelain sculpture of a horse and smashing it over Chardin's head, then strangling him. It had been an ugly scrap. But was there any appreciation from Carlisle? *Why*, Jean-Phillippe thought, *does Carlisle continue with these little digs of his?*

The truck was parked inside a garage that faced an alley running from Rue de Bellechasse, a fifteen-minute drive to the target location. Two large men stood guard at the open door, intrigued by the work of the men inside the warehouse, but smart enough to know not to ask questions.

"How close do you think we'll be able to get to the target?" asked Jean-Philippe, looking to change the subject.

"We'll be right in front of it," said Carlisle. "Right in front of it." Carlisle didn't especially like Jean-Phillipe. He didn't care for his obsequiousness, nor his lack of mental acuity, but the latter was a problem he found with everyone. At least Ivan Yanovich could keep up with Carlisle's quick mind. But even Yanovich had his mental weaknesses. He was, as they say, book smart. But he was no good with strategy. He was the type who could never seem to grasp the larger picture. Never in a million years could he have hatched a plan like this one by himself. The very idea would never have occurred to him in the first place. The *idea*. *That's* what Yanovich could never do on his own.

Some people are detail people, some are concept people. Yanovich was all detail. *Just as well*, figured Carlisle. Too many concept people in the same room can lead to arguments over objectives and direction.

"But the nearest parking is some 500 meters away," said Jean-Phillippe. "I know that area well. And even then, how do you know there will be a place for a truck?"

"First of all, Jean-Phillippe, 500 meters is more than sufficient," replied Carlisle. "Wouldn't you agree, Ivan?"

"Yes, quite," said Yanovich. "The target would be rendered a melted mass of metal from ten times that distance."

"And second of all," continued Carlisle, "it so happens that there is plenty of room along Quai Branly, which runs right in front of it."

"Parking is not allowed there," said Jean-Phillippe.

"I'm pretty sure you're not allowed to detonate a nuclear device within the city limits, either, Jean-Phillippe."

"That's not what I meant, of course," smiled Jean-Phillippe, suddenly cognizant of the fact that he was, perhaps, pushing things a bit far with his questioning. "I'm sure you have things well thought out and quite in hand."

"I do. If you must know, I have a man there. A gendarme. He will allow us to park the truck directly in front. He will, in fact, be saving us a parking space to do just that."

Detail person or concept person, Yanovich never tried Carlisle's patience as much as Jean-Phillipe had. But finding a good actor who also happened to be a sociopathic anarchist had proved harder than he thought, especially since he'd had to find him at the last minute. Carlisle prided himself on his preparedness, but how in God's name did Rampart find out about Paris? He'd had people in Washington making it look like the bomb was going to go off there. And none of them even knew about Paris. And when they'd left Tel Aviv, Carlisle had made sure not to leave anyone behind who could talk. That's why he'd ordered the death of Jael Roth. "Shot and left for dead," said the Tel Aviv hitman he'd hired to carry out the murder. Carlisle would have carried it out himself, but he'd been working so closely with Yanovich, that Yanovich would have found out. And Yanovich, unable to see the big picture, would certainly have resented the killing of his brother-in-law. They weren't close exactly, but there seemed to be some mutual respect between the two, and family is family, even if the family member in question is an in-law of a failing marriage. At any rate, Roth was dead. So how was it that that bitch Kori Briggs was suddenly on a plane to Paris? Something had slipped through the cracks. Someone had talked. He'd have to figure out who later. There were other issues just now. Besides, Briggs and her friend were surely dead by now, anyway.

"A gendarme working for us. Great plan, Efron," said Jean-Phillippe, nodding in approval, as if Carlisle needed it.

However Briggs found out about Paris, Carlisle had sufficiently thrown her and her Russian friend off the trail.

257

Thankfully, he had eyes at Ronald Reagan International in DC as well as Charles de Gaulle airport in Paris. He knew every move Rampart was making. And it wasn't hard to figure out that Agent Blake would most likely get in touch with his friend Director Chardin. A simple wiretap on Chardin's phone and the rest fell into place. Briggs and the Russian had set up a meeting at the Eiffel Tower with Director Chardin, so, they would get their meeting. All Carlisle needed to do was find another Director Chardin. Fortunately, Gustave Trémaux knew Jean-Phillippe, an actor and fellow anarchist with a streak of sociopathy, who bought into the fiction that Carlisle was looking to make a political statement. In truth, that was the furthest thing from Carlisle's mind. What political statement? A combination of death and mayhem. That was the goal. *For its own sake.* Why complicate things with political statements? *This was the problem with the modern world,* thought Carlisle. *Too complicated. It's the sheer purity of the act—that's the objective. It isn't politics. It's art.*

"Okay, let's hammer the lid onto this beautiful crate," said Carlisle.

"Very carefully, I would think," said Jean-Phillippe, trying not to appear too nervous in front of a nuclear bomb that was now armed.

"Unnecessary," Yanovich said brusquely. "The uranium is completely inert and harmless housed, as it is, in the lead canisters. The only thing that will activate it is the collision of the canisters at high speed."

"Yes, Jean-Phillippe," said Carlisle. "Get a hold of yourself. Ivan's uranium is just fine, I'm sure. Of course, we could be in for trouble if you rigged the detonation bomb errantly. Should we be worried about that?"

"Of course not," Jean-Phillippe huffed. "I know what I am doing."

"I certainly hope so."

Jean-Phillippe had at least proved somewhat useful. He had had no compunction about doing away with the real Chardin and becoming the new one. But how could he have allowed the women to get away that night? The plan was straightforward. Throw them off the track by having them follow some unwitting student, let them report back to Rampart with their findings, then take them out of the equation permanently. The other agents at Rampart, having lost communication with the women, would come to Paris, yes. But, then they would get bogged down following up on the bogus trail that led to the student. But Jean-Phillippe had let the women slip away that night and somehow they had learned about the chateau, forcing Carlisle to go to plan B, taking the bomb elsewhere and leaving Trémaux behind to take care of Briggs and her Russian friend. If that failed, there would be the tunnel trap. In the meantime, the Gulfstream would keep everyone else busy and buy Carlisle precious time, time that he was now putting to good use by having Jean-Phillippe apply the finishing mechanical touches on the firing mechanism and detonator.

Frankly, Jean-Phillippe's knowledge of bombs was the only thing that had kept Carlisle from killing him for his bungling. Not that Yanovich couldn't have set up the detonation device, but the phone-activated firing mechanism had been Jean-Phillippe's idea. He had rigged up something like it before on a small bomb he'd set off at an anti-government rally in 2019, destroying a car, but harming nobody. The phone activation was a last minute addition to the plan, but Carlisle liked it very much. He had planned on using a standard time delay, but too many things can go wrong. You have to set the delay with enough time to get clear of the bomb—not an easy thing to do with a bomb that destroys such a wide area—yet not too much time to where somebody can find it and disarm it. With the phone activation, he could have his goons drive the truck right past the target and, as they do so, make the phone call.

That was the real beauty of it. The truck didn't even need to be parked. Nor would it be. There was, in point of fact, no gendarme and no place to park. Carlisle would have the large men at the garage door drive the truck past the target looking for the fictional gendarme and supposed parking spot. He would convince them that a getaway vehicle would be awaiting them once they parked. In reality, Carlisle would follow the progress of the truck by GPS and, when it got to the target, he'd place the phone call that would cause the detonation. Simple. *Art.*

Carlisle, Yanovich, and Jean-Phillippe affixed boards to the top of the crate and then hopped down from the bed of the truck. "So we're all set," said Carlisle. "I don't need to ask you again, Ivan. You know I trust you. However, please understand, this had been my dream now for some time. You are certain you have configured the bomb correctly? Assuming the detonation bomb goes off, the chain reaction will occur and a nuclear explosion will take place, yes?"

Yanovich scoffed. "Please. This is basic nuclear science. I could have done this in my sleep. Even with the rudimentary tools you were able to provide in that drafty monstrosity of a house."

"Yes, well, sorry about that, old sport. One does what one can. The chateau saved us from having to rent warehouse space with potentially nosey neighbors or, perhaps, a meddlesome landlord. Personally, I found the chateau very comfortable."

"That makes one of us."

"Regardless, here we are. And if you say you are certain of this device, Ivan, then that is good enough for me."

Yanovich permitted himself a half-smile. In truth, he didn't care at all for Efron Carlisle. Carlisle's reputation had, of course, preceded him. He was, in a word, insane. Yanovich was a lot of things, but he would never describe himself as being mentally unstable. Indeed, he was one of the most logical, rational people he knew. Carlisle's insanity made him uncomfortable. And the most uncomfortable thing about it was how hidden it was. Carlisle spoke with reason. He could communicate with charm. Yanovich remembered the way Carlisle flirted with Madame Duchamp at the restaurant in the village, convincing her to contact him should any strangers come into the place asking suspicious questions. He didn't seem insane. *But,* Yanovich thought, *being insane while not appearing insane was surely the hallmark of insanity.*

"The way I calculate it," said Carlisle, "everybody is by now chasing the plane somewhere over the Atlantic. We are free to drive the truck to the target, park it, and get ourselves back to the chateau airstrip where my pilot will be waiting for us with the second plane. From there, I will call the number of the phone in the crate and we will … complete the plan." Carlisle smiled broadly. "I trust there are no questions? Good."

Yanovich had to hand it to him. Carlisle really did seem to know how to put together a plan. But of course, that was no sign of genius. In fact, Carlisle's plan had been based almost entirely, it seemed to Yanovich, on having the right people in place along the way. And that was a result of his money. Yanovich knew that if he'd had Carlisle's money, he too could have orchestrated something this bold. But wealth isn't the same thing as intelligence. What Yanovich had in pure brain power, Carlisle could only envy. Carlisle would never admit it, but he had to know that his idea, which an eight-year-old child could have thought of, was only going to be made possible by Yanovich's knowledge. The *details.* Understanding those—*that's* what Carlisle could never do on his own.

"Now," continued Carlisle, "you two gentlemen." Carlisle was looking at the guards by the door. "It's Nicolas and Paul, is it not?"

"*Oui*," said one of the men, a large, bald man.

"Well, *monsieurs*, here is what you are to do. You will drive this truck down Quai Branly. Directly in front of the target, you will see a gendarme. He will be ... tall, with a beard. Yes, tall with a beard. His name is Pierre. He will be on the lookout for you, so you won't miss him. He'll see the truck and throw you a wave. Then he'll direct you to park right there, up against the security bollards. Pierre will put a special tag on the truck, which, to anybody else, will make the truck look as if it is a typical maintenance–vendor type truck, authorized to park there. Now, Pierre will have a car close by. You two and he will get into the car and meet us back at the chateau. Call me when you are out of the city limits, at a safe distance, and I will make the detonation phone call. Do you understand?"

"*Oui, monsieur*," said the large, bald man.

"Here is a little something extra for your trouble." Carlisle stuffed a wad of bills into each man's hand.

"*Merci*," the men said in unison.

"Think nothing of it. Now, here are the keys. I will call you when it is time for you to leave. So, you will wait here until you hear from me. Probably about fifteen minutes from now. Ivan, Jean-Phillippe, and I have something we need to take care of first. Is everything clear?"

"*Oui, monsieur*," both men said.

263

"*Merci*. Good luck, gentlemen. The operation now hinges entirely on you. I can't overemphasize the importance of your role. Remember, wait for my call before you leave." Then turning toward Ivan and Jean-Phillippe, Carlisle said, "Okay, let's go, fellows."

The three piled into Jean-Phillippe's Peugeot, which was parked out on the street, with Jean-Phillippe behind the wheel and Yanovich in the back seat. Soon they left the garage behind.

"Where am I driving?" said Jean-Phillippe.

"To the chateau, of course," said Carlisle.

"But you told them that we needed to take care of something."

"Yes. Indeed we do. We need to get the hell out of Paris, Jean-Phillippe! Haven't you heard? There is a nuclear bomb about to go off!" Then Carlisle began to laugh—a long, loud, maniacal laugh. Jean-Phillippe, the actor, thought that the laugh seemed too clichéd, too forced. It was the laugh of every evil bad guy in every mediocre thriller ever made. And yet, the more he listened to it, the more he realized that there was nothing disingenuous about Carlisle's laugh. His was the real deal. The nuclear device was all set, the men back at the garage would drive it past the target where it would go off—taking the men with it—Jean-Phillippe now realized, along with most of Paris. And Carlisle was in a state of pure, joyous rapture.

CHAPTER 29

Kori took a taxi from Vélizy-Villacoublay Air Base back to Boffrand's office to rendezvous with Anya. Along the way, she got a call from Eaglethorpe. "We're in the air, Agent Briggs," he said. "I'm with Cooper and Foster. The president cleared the use of a C-20 for us and we're on our way."

"So the cavalry is coming, eh?"

"Yes, but it'll be a couple of hours before we get there."

Kori filled the chief in on the shooting down of the Gulfstream.

"Obviously, it wasn't Carlisle," said Eaglethorpe, "but whoever it was, why in God's name would they allow themselves to be shot out of the sky? For what purpose? To die for Carlisle?"

"I have a theory about that, Chief. The figures in the plane seemed strange to me."

"Strange how?"

"Lifeless. Still. I'm racking my brain trying to remember exactly what I saw, but I swear they never moved."

"Dummies?"

"Yeah, like store mannequins or something."

"Flying a plane?"

"I'm thinking maybe Carlisle rigged up some kind of remote control system. He could do it. He has the know-how. Or maybe Yanovich did it. He's a pretty smart guy, after all."

"I don't know, Kori. Remotely operating a drone is one thing, but a Gulfstream 500? I'd have to say that's close to impossible."

"Well, it wouldn't have to be that sophisticated. All he needed to do was design a system that would allow for an unmanned takeoff. He could plug a preset route into the Gulfstream's nav system and then send it into the air. Remember, he wasn't expecting that he'd have to land it. All it needed to do was take off and head west. The technology exists, Chief. Airbus has been experimenting with auto takeoff for jumbo jets. Surely, Carlisle could improvise something for a small plane."

"All to make us spin our wheels while he got closer to setting the bomb off somewhere else. I'll say one thing for Carlisle. He's full of surprises. So what's your plan now, Kori?"

"I'm going to meet up with Agent Kovalev. I think we need to go back to the last place we believe the bomb was. Gustave Trémaux's chateau. There's got to be a clue there. There has to be something we missed. I just know it. And frankly Chief, I don't know what else to try. We're kind of running out of ideas."

"And time, I'm afraid."

"I know, Chief. And time. We've had some close ones before, but this is coming down to the wire."

"Do what you can, Kori. And stay safe. We'll be there soon."

"Roger, Chief."

Boffrand's office was a flurry of activity. After it was determined the Gulfstream didn't contain the bomb, Boffrand had called in all the high-ranking staff members of intelligence and security, and loud discussions were ringing out regarding the best course of action. The idea wasn't his. He still only partly believed Kori and Eaglethorpe's tale about Carlisle come back to life with a nuclear bomb. But the French president was insistent. He'd gotten intelligence from the US president, who had assured the French president that it was credible. Boffrand wasn't so sure.

In the interim, the GIGN, France's elite tactical unit, had been dispatched in substantial numbers all over the city. The national police had been notified and were routing traffic around all major government buildings, the line of thinking being that Carlisle, in true anarchy fashion, would look to set off his bomb in front of something like the Palais Bourbon, where the French National Assembly met, or, perhaps, the Élysée Palace, the official residence of the French president. These and other governmental buildings were being hastily evacuated. Bomb-sniffing dogs were being led around seemingly everywhere. All suspicious vehicles were being searched. Boffrand wondered at the point of the evacuations. Assuming the bomb was a nuclear one, which, in Boffrand's mind, was still a huge assumption, what good would it do to evacuate? He knew that if the searching didn't work, they'd all be screwed.

Meanwhile, with the sudden, city-wide commotion, questions were being asked. The media, some of the same reporters who had broken the story of Director Chardin's murder, were now reporting on what seemed like an obvious terrorist threat. Boffrand's phone was ringing incessantly, his personal secretary saying the same thing to everyone who called: "Certain actions are being taken around the city out of an abundance of caution. The acting director has no further comment at this time." Boffrand's head was hurting. He had searched in vain for a bottle of aspirin he was certain was in his desk. Assuming he survived the day, his plan was to reach into the desk for his bottle of bourbon.

Kori found Anya in the hallway outside of Boffrand's office and Anya filled her in on the actions the French authorities were taking.

"Sounds like the right plan," said Kori, although, like Boffrand, she, too, wondered about the effectiveness of the evacuations, given the damaging potential of the bomb.

"What about us?" said Anya. "Back to the chateau?"

"You read my mind. I just told the chief that's where we were headed."

"Think we can prevail upon the inspector to provide us with a car and a driver once more?"

"Never hurts to ask. This probably wouldn't be the best time to commandeer a police vehicle on our own, even if we could find one that isn't currently in use." Kori stuck her head into Boffrand's office, where the noisy conversation with seven of his staff members was continuing, all of them leaning over city maps and floor plans of various buildings. "Excuse me, Inspector?"

"You!" bellowed Boffrand, turning toward Kori and glaring at her. "You're the reason we are in this mess." The rest of the room fell silent and Kori felt the eyes of all eight governmental authorities.

"Me?"

"Carlisle is your man, is he not?"

"My man? He's a psycho, Director. I think that makes him a man of the world, no?"

"*Your* man," Boffrand continued, "is on the loose. Obviously, he was not on the plane, where you thought he was."

"I didn't—"

269

"We are mobilizing here, as you can see, doing everything we can with the severely limited information you have been able to provide. Might I ask what *you* plan on doing about this unfortunate situation that you have brought to our nation and city?"

"Yes, well, as it happens, Director, Agent Kovalev and I believe we can best be of service by following up on some clues where we think Carlisle and Yanovich built the bomb. That's a chateau about an hour from here."

"And?"

"And ... well, we were hoping maybe you could spare a vehicle?"

"I see. Oh, I will spare a vehicle, all right. And several police officers. You see, Agent Briggs, you and Agent Kovalev are not going to be out of our sight again. You are working for us now. You are on French soil, and from this point forward, your only mission in life will be to help us find this maniac of yours. And in the carrying out of this mission, you will report directly to me."

"Gee, Director, I'm flattered that you're so enamored with us."

Boffrand continued to glare at Kori but said nothing.

"Well, anyway," said Kori, "about that lift to the chateau ... "

Boffrand picked up his phone and rang for his assistant who immediately came trotting in. "Please have these two mademoiselles driven where they wish to go," said Boffrand. "Place them under the supervision of Capitaine

LeClair and his men. Instruct him to report to me on their actions every fifteen minutes. Whatever information they stumble upon, I want to know about it immediately."

"*Oui, monsieur.*"

"Thanks, Director," smiled Kori broadly. "Your concern for us is touching." She turned to leave with Boffrand's assistant, feeling the glare from Boffrand all the way out the door and down the hallway.

Capitaine Matthieu LeClair was a thirty-year, no-nonsense veteran of the national police. He was tall, with a thin nose, silver hair, and a matching silver mustache. Kori and Anya filled him in on their idea of returning to the chateau to dig around some more for clues on the possible whereabouts of the bomb. In turn, he ushered them into the backseat of his police car and they sped off, with two additional police cars in tow, each with a pair of officers. The convoy navigated swiftly around the Paris traffic and was on the main road to the village in short order.

"The details of all of this are sketchy to me, *mademoiselles*," said LeClair, glancing at the Rampart agents in his rearview mirror as he drove. "Acting Director Boffrand's instructions are apparently to escort you to where you wish to go, and to lend you assistance. However, I am also supposed to report to him every quarter hour on your activities. This seems strange to me."

"Yes, well, Captain," Kori said, "I get the feeling Director Boffrand isn't too happy with us."

"Then you are not alone, *mademoiselle*. It is Boffrand's nature to not be happy with anyone. Himself included, I'm afraid. He has been married and divorced four times, if that tells you anything. Some men are simply hard to get along with."

Captain LeClair smiled as he spoke. Kori caught his eyes in the mirror and sensed a man with a lot of wisdom and life experience. She imagined the captain to be the trustworthy, dependable kind. Kori decided that she liked Captain LeClair. "Yes, but you see we've given him especially good reason for his antipathy. You see, we seem to have loosed a madman on your fine city."

"Yes, we were informed that a bomb is planted somewhere," said LeClair. "But that is about all we were told."

"It is not just any bomb," said Anya. "It is, in fact, a nuclear device."

Captain LeClair's eyebrows went up but if there was any further hint of alarm, he hid it well. "I see. And may I ask who you are and what the nature of your involvement is with this nuclear bomb?"

"I'm Kori Briggs, this is Anya Kovalev. We are agents with the United States government."

"CIA?"

"Something like that."

"And who is this madman of which you speak?"

"Does the name Efron Carlisle mean anything to you?" asked Kori.

"But of course. Grover Carlisle's son. The One Hundred Bombs plan in your country. That was quite a frightening time. Efron Carlisle escaped from prison, as I recall, and was found dead some time later in his private plane."

"That's what we thought, too. Turns out the body wasn't Carlisle's. Turns out Carlisle faked his own death."

"Carlisle is alive? *He* is the madman?"

"Yep. And he has some help. He recruited a scientist who used to be with the Russian Ministry of Atomic Energy. Ivan Yanovich. They met through Yanovich's brother-in-law, Jael Roth, an anarchist in Tel Aviv. They broke into the Bayanovka nuclear storage facility in the Ural Mountains in Russia and made off with a hundred pounds of uranium. We believe Carlisle bribed airport officials, and probably air traffic controllers in several countries along the way, to land his private jet here, in France."

"This seems unlikely," LeClair interrupted. "Our borders are very secure, *mademoiselle*. It would be exceedingly difficult to enter our country with nuclear material."

"You don't know Carlisle, Captain. He's been working on this plan since he broke out of a federal correctional institute. He's a loon, but he's also a genius. Not only that, we believe the man still had millions, if not billions, of dollars secreted away. In fact, we believe that he not only bribed the right people, he might have even planted them in their positions in the first place, years ago, to place them beyond suspicion."

"I see."

"There is a makeshift airstrip near the chateau we are going to," added Anya. "We believe he landed there with the uranium. He left Tel Aviv, his base of operations, on a cargo plane, probably landed at a small airport somewhere in France, transferred the uranium to his Gulfstream, then flew to the chateau where Yanovich began working on the bomb."

"Yes," said Kori, "and the chateau is owned by Gustave Trémaux."

"The anarchist?" asked LeClair. "The one we have taken into custody?"

"One and the same."

"With *Le Désordre*?"

"He's not with them anymore," said Anya.

"Got bounced out for being too violent," Kori added. "In fact, it was *Le Désordre* that tipped us off about the chateau. If we manage to stop Carlisle in time, you'll have to make sure a man by the name of Léon Millet gets the Legion of Honor or something."

"The highest French governmental award to an anarchist?" said LeClair. "That would be, how do you say, ironic?"

"Yeah, maybe too ironic," Kori agreed. "Well, perhaps a nice blue ribbon. Or at least a framed certificate he can hang on his office wall."

"I must say, I wondered why Trémaux had been arrested. That is not my department, but I heard of the arrest. Was he interrogated?"

"Yes," said Kori. "We took care of that ourselves. He knows nothing. Carlisle left him in the dark."

"And who else is Carlisle with?" LeClair asked.

"Besides Yanovich, probably a couple of goons," replied Kori.

"And one man who pretended to be Director Chardin a couple of nights ago," added Anya.

"Yes," said Kori, "and I'm afraid we have no idea who he is or exactly what his involvement is."

The three drove through the French countryside on the same road Kori and Anya had been on the day before. Kori glanced out of the window as the scenery passed by. She hadn't had the chance to take notice of it the day before from behind the wheel of the borrowed police vehicle. It had turned out to be a sun-filled day and the green fields of France seemed especially serene. They passed vineyards and small farms and tiny villages with medieval churches.

"So what more can you tell me about the chateau?" LeClair asked after a while.

"Well, there is a cellar," replied Anya, "where Yanovich apparently built the bomb."

"Yes, but besides Trémaux, there was nobody else around," said Kori. "They took off when Carlisle suspected we were on his trail. At the airstrip, Carlisle rigged his private jet to take off and head west, allowing us to believe the bomb was airborne and potentially heading across the Atlantic. We chased it and shot it down this morning. Of course, it was only a diversion. A complete waste of time."

Then Kori thought of Captain Shane Scott in his flight suit, his wavy blond hair and his clear blue eyes. "Well, maybe not a complete waste," she added.

"And you believe there might be a clue back at the chateau?" said LeClair.

"Frankly, it's all we've got, Captain. We know it's a long shot, but we're kind of grasping at straws."

"How do you know the bomb is not still there?"

"We searched the chateau thoroughly," replied Anya. "And there was nothing of it in the cellar, just the tools to produce it."

"Although, admittedly, we're a little hazy on how they got the bomb out of the cellar," Kori added. "Regardless, we think Carlisle moved the bomb to its ultimate destination after setting us on the trail of the jet."

"Well, in the meantime," said LeClair, "I believe our people in Paris are up to the task. I understand that our tactical units and our police have been completely mobilized. All the major governmental buildings are being evacuated and searched. Boffrand is disagreeable, but he is efficient. But tell me, why do you think he holds you responsible for Carlisle being here?"

"Well, you know—we're Americans, Carlisle is an American. He escaped from an American prison, he faked an American death, he even flew an American plane into your country. In the meantime, in Boffrand's defense, we were a little slow to inform your government of the extent of the danger. Then again, we didn't know ourselves. And we couldn't take a chance. Carlisle thrives on panic and fear. It's what motivates him. We had to make a tactical decision."

"For what it's worth," said LeClair, "it is my experience that no one can be blamed for the actions of a madman, except the madman himself. A madman will do what a madman will do. Unpredictability is the primary hallmark."

"You said it, Captain," said Kori. "Truth be told, we don't even know why Carlisle is targeting France in the first place."

"Hmm … well, I can think of one potential connection," said LeClair. "His father was quite fond of Paris, you see."

"Oh? We were not aware."

"Oh, yes. Grover Carlisle was frequently in the papers over here. He and his wife were always attending this or that theater show or gala event. Any time Grover would speak to the media over here, he would talk about his beloved Paris. It seemed like a second home to the man."

"Interesting," said Kori. "A psychiatrist might have a field day with that. Efron hated his father, you know."

The captain continued. "Yes, apparently, Grover Carlisle's love affair with our city started many, many years ago. He came here for a summer as a student. It's where he met his wife. She, too, was here on a student visa. I heard one time that Grover proposed to her at the Eiffel Tower."

Kori bolted upright in the backseat of the police car. "Of course!" she exclaimed. Turning to Anya, she said,

"Anya, why did you set up the meeting with the fake director at the Eiffel Tower?"

"Because of its popularity," Anya replied. "Its high profile. It would be the last place Carlisle would expect us to meet." As she said the words out loud, Anya knew immediately what Kori was thinking.

"We know where the bomb is, Captain LeClair," said Kori. "Turn us around. Screw the chateau. How fast can you get us to the Eiffel Tower?"

CHAPTER 30

"Turn right here," said the large, balding man in the passenger seat of the truck.

"I know my way around Paris, Nicolas." The man in the driver's seat, a barrel-chested man with dark stringy hair, was frowning.

"Just making sure, Paul. You seem ... agitated. Nervous."

"I am not nervous," Paul snapped back. "It is just, well, you must admit, this whole thing is a bit ... what is the word? Overwhelming?"

"What? Overwhelming? We drive the truck to a spot in front of the Tower, park, get in a car, return to the chateau, and collect 50,000 euros apiece. How is this overwhelming? We should be overwhelmed more often."

"Why could he not have done this himself? Or Jean-Phillippe or the professor? Doesn't that seem strange to you? Why does he need us to drive the truck?"

"Efron Carlisle is a genius. I would not second-guess his plans. He does everything for a reason."

"Yes … yes, I suppose so."

"Relax, *mon ami*. You worry too much. This plan is brilliant in its simplicity. We are lucky to be a part of it. Here, take a swig of this." Nicolas pulled out a small bottle of bourbon and handed it to Paul.

"*Merci*. But do you not worry that this … this bomb … well, it's a bit over the top, no?" said Paul, taking a large gulp from the bottle and passing it back to Nicolas.

"I'm sure it is all for good reasons. You heard Gustave Trémaux back at the chateau speaking of things like emancipation of workers and freedom from repressive governments, and so forth. He spoke with passion, that man. I don't pretend to understand everything about the movement, but I trust that people with that kind of passion do things for good reasons. This feels … important. We are doing good work here, I believe."

"Yes, that may all be true, but did you notice that only Trémaux and Jean-Phillippe spoke like that? Carlisle and the professor never joined those conversations. Carlisle's mind always seemed to be elsewhere. I tell you, Nicolas, he has a strange look in his eyes, that one."

"Are you a psychologist now, Paul?"

"I know what I know. That man cares nothing for the so-called movement. I don't know what his reasons are, but he just comes across to me as being a bit … unhinged, perhaps."

"Nonsense. And what difference does it make? The job will still get done. And we will have ourselves a pretty good payday. Or do you want to continue to work as a bouncer all your life in cheap bars? Don't you see? This is a second chance for us both."

"Yes, maybe, but Nicolas, you heard them talking. This is no ordinary bomb."

"No. It's not. It's big enough to take the Eiffel Tower down. *Good*, I say. I always hated that monstrosity."

"I fear it's bigger than that. You heard what the professor said. This bomb could take out the Tower from a distance of ten times where we are going to park."

"Paul, Paul, Paul," said Nicolas, shaking his head. "You think too much. And if you think too much, you worry too much. These are very smart people we are working for. They know what they are doing. You need to have a little faith."

The two drove in silence for a few blocks until traffic suddenly came to a standstill. The traffic light in front of them changed twice without a single car moving through it.

"What is all this?" said Nicolas, craning his head to get a better look at the line of traffic ahead.

"Rush hour?" said Paul. "It is getting late in the day."

"If we were in the business district, I would agree. This is something else. Look. There are police lights flashing up ahead."

Two blocks in front was the Palais Bourbon. From the cab of the truck, Nicolas and Paul could see the flashing lights of what looked like multiple police cars.

"An accident?" said Paul.

"It must be a big one. Let me go see. Here, hold the bottle." Nicolas opened the cab door and jumped down from the truck. He jogged down the sidewalk for a block then quickly spun around and made his way back to the truck. Climbing back in, out of breath, he said, "We've got to get out of here, Paul."

"Why? What is it?"

"They are not letting anyone drive past that building. In fact, the police are stopping and searching vehicles."

"What?! Why? What is that building?"

"The National Assembly building, I think. Take a right at this intersection. We'll have to go around. We'll have to take Rue de Lille, which, unfortunately, will actually take us in the other direction for several blocks. Then we'll have to find a way to cut across to Rue de Grenelle. That will take us to the Tower."

"Yes, but we'll be late. Damn. Perhaps you should call Carlisle and tell him."

"You have the phone, Paul. Why don't you call him?"

"But I am driving, Nicolas."

"But we are stopped, Paul."

The two glanced sideways at each other and said nothing for several moments. Finally, Paul grumbled, "Okay, okay, I'll call him. But he will not be pleased."

Paul pulled out the phone and dialed Carlisle's number, taking a deep breath as he did so. "Boss?" he said when Carlisle answered, "we have run into a small snag ... Yes, sir ... Well, it seems there is an incident at the National Assembly building ... No, I don't know what it is, but traffic is stopped. The police are searching vehicles ... no, no, they have not searched ours. We are going to go around the roadblock. In fact, cars are now starting to move through the intersection in front of us. Everybody is turning right. Nobody is going past the building. But it is very slow. We will turn right but we will lose time, I'm afraid. All the traffic is now going that way. At this rate, by the time we get turned around and find another route, it might be an additional forty-five minutes before we get to the Tower. And then by the time we park and get far enough away ... *Pardon?* Yes, of course we will call you the moment we are parked ... Yes, boss. *Merci.*"

"What did he say?" said Nicolas.

"Well, he was surprisingly calm about the delay."

"See? And you were afraid to call him."

"And you were not?"

"I knew it would be okay. After all, so what if we're a little late? I can't imagine it would make a difference."

One by one, cars began moving through the intersection ahead until, finally, the truck made it to the light. Paul made the right turn while looking over his left shoulder toward the assembly building and the line of police cars. "I wonder what is going on there?" he said.

"I have only seen roadblocks and vehicle searches like that during bomb scares," said Nicolas.

"Do you suppose?"

"What a coincidence!" said Nicolas and both men began to laugh. "What are the odds that someone else would be planting a bomb today?"

"Remarkable," Paul agreed. "Absolutely remarkable."

"Of course, their bomb will be nothing like ours."

Paul frowned again. "Yes, I suppose that is true."

The traffic crawled along. Each man took another swig from the bottle of bourbon. Neither spoke for quite a while.

"Here, take a right here," Nicolas said at last. "And then another right should put us on Rue de Grenelle." The traffic eased when they got on Rue de Grenelle. Finally, they could see the Tower in the distance. "We are only fifteen minutes away now. I'll be glad when we get there."

"Nicolas," said Paul, "why do you think Carlisle was not displeased by the delay?"

"Hmm? Why would he be? He's a reasonable man. He knows delays happen. And what's forty-five minutes or an hour in the grand scheme of things?"

"Yes, he is reasonable, but he is also a careful, deliberate man. Everything so far has been planned out very meticulously."

"What are you saying, Paul?"

"He has plans for all of us to get away, yes?"

"That is what he said. He has another plane back at the chateau. My understanding is that we will fly from the chateau to an airport near Lyon. We will get our 50,000 euros and say *au revoir*. A new start, Paul."

"But, Nicolas, why would he wait around for us? Especially if we are late to deliver the bomb. Who are we to him? Why would he go out of his way to help us escape with him to Lyon? He barely knows our names."

Nicolas was quiet for several moments. "I don't like what you are saying, Paul," he said finally.

"Neither do I, *mon ami*. But think, Nicolas. Think! We are each 50,000-euro liabilities to him now. Worse, we know who he is, where he can be found. We are witnesses to a monumental crime."

"I don't like what you are saying, Paul," Nicolas repeated.

"Nicolas, he is waiting for us to arrive in front of the Tower. He made sure to remind me to call him when we arrived. He can detonate the bomb remotely anytime he likes. Can you honestly think of a single reason why he would wait for us? Why he wouldn't simply detonate it the moment I call him? I wonder if there is even a getaway car for us. The parking spot, the gendarme ... "

Nicolas took another hit of the bourbon and in a low, resigned whisper, he said once more, "I do *not* like what you are saying, Paul."

285

"Nicolas, he might not even wait for our call. He is probably following our progress by GPS. We have to park this thing and get the hell out of here. *Now.*"

"There," said Nicolas, snapping to attention. "The circle in front of the military museum. Quickly, Paul."

Paul wheeled the truck into the center of the roundabout across from Les Invalides, a complex of buildings that included the military museum of the Army of France. He shifted the truck into park and jumped out. Nicolas likewise jumped and the pair began running in the opposite direction of the Eiffel Tower.

At a stoplight, Nicolas ran up to the driver's side window of a waiting car, pulled out his gun, and pointed it at the alarmed driver, an elderly man wearing a herringbone Kangol hat. "Out!" Nicolas yelled. The old man opened the door of his Renault and stumbled out of the car, Nicolas pushing him aside and climbing in. Paul jumped into the passenger side of the car and Nicolas floored the gas pedal, squealing the tires and leaving the man sitting on the street.

"*T'es une raclure de bidet!*" the man screamed at the quickly departing car, shaking his fist with one hand and clutching his Kangol in the other.

Thirty-five minutes later, the Renault was on A12 on the outskirts of Paris, zipping west at twice the speed limit and weaving in and out of traffic. Neither man noticed the three police cars heading east, lights flashing—a median divided the road—nor would that observation have slowed them down. More importantly, a bomb, neither one knew much about it, other than it was a *big* bomb, was behind them in a parked truck and they had to get the hell away from it, whatever the cost.

CHAPTER 31

Capitaine LeClair didn't notice the fast-moving Renault in the westbound lane, nor would that observation have slowed him down. A bomb—a nuclear bomb, he now understood—was most likely sitting within mere blocks of the Eiffel Tower.

The three occupants of the car—Kori and Anya in the back seat with LeClair driving—stared straight ahead, saying nothing. The two other cars in LeClair's unit were following close behind, lights flashing. LeClair had called in the probable location of Carlisle's nuclear device and the elite GIGN was swarming to the Eiffel Tower, bomb squads in tow. The Paris police, in the meantime, were closing off the area around the Tower. There had been some discussion in Boffrand's office about evacuating the area, but the officials had all decided the effort would be futile. The bomb was going to irradiate anyone within the city limits, anyway. A city the size of Paris simply could not be evacuated. That, of course, had been part of Carlisle's plan all along. Hope now rested on the expertise of the bomb squad personnel, none of whom had been schooled in the dismantling of a nuclear bomb. Then again, it was the detonation bomb that they would need to disarm. Without the small detonation, there would be no bigger detonation. But time was running out.

LeClair's police radio was crackling with activity. Every law enforcement agency in France seemed to be involved. Over the static and the voices, Kori heard her phone ring. "Briggs here," she answered.

"Kori, status update," came the voice of Eaglethorpe. "What's going on? Cooper and Foster and I are landing in forty minutes."

"Chief, I'm afraid status-wise we're in a bit of a pickle. The nuclear device is in the city. We believe it's at the Eiffel Tower. I'm in a car with Captain LeClair of the national police. Agent Kovalev is with me. We're heading there now. So are the bomb squad units of the *Groupe d'intervention de la Gendarmerie nationale*. I can't promise we'll be in time, Chief, but we're sure going to try."

Eaglethorpe was quiet for a moment, taking in the enormity of what Kori was telling him. Then he collected himself and said, "We'll meet you there, Kori. Soon as we land."

"Negative, Chief."

"*Excuse* me, Agent Briggs?"

"I'm sorry, Chief. I'm not trying to be insubordinate. But the truth is, there's nothing you guys can do at this point. My advice is to turn your plane around and land elsewhere. If this thing goes off, it's not going to do the world any good to lose the chief of Rampart and two of his best men. Sorry, Chief, but I guess we're going to have to go without the cavalry this time."

"Then you should get out, too, Kori. What are you hoping to accomplish? Leave it for the bomb squad. That's what they do."

"We have to see it through, Chief. We've come too far." She turned toward Anya and held her eyes for a moment, seeking confirmation, which came by way of a determined nod. "Besides, I'm sure we'll be able to do something when we get there. I don't know what yet, but I feel it in my bones. We can fix this thing. I know we can. We need to be there, Chief."

Eaglethorpe knew there was no talking Kori into giving up her pursuit of the bomb. She was going to do what she felt she needed to do, even if, at that moment, she had no real idea as to what that would be. As more of a plea than an order, Eaglethorpe finally said, "Kori, just get there in time. Okay?"

"Roger that, Chief. I'll keep you posted."

She hung up the phone and LeClair said, "So who is this Rampart of which you speak?"

"Sorry, Captain," said Kori, "I'm afraid I'm going to have to ask that you forget I mentioned that word."

LeClair smiled. "Consider it forgotten. If you can help us with this *pickle* we are in, I do not care who you are with, mademoiselle."

"Thank you. In the meantime, Captain, there is no reason for you or your men to put yourselves at risk. Why don't you pull over and let Agent Kovalev and I take the car. Keep yourselves out of harm's way."

"I'm afraid I cannot do that, Agent Briggs."

"Why not? I promise we'll bring it back in one piece."

"It is my sworn duty as an officer of the law to remain engaged in the pursuit of a successful outcome to this case. I cannot turn away from this now any more than you can."

Kori smiled. "You're a good man, Capitaine."

"*Merci.* You do bring up a good point, however. My men, as much as I'm sure they feel the same way, are under my orders. And I do believe we can proceed without them. They have families, after all." The captain got on his radio to the two cars behind them and ordered the officers to stand down, indeed suggesting they reverse course. Now, it was just the captain, Kori, and Anya moving forward, moving toward the city.

Before long, they crossed the Seine and were within mere miles of the Tower, able to see it in the distance, above the landscape of Paris. The three remained quiet, listening to the crackling voices over the radio. Several blocks around the Tower had been searched and nothing had yet been found. Bomb-sniffing dogs had been sent up and down the surrounding avenues, all through the Champs-de-Mars and along the footpaths and gardens at the base of the Tower. Police units had walked the area thoroughly. Nobody had yet reported anything.

"What do you think?" said Anya, after listening to the various units reporting in. "Something should have been discovered by now. They seem to have covered every inch."

"Maybe my hunch was wrong," said Kori. "But if it's not the Eiffel Tower, then we have a pretty large area to search. All of Paris. Maybe all of France."

The radio came alive just then with the sound of Acting Director Bernard Boffrand's voice: "Capitaine LeClair?"

"Yes, sir," LeClair answered over the open speaker.

"Would you mind telling me why I have every law enforcement agency in France patrolling the Eiffel Tower? You called in to report that the presumed nuclear bomb was at the Eiffel Tower, did you not?"

"Yes, I—"

"And yet, we have turned up nothing. Not so much as a firecracker."

Kori broke in. "The report of the Eiffel Tower was my idea, Director."

"Ms. Briggs, is that you?"

"Yes, sir."

"Why am I not surprised that you have further inserted yourself into this matter? May I ask upon what information you have caused such a wasted use of police resources?"

"Um … a hunch?"

This was followed by several seconds of silence. Finally, "A hunch, Ms. Briggs? A *hunch?!*"

"An educated hunch, Director."

"Well, I am afraid your educated hunch has come to nothing. And I remain unconvinced that the threat is even real."

"It's real, Director. Believe me. Efron Carlisle is out there somewhere with a nuclear—"

"Enough, Ms. Briggs! I have heard everything from you about this alleged bomb that I care to hear. Capitaine LeClair?"

"Yes, sir?"

"Bring Ms. Briggs and her friend to my office immediately."

"Director," said Kori, "if you'll just let us—"

"Ms. Briggs, do you have any idea what the penalty is for creating a false alarm the magnitude of this one? If not, do not worry. I will explain all of that to you when you arrive. That is all."

The radio went silent. "Looks like we're being sent to the principal's office, Anya," said Kori.

And then the radio came alive again, this time with the voice of a Paris police officer in front of Les Invalides. "Suspicious vehicle," declared the officer. "I repeat, a suspicious vehicle. A flatbed truck, abandoned in the roundabout. There is a large wooden crate on the bed of the truck."

"That's just three blocks from here," said LeClair.

"Take us there!" said Kori.

LeClair picked up the mic. "Officer, this is Capitaine LeClair responding. Route all traffic away from the truck. We are on our way."

The speaker crackled once more with the sound of Acting Director Boffrand's voice. "No, Capitaine LeClair! You have your orders to report back to me at once. Do not disobey my—"

Capitaine Matthieu LeClair reached up to the dashboard and switched off the radio and Boffrand's voice was heard no more.

CHAPTER 32

Three-quarters of the way to the chateau, Efron Carlisle was following the progress of the truck on his GPS. In the passenger seat of Jean-Phillippe's car, he looked at the GPS screen with some exasperation. The men had successfully navigated around the roadblock in front of the Palais Bourbon and gotten themselves back on track, but now they were stopped again, still many blocks from the target. Traffic?

Carlisle stroked his chin and thought for a second, finally deciding that he'd wait a little longer. But not too much longer. Turning to Jean-Phillippe and Yanovich, he said, "Ten more minutes, gentlemen. We'll be far enough away by then. Hopefully, the truck will be at the Tower.

If not? Well, not everything can be perfect, I suppose. Besides, you know the old saying. Close only counts in horseshoes and nuclear bombs!" Then he laughed again, that same loud, maniacal laugh.

LeClair pulled up to the roundabout and Kori and Anya spilled out of the car. The truck sat in the center of the circle, a long wooden crate resting in the back. Kori jumped up onto the bed of the truck, followed by Anya, and the two peered in between the slats of the crate. Two large metal containers sat about four feet apart, a small cannon-like apparatus behind one of them and a long wire rigged to something, though the end of it was not visible.

"I think we have our bomb," said Kori. "Ever been this close to a nuclear device?"

"Can't say that I have," said Anya.

"Me neither. They say you never forget your first. Any ideas?"

"Let's pry the top boards off and get a better look. And I suggest we move with some rapidity."

"I'm all in favor of that. Captain LeClair? Do you have something like a crowbar?"

LeClair popped open his car's trunk and grabbed what he wanted, then dashed over to the truck and handed it to Kori. "Here, *mademoiselle*, this is better than *like* a crowbar. It's an actual crowbar."

"I'm going to buy you a drink when this is all over, Captain," Kori said.

"I'm afraid I do not drink, Ms. Briggs."

"Well then you can buy me one."

"It would be my pleasure, Ms. Briggs."

Kori stuck the crowbar between two boards across the top of the crate and began to pry one of them off.

"Gently," said Anya.

"Gentleness isn't exactly my strong suit, Anya, but I'll try." The board came loose and Anya pulled it out of the way. Then Kori yanked off the adjacent board, giving them access to the contraption below.

"Now what?" asked Anya.

"Beats me. We need someone who knows bombs." Kori pulled her phone out and called Eaglethorpe.

"Kori, we're on our approach," Eaglethorpe answered. "What's the scoop?"

"No time to explain, Chief. I need Cooper. ASAP."

"Right. Here he is."

Darren Cooper got on the phone. "Kori?"

"Listen, Coop, I'm sitting on top of the bomb. It's just how you described it. So what do I do?"

"Cripes!" said Cooper. "You found the bomb? Holy cow! Chief, Briggs found the bomb."

"Coop!" yelled Kori into her phone. "Focus, would you? This thing could go off any moment."

"Right, sorry. Okay, so let's see. First things first, do you see any kind of detonating device?"

"I don't know. What would a detonating device look like?"

"Well, it's going to be activated by some sort of electrical connection. So look for some wires."

"There's a single wire."

"Really? Just one?"

"Just one."

"Are you sure?"

"I can count to one, Coop."

"Sure, of course. Well, where does it lead?"

"It runs from the cannon thing to underneath one of the main containers."

"Okay, that's probably it. You need to follow it, Kori. You need to see where it goes."

"I'll have to lift the container."

"Do it. But be careful."

Kori put the phone on speaker and laid it down. Then she put her hands underneath the container and tried to lift it. "Man, what is this made out of?" she said, "lead?"

"Yes, of course," came Cooper's voice over the speaker. "There's uranium in there, you know."

"So I've been told."

Anya reached down into the crate and with her and Kori working together, they managed to lift the container up a couple of inches, enough for Kori to see that the wire led into a cell phone. Then they slowly lowered the container back down.

"Coop, the wire leads into a phone."

"Okay, great," said Cooper, "then we know the detonator is remote activated by a phone call."

"So what do I do?"

"Easy. Just cut the wire."

"Are you sure?"

"Sure, I'm sure."

"But in all the movies there's always a couple of wires. One's always red and one's always black and the hero's never sure which one to cut."

"Kori, this isn't a movie! Cut the damn wire!"

"Right, Coop. Captain! Do you happen to have a—"

"Wire cutter?" the captain said, standing next to the bed of the truck. And then he handed one to Kori that he'd already fished out of his trunk.

"What a guy," said Kori. She took the cutter and brought it up to the wire preparing to cut it. "Okay, Coop, I hope to God you're right. Here goes nothing."

CHAPTER 33

"Well, that's ten minutes," said Carlisle. "Jean-Philippe, pull the car over at the top of this rise. We're going to want to see this. We should be able to observe the mushroom cloud from here, correct Ivan?"

"Oh, yes," Yanovich replied from the back seat. "There will be a rather strong updraft. The gases will spin in a vortex, drawing debris upwards probably to at least 10,000 feet. Perhaps more. It should be quite spectacular."

"Excellent!"

Jean-Phillippe pulled over and they all got out of the car. Carlisle stood on the hood of the Peugeot to get a clearer look toward the sky over Paris in the distance. Then he took out his phone. "Ready, gentlemen?" he beamed. "Behold the hand of death!" Then he dialed the number to the bomb.

CHAPTER 34

"Ivan?" said Carlisle, his voice rising. "I'm not seeing a mushroom cloud. Ivan?!"

"Perhaps you misdialed," said Yanovich.

"I know how to dial a phone number. Could there be some sort of delay?"

"No. The explosion should be instantaneous. Dial it again."

Carlisle sneered and redialed the number and all three looked expectantly toward the sky over Paris.

Nothing.

"Something is not working," said Carlisle. "Something. Is. Not. *Working!*"

"There was nothing wrong with my beautiful nuclear

bomb," said Yanovich. "Might I point out that it was not me who rigged the detonator?"

"Ah, that's true!" said Carlisle. "Jean-Phillippe? Why is my bomb not going off?"

"I don't know, Efron," a nervous Jean-Phillippe replied. "There's no reason it shouldn't. I swear, I rigged it correctly. Try it once more."

Carlisle dialed yet again. Still nothing.

Silently, Carlisle seethed, but it was Ivan Yanovich who voiced the anger. "You idiot!" screamed Yanovich to Jean-Phillippe. "All of my work! Do you understand what went into making that bomb? Do you?!"

"Well, I—"

"A lifetime of knowledge, that is what! Not to mention a hundred pounds of uranium that the Russian authorities would have executed me for, had they caught us at Bayanovka. The risk! The time! I knew I should have rigged the detonator myself. You fool!"

Jean-Phillippe thrust his shoulders back and decided to go on the offensive. "There was nothing wrong with my detonator, professor! It was rigged perfectly. It worked. I have no doubt that it worked. The detonation happened. What occurred, or did not occur, after that is your responsibility, professor, not mine!"

"If your detonation happened, then why did the bomb not go off?! It would have been impossible! A simple detonation would have fired the cannisters into each other and no other possible result could have occurred!"

"So you say. But how are we to know that? Perhaps you did not use enough uranium. Perhaps you built the cannisters wrong. Perhaps you are not as smart as you have been claiming you are. Perhaps you think you know what you are doing when, in reality, you do not!"

Yanovich sprang at Jean-Phillippe, clutching his throat with his hands. The two wrestled, knocking into the car and then falling onto the ground and rolling toward the brush near a grove of trees. Jean-Phillippe was the stronger of the men and was soon on top of Yanovich, punching at his face.

Carlisle glanced at the road and saw no cars coming in either direction. He took the opportunity to end the fight, pulling out his gun and firing twice. Two men, two shots. Carlisle always valued efficiency. He fished the car keys out of Jean-Phillippe's pocket, rolled the bodies into the brush, and was soon driving west again.

Kori held her breath and cut the wire. Nothing happened. She started to exhale when an instant later, the cell phone beneath the bomb rang, causing her and Anya to both recoil with Anya losing her balance and tumbling off the back of the truck. LeClair helped her to her feet.

"Was that it?" she said. "The phone call to set the bomb off? Kori you cut the wire just in time!"

"Way to go!" came Cooper's voice through the speaker on Kori's phone.

"Thanks, Coop," said Kori. She sat on the bed of the truck, wire cutters in hand, trying to collect herself. And then the phone rang a second time and Kori snapped to attention. "Anya, help me lift this again. We have to see where the call is coming from."

"Here, let me help," said LeClair and he and Anya both hopped onto the bed of the truck. While they lifted the heavy lead container, Kori dug out the phone. It rang a third time and Kori could see the number.

"Paris phone number," she said. "No surprise. Carlisle probably bought both phones here. They're most likely prepaid phones so there will be no record of any attached account."

"Doesn't matter," came Cooper's voice. "Tell me the phone number. We can access the network and run a tri-angulation. We won't be able to pinpoint an exact location, but we'll be able to identify the nearest cell tower that was used. France's telecommunications system is pretty elab-orate. Cell towers are close together. We can get awfully close to where the call came from."

"Do it, Coop," said Kori and then she relayed the number to him. "And hurry. We've disarmed that maniac, but he's still out there."

"Shouldn't take me more than five minutes."

LeClair used the time to call Acting Director Boffrand, who, after hearing the captain's report, grudgingly agreed that the captain had made the right decision by going to the truck, but who, nevertheless, wanted the captain to know that refusing an order was still insubordination regardless of motive. Furthermore, he wanted the captain to know that, when this whole thing was over, the two were going to sit down and have a very long, very serious chat. "I will look forward to it, Director," said LeClair curtly before hanging up.

By then, the bomb squad had arrived and several members had gathered on the back of the truck to inspect the contents of the crate. The hazardous materials unit of the national police was on its way, as were two engineers from the Dampierre Nuclear Power Plant to help with disposal. Before long, the bomb squad would remove the detonating explosive device and disassemble the cannon apparatus. The bomb would no longer be a bomb. Just two lead cannisters of uranium.

In the meanwhile, Cooper was back on the phone with coordinates. The call had come from just a few miles east of Gustave Trémaux's chateau.

"Of course," said Kori. "The landing strip. He's probably got another plane coming in for him from somewhere. Coop, let me talk to the chief."

Eaglethorpe got on the phone. "Congratulations, Kori. We're all breathing again. A round of beers on me."

"Don't congratulate me yet, Chief. We still need to get that son of a bitch. If we lose him now, he'll just set up shop again somewhere else. As long as he's around, this world isn't safe. He's probably on his way out of the country. Most likely, he's planning on leaving by way of the same landing strip he sent the Gulfstream out of. My guess is that another plane is coming in for him."

"Roger that, Kori. What do you need?"

"Well, I hate to say it, but I'm afraid we're going to have to notify EUROCONTROL again. They need to start searching the skies once more, starting near the coordinates that Cooper has."

"I understand. I'll make the call. What are you going to do?"

"Agent Kovalev and I are going to drive out there with the captain."

"Kori, please wait for us. We're almost there." Then he caught himself. "What am I even saying? As if I'm going to be able to stop you. Go. But be safe."

"I will, Chief. After all, it's not every day you offer to pay for a round of beers."

"You find Carlisle, I might even pay for second round."

"I'm holding you to that, Chief." She hung up the phone and turned toward Captain LeClair. "Any interest in meeting the man who paid to have this bomb put together?"

"I insist upon it," the captain replied.

Moments later, Kori and Anya and LeClair were speeding back toward the chateau. There were still a couple of hours of daylight remaining and Kori knew their chances of finding Carlisle would take a nosedive after dark. Along the way, LeClair called the national police, bypassing Boffrand and the intelligence department altogether, and requested roadblocks within a ten-mile radius of the chateau.

"I'd love to be a fly on the wall when you finally sit down with Boffrand," Kori said to LeClair.

"Yes, I don't imagine it will be pleasant," said LeClair. "For either of us. I have been doing this much too long to take guff from someone like Boffrand. If he so much as threatens me with a suspension, I believe I will resign."

"Really, Captain? That would be a big loss for the department, I'm sure. They'd be losing a good man."

"That is kind of you to say."

"And wouldn't you miss it?"

"Perhaps. But retirement is something I have been considering for some time now. My daughter is grown, and it is just me and my wife. We have talked about doing some traveling."

"Sounds nice."

"Yes, I think it would be. My wife has been a very patient woman."

Within an hour, they were at the main road where it ran past the long driveway of the chateau. "Park here, Captain," said Kori. "There's no access road to the airfield. The best way to access the field is to walk through that grove of trees over there, beyond the house."

LeClair parked and the three began hiking toward the trees that ringed the airfield. Once through the grove, they drew their guns and looked around at the empty field.

"No signs of a plane or of Carlisle," said Anya.

"And yet the latest report from the chief is that EUROCONTROL has reported no flight activity out this way," said Kori. "So he hasn't taken off from here, at least not yet."

"Then, assuming he came back here, he might be holed up in the chateau."

Kori nodded. "Yep. Waiting for dark to make his move."

"Then I suggest we search the chateau, *mademoiselles*," said Captain LeClair, looking back over his shoulder at the house through the trees. "But let me call in the GIGN tactical unit first."

"Yes, by all means, call them," said Kori. "But it might take them awhile to get here. We'll soon be losing daylight. As Anya and I know, that chateau can be a pretty foreboding place in the dark. We need to go in now, Captain."

"I understand, Ms. Briggs," said LeClair. "Lead the way."

With LeClair following on their heels, the Rampart agents scrambled through the woods to the far side of the chateau and around toward the rear veranda where they had entered the house the night before. They crouched down at the edge of the trees. The daylight meant they could see the house better, but Kori also knew that it meant that anyone inside could see them better, too.

Kori was about to point out the balustrade they had climbed, when she suddenly sensed movement in one of the upstairs windows. Then a flash, followed immediately by the sound of a gunshot. Something whizzed past her and the next sound she heard was a loud grunt by LeClair.

"Gunfire!" she yelled, flattening out on the ground. "Second floor window!"

"Got it!" said Anya, who spun around from behind a tree and returned fire at the window, getting off several rounds. Then silence. When Anya turned back around she saw Kori kneeling over LeClair, blood oozing out of the captain's body.

CHAPTER 35

"Captain!" said Kori.

"It is nothing," said LeClair, trying to push himself up to a seated position behind a tree. "My shoulder."

While Anya kept a lookout on the chateau, Kori applied pressure to the shoulder wound. She ripped the captain's shirt to get a better look. "Looks like it got you pretty good, Captain, but I've seen worse." Then she ripped off the rest of the sleeve, wadded it into a ball, put it on the wound, and took the captain's opposite hand, placing it over the balled up fabric. "There. Keep pressure on it. You'll be fine, but you're going to need some medical attention. Here, let me use your radio."

Kori took the captain's radio and called for an ambulance.

"Kori, it won't be safe for the medical crew when they get here," said Anya, still watching the windows. "We need to go in now and get Carlisle. Otherwise, he might try to pick them off. As well as us, of course."

"Agreed," said Kori. "We can't stay here. We need to go in now."

"Wait," said LeClair. "I'll be fine here, *mademoiselles*. Forget the ambulance. I do not need one. We need to wait for the tactical squad."

"We could wait for the tactical squad, Captain, but that rather interferes with my plans," said Kori with a grim smile. "You see, I was planning on getting this son of a bitch myself. Agent Kovalev?"

"I'm with you, Agent Briggs."

"Now, Captain, stay here, against this tree, out of sight. By the time the paramedics get here, we'll have resolved this whole thing."

"*Mademoiselles, s'il vous plaît*, it is much too dangerous for you to go in by yourselves."

"Save your strength, Captain," said Kori. "And keep pressure on that wound. Anya, ready?"

"Ready."

"*Go!*"

The agents spun toward the chateau, fired several shots at the window, and then sprinted toward the building, diving behind the shrubs next to the side of the veranda. Kori peered over the shrubs. "There's our window," she whispered, pointing to the tall, arched window they had accessed the night before. "Shall we?"

"Anytime you're ready."

Anya gave Kori a boost and Kori clambered over the balustrade. She turned and helped pull Anya up, and then both agents, crouching and with guns drawn, moved toward the window. Anya glanced between the open curtains and saw nothing. "It's still unlocked from last night," she whispered.

"Then we might as well make a grand entrance."

Anya nodded. Kori said, "Now," and they each took a window, threw it open, jumped up on the sill, and then leapt into the chateau. Landing on the hallway floor, Anya had her gun pointed in one direction and Kori the other. But the hallway was empty.

The two remained stationary, listening for any noise at all, but the chateau was quiet.

"Anya," whispered Kori, "do you think it's possible that you hit him when you shot at the second-floor window?"

"If he was standing there, yes, of course. It is more than possible. It is certain. My bullets go where I aim them."

Kori smiled at Anya's quiet conviction, knowing she wasn't saying it to brag, but merely to relate a salient fact. "Then I suggest we start with that room," she said.

The two made their way quietly up the staircase. It was now approaching early evening and the light from the outside windows was growing weaker, creating eerie shadows. At the top of the stairs, they paused and counted the doors from the end of the hallway, determining which room the shot had come from. As Kori recalled, this was the music room, the large room with the baby grand piano and the harp. The door was open. Both agents stormed through the doorway, ready to shoot, but nobody was there. Kori moved around the piano to the tall window and saw a shell casing on the floor. "It was definitely this room," she whispered. "I wonder why he only shot once." Then she noticed several bullet holes through the curtains, dead center of the window. "You weren't lying about your aim," she said. "No wonder he only shot once. You didn't give him a second chance."

"But where in this house could he be?" asked Anya, joining Kori by the window.

Kori was ready to make a guess when she heard the sound of metal on metal, then felt the floor abruptly shift below her. For a millisecond, she imagined an earthquake, but before she could gain any conscious recognition of what was happening, the floor was suddenly gone. The only sense she had then was one of falling. Helplessly.

She landed hard on the floor below, joined by Anya, and the first thing both agents saw was the twisted, smiling face of Efron Carlisle, holding a Smith & Wesson 500. "Welcome, ladies," he said. "Nice of you to drop in!"

"Well, what do you know, Anya?" said Kori, sitting up and taking mental inventory of her condition: bruised, certainly, but no breaks. "The nutjob himself. That's a hell of gun you've got there, Carlisle. I can only guess at what you're compensating for."

"Speaking of which," said Carlisle, "you'll be so kind as to slide your weapons over to me, won't you? Yes, that's good. Thank you. Interesting house, isn't it? Would you believe I didn't even have to make that trap door? Gustave told me that it's been here for decades. Apparently, at one time, the lady of the house insisted on making the room above us into a music room, over her husband's objections, who, naturally, suggested that a first floor room was more suitable, given the difficulties of getting the piano upstairs. But of course the lady would get her way and it was decided that the easiest manner of transport would be to actually remove part of the floor and use a crane to hoist the piano up. Rather than tear apart and rebuild the floor, they simply cut out a section of it, putting one end of the section on hinges, thereby allowing for future deliveries to the room and, in fact, to the entire second floor. It was actually a smart idea, don't you think? More homes should come with trap doors. Obviously, there are a myriad of uses. Anyway, I merely moved the piano off the hinged section, leaving it for you to stand on. The side that swings open is held in place by a steel pin. All I needed to do was knock the pin out and *voilà*. Here you are."

"So you shot out of that particular window on purpose, knowing that's where we would go first," said Kori.

"Indeed."

"You'll be disappointed to learn that you didn't kill your target, by the way."

315

"No matter. I didn't want him anyway. It's you two that I want. That's why I've stayed around. That's why I haven't yet made my getaway. There will be a plane landing here soon." And then the smile was gone and the face of Efron Carlisle turned red and wrathful. "I wanted you two," he seethed, "because it was you two who *screwed up my beautiful plan!*"

"Oh, yeah, it was beautiful all right," said Kori. "A plan to destroy the Eiffel Tower and most of Paris and potentially kill millions of people in the process. Lovely. Tell me Carlisle, do insane people know they're insane? I mean, do you have any idea how far off the wacko scale you really are?"

Carlisle comported himself and replied, "Oh, but my dear, it is the world that is insane."

"No, I'm pretty sure it's just you, babe. By the way, I know all about your daddy and mommy issues. They didn't give you enough love, blah, blah, blah. And so you want to get back at them by destroying the world, especially a place that meant so much to them. Congratulations. You'll probably be a case study in a psychiatry textbook someday."

"Well, that is where you are wrong, Ms. Briggs. I dealt with my parents a long time ago. Paris was just convenient. In the beginning, it was to be DC. I had my people in place there, as I believe you know."

"I assumed that was to throw us off the track."

"Well, it turned out that way, but, no, that was where I had originally envisioned my beautiful bomb going off.

Right at the Lincoln Memorial, as a matter of fact. You see? It's not 'daddy and mommy issues,' as you so inelegantly put it. What I do is art. I am an artist first and foremost. This would have been a masterpiece that no one would have ever forgotten."

"Yeah, well, you'll have plenty of time for art where you're going. You like basket weaving? How about water-colors? You're under arrest, by the way."

Carlisle laughed. "Too bad you won't have time to read me my rights, Ms. Briggs."

"So why didn't you go through with your DC plans?"

"Well, I knew from my people there that you and your Rampart pals were hot on my trail and I decided not to take the extra time. We let you believe we were there, but I routed a cargo plane to Paris and then came here."

"Where you had a friend."

"Gustave Trémaux is not a friend. He was a tool for my use. And not a very good one, as it turns out. Anyway, I will have to confess that the Eifel Tower idea was a sort of nod to my parents, yes."

"Wait a minute," interjected Anya, "what did you mean when you said you 'dealt with' your parents a long time ago?"

"Why, the fire, my dear. It was in all the papers. I made it look like a gas leak. Even fooled the insurance investigators."

"Wow, you really are a sicko," said Kori.

"Be that as it may, it is my turn to ask a question." Then Carlisle looked at Anya and smiled. "I know you have been tagging along with Ms. Briggs here, but I'm afraid I must confess that I am not entirely sure who you are, my lovely."

"My name is Kovalev."

"That is quite impossible. My father's notes mentioned a Rampart connection in Russia named Kovalev, but Kovalev is an older man."

"Your father's notes are correct. But they are incomplete."

"I see. A daughter, perhaps?"

"Something like that."

"How nice. I am sure that when he hears of your death, he will be proud that you died in the line of duty."

"Your father's notes," said Kori. "When did you stumble upon those?"

"Ms. Briggs, I don't *stumble* upon things. I knew my father had political connections and I suspected all along that those connections went as high as the White House and included national security interests. I have to confess I didn't know of Rampart, however, until after my father's death. Among other things, I inherited a key to a certain safe deposit box with all of his records on your organization. The records were quite detailed. I knew I could use my knowledge of your agency's existence to my ends. I could make you believe that the uranium was stolen by Alfawda. We set up the raid in Bayanovka to look like it."

"But Hasan el-Sadek learned it wasn't and you had him killed."

"That is correct, Ms. Briggs."

"Hasan was a friend of mine."

"Pity. In truth, it wasn't easy to identify him. I had my best man in New York searching for him for quite some time. When he found him, he followed him for a day, to be certain. Sure enough, he followed el-Sadek to Central Park where you happened to be waiting for him."

"Impossible. Nobody followed Hasan to the park that day. I was watching."

"Perhaps you remember an old woman walking through the park?"

"Don't tell me. Your man?"

"A master of disguises. But, tell me, how did you learn I was in Paris?"

"Jael Roth told me," said Anya. "Your hit man left him alive."

"Hmm … I knew I should have taken care of that little detail myself. Apparently, I can trust no one."

"All right," said Kori. "One more question before you kill us, you cretin. How did you get the bomb into the city? We followed your tunnel to the airfield, but there are no access roads there."

"You assumed we took it out through the tunnel."

"Of course."

"But, you see, your assumption is wrong. We took it out through the front door."

319

"But how could you have gotten it out of the cellar?" asked Anya.

"We didn't, my dear," Carlisle grinned. "You see, we didn't build it in the cellar. We built it in the room above you. Then we lowered it down through the very trap door you fell through."

"Aha," said Kori. "And then you took all the tools and everything down to the cellar to make it look as if you'd built it there."

"Exactly."

"I thought the music room looked a little too clean."

"You wanted us to enter the tunnel," said Anya.

"Precisely. Meanwhile, we were long gone by then."

"Then who blew up the tunnel?" said Kori.

"It was rigged to cave in when you reached a certain point. It was, in actuality, a backup plan. Trémaux was supposed to have taken care of you long before you entered the tunnel. How did you get away from him, anyway?"

"Let's just say these boots are made for more than walking," said Kori.

"I see. More incompetence on the part of my people. The tunnel is a job I left to Jean-Phillippe. You might remember him as the fake Director Chardin. But he apparently screwed up his job, too. Both of you, by all rights, should be buried in that tunnel right now."

"Hard to find good help these days, eh, Efron?"

"Apparently he screwed up the detonator on the bomb, too."

"Well, I'm afraid I'm going to have to defend him on that one," said Kori, pulling the detonator cell phone out of her pocket. "This belongs to you, I believe. You'll be pleased to know that it worked just fine. This phone rang and rang. Unfortunately for you, someone cut the wire from this phone to the detonator."

"And can I presume that someone was you, Ms. Briggs?" Carlisle said, beginning to seethe once more.

"Guilty as charged." Then Kori laughed. "Oh, man, you were close, too. Wasn't he, Anya?"

"Probably not even two seconds off," Anya grinned. "Damn shame. All that work."

Carlisle said nothing, once again composing himself.

"But speaking of deranged people," said Kori, "where is this Jean-Phillippe? And where is Ivan Yanovich?"

"Let's just say I terminated their employment," said Carlisle.

"I see. And what about the Gulfstream? How did you know we'd find the airfield? We were supposed to have been killed in the tunnel collapse."

"Yes, but I assumed your people would come to the chateau, search the grounds, and come upon the airfield. And your dead bodies, by the way. The airborne plane was designed to keep everyone busy searching for hours. I had hoped it would be practically across the Atlantic before being spotted."

"It almost worked, Efron. But we survived your stupid tunnel, found the airstrip, and eliminated the plane in no time. From there, it was easy. You shouldn't leave flatbed trucks with suspicious packages parked in tow-away zones."

"Be that as it may, I believe I have answered enough of your questions. The time has come to deal with the both of you. Ms. Briggs, you seem to be the one who has been the biggest thorn in my side, the one who has tried my patience the most and is who is even now trying my patience. Congratulations; you'll be first. Ms. Kovalev, I'll understand if you want to turn your head away. This will not be very pretty, I'm afraid."

Carlisle took a step toward Kori and raised his gun, aiming dead center at her forehead. "Any last words, my dear?"

"Sure, I've got some last words: *Screw you, you freaking loon!*"

CHAPTER 36

"Yoo-hoo! Mr. Trémaux? Are you home? Yoo-hoo!"

It was the unmistakable voice of Madame Duchamp and it seemed to be coming from the foyer. Carlisle, gun still trained on Kori's forehead, instinctively turned ever so slightly toward the sound.

It was just enough.

Efron Carlisle never saw it coming. The bullet hit him squarely in the temple and he dropped in a heap, dead before he hit the floor. Kori turned toward Anya who was holding a pistol that was no bigger than her hand.

"Nice," said Kori, breathing a sigh of relief and getting to her feet. "What have you got there?"

"Colt Mustang," said Anya. "I keep it taped to my ankle. Do you not have one of these?"

"Nope. I guess that's just one more thing I need to add to my Christmas list."

"I highly recommend it. It's gotten me out of some jams before."

The agents walked over to Carlisle's body to confirm the kill. "You hit him perfectly," said Kori.

"I told you," smiled Anya. "My bullets go where I aim them." This time, it seemed just a little like bragging, but that was quite all right with Kori.

"Looks like I owe you one, my Russian friend."

"Happy to help, my American friend."

Sweeping into the room just then was a smiling Madame Duchamp, whose smile withered the moment she gazed upon the dead body of Carlisle, blood pooling under his head. "Oh, my!" she gasped. "What has happened here? I came to see Mr. Trémaux. To invite him and his friends to our wine and cheese party tomorrow evening. The door was open and I ... oh, my, I think I'm going to faint ... "

Kori ran over to Madame Duchamp and helped her into a chair. "There, there, Madame Duchamp. Just breathe. You'll be fine. But I'm afraid neither Mr. Trémaux nor his friends will be able to attend your party tomorrow."

Outside, the sound of a siren indicated that the paramedics had arrived. Kori turned to Anya. "Stay with her, okay? I'll run out and point the paramedics to Captain LeClair."

"Of course."

Kori ran through the house and out the front door and down the steps of the portico just as the ambulance pulled up. "He's around the rear of the house," Kori told the two medics in French. "You'll find him just at the tree line. Gunshot wound to the shoulder. Quickest way is through the house and out the back. Oh, and in the rear room, you'll see a body, too. Plus a woman who's feeling a little faint."

The paramedics looked at each other quizzically, shrugged, and then dashed inside the chateau with a stretcher. Kori glanced down the long driveway and spotted two police cars speeding toward the house followed by a third, unmarked car. The convoy pulled up beside the ambulance, two officers rolling out of each police car. To Kori's surprise, out of the third car poured Eaglethorpe, Cooper, and Foster, all with guns drawn.

"Briggs!" exclaimed Eaglethorpe. "Are you okay?"

"Chief! Guys! Boy are you all a sight for sore eyes. Yes, I'm fine. You can put your guns away." Then, turning toward the officers, she said, "The scene is secure, fellas. Check out the back room. And then, get on the radio and call in some reinforcements. Have them stationed out back beyond the grove of trees. A plane will be landing on a grass airstrip soon. You might want to arrest the pilot and take him in for questioning." The officers nodded and rushed inside. "Hey, Chief," said Kori, "I thought the cavalry was supposed to arrive *before* the big life-and-death moment."

"Got here as fast as we could," said Eaglethorpe. "Where's Carlisle?"

"He's in the back. Dead. Agent Kovalev shot him."

"Great! Where is that old Russian mug? I'd sure like to shake his hand."

"*He* is right here," came Anya's voice as she walked out onto the portico, Madame Duchamp leaning on her arm.

Eaglethorpe looked bewildered.

"Chief," said Kori, trying to contain her amusement, "allow me to introduce you to Agent Anya Kovalev."

"You … you're Kovalev?"

"Yes, sir," smiled Anya. "At your service."

"Are … are you sure?"

"Yes," Anya snickered. "At least I think so."

"Well, I'll be damned."

Kori and Anya both broke into laughter. Then Kori said, "Listen, Chief, what do you say after we wrap up here that we hold our debriefing at a charming little inn that happens to be nearby? Agent Kovalev and I can vouch for the place. They have a marvelous duck, as it happens, and a pretty solid wine list. Is that okay with you, Madame Duchamp?"

Madame Duchamp meekly nodded. "I do hope someone explains all of this to me at some point," she said.

"Don't worry. We'll give you a ride back and explain on the way. Oh, and guys, after dinner, let's head back to the city. Anya and I happen to know of a nice little jazz place. Chief, I believe you said something about buying the beers? At least two rounds of them, as I recall."

"It would be my pleasure, Agent Briggs," said Eaglethorpe. Then, pulling out his cell phone, he said, "I'd better call POTUS in the meantime. He's expecting a report."

As Eaglethorpe briefed a much-relieved president, Cooper and Foster introduced themselves to Anya. Kori then gave them the blow by blow account from the defusing of the bomb to the shooting of Carlisle.

"Wow, two close ones in a single day," said Foster. "You're really earning your paycheck, Briggs."

"Tell me about it," said Kori.

Eaglethorpe finished his call with the president just as the paramedics came through the front door with Captain LeClair on the stretcher, his shoulder bandaged.

"Chief, this is Captain LeClair of the national police," said Kori, stopping the paramedics. "He was of immense help to us."

"*Monsieur*," said LeClair. "I take it you are the superior of these two *mademoiselles*?"

"Superior?" said Eaglethorpe. "Well, I wouldn't put it like that exactly. Let's just say one of them works for me."

"Actually, Chief," said Kori, "both of us work for you."

"Huh?"

"It's true," said Anya, smiling. "Blake, your man in Russia, hired me years ago. I believe that makes me an employee of yours, at least indirectly."

"Cripes, nobody ever tells me anything," said Eaglethorpe, shaking his head. "Well, a belated welcome aboard, I guess."

"Thank you."

Eaglethorpe shook his head again and then turned toward LeClair. "Well, it seems as if both of these agents *do* work for me, Captain. I trust they represented themselves well."

"Represented themselves well?" said LeClair. "I want you to know that I will be speaking to my superiors about their bravery. Paris thanks them. All of France thanks them. It has been my pleasure to have worked with them today. You have two of the very finest here, *monsieur*."

"Thank you, Captain," said Eaglethorpe. "I know. Believe me, I know."

The paramedics continued carrying LeClair to the ambulance.

"Take care of yourself, Capitaine," Kori called after him. "And don't take any crap from that pinhead Boffrand!"

Captain LeClair managed a smile before the paramedics slid the stretcher into the back of the ambulance.

"Okay, Agent Briggs," said Eaglethorpe. "Take me to Carlisle's body. Let's get this thing turned over to the national police and move forward with dinner. That duck sounds good."

"Sounds like a plan, Chief."

CHAPTER 37

After dinner, the group celebrated at the jazz club until the wee hours of the morning. Eaglethorpe bought the beers and then some. Then, in accordance with Rampart procedure, they left for the airport, quietly leaving France behind. Boffrand's people searched in vain for them the next day. There were many questions that needed answering. Paperwork to be completed. Reports filled out. Witness statements to be entered into the record. Two days later, Boffrand would receive a package with a full and complete accounting of the events. There was no return address. Boffrand would have everything he would need to close the case, but he'd never discover who the agents were. Rampart would keep its anonymity.

Most Parisiennes would never know the extent of the danger their city had faced. They knew only that "a large bomb" had been disarmed in front of Les Invalides, but Paris intelligence released no details to indicate it had been a nuclear bomb. A hero was needed, and so the national police chose Capitaine Matthieu LeClair to receive a medal of valor, over the protestations of Acting Directorate of Intelligence and Security of Defense Bernard Boffrand. LeClair reluctantly accepted the medal, making a very brief speech, his arm in a sling, thanking "the two amazing women who made this possible." Everyone assumed he was honoring his wife and daughter.

The morning Rampart left Paris, Kori and Anya said their goodbyes at the airport before Anya boarded her plane for Moscow.

"Take good care of yourself, my Russian friend," said Kori. "It's been a hell of a ride. Thank you for everything."

"Take good care of yourself, my American friend," said Anya. "It has been my pleasure. Perhaps someday we'll work together again."

"I hope so."

"Me, too."

They embraced and Anya turned and headed for her gate, looking back once and throwing a quick wave to Kori. Kori waved back and watched Anya disappear into the airport crowd. There was so much she would have liked to have said to her. But after what the two had been through together, she also knew that no words could do justice to what either one was feeling.

Two weeks later, Kori found herself sitting in the Oval Office with Eaglethorpe, Cooper, and Foster. They had met with the president for a full debriefing the day after they'd arrived, but he had called them back in for a special meeting. None of the agents knew the reason.

"Folks, first of all," said the president behind his desk. "I want you to know that the CIA is now busy tracking down every lead that can help us find anybody whatsoever who was even remotely connected to Carlisle. I just got off the phone with the director and she was very resolute, assuring me of the efforts being made. As we know, Carlisle had to have had a lot of help to pull this off. The CIA is tracing his route from Bayanovka to Tel Aviv to Paris and interrogating anyone who might have been involved. I'm happy to report that the French police have apprehended the drivers of the truck. They've turned themselves in and have been spilling the beans about everything they know. The pilot of Carlisle's getaway plane has been talking, too. And of course, you already know that the body of Ivan Yanovich was found, along with the man who pretended to be directorate of intelligence Marc Chardin. The French ballistics report has matched their gunshot wounds to Carlisle's gun."

Kori thought about Olga—Yanovich's sister in St. Petersburg, and the honey cake she had offered her and Anya that day. Yanovich might have gone off the deep end, but he had a caring sister who still loved him. Kori made a mental note to send flowers. She was going to send some to the Roths as well. Jael had indeed died of his gunshot wounds. Kori thought of his father, declaring "I have no son," but she knew better. She remembered him looking at her with pleading eyes. *Do you think you can help us find our boy?*

The president continued. "Also, in conjunction with the FBI, the CIA director is following up on any lead that can help us locate Carlisle's men here in Washington; the ones who were following Agent Briggs in that BMW that day. We're trying to find Carlisle's contacts in New York, too. In particular, whoever it was that killed Hasan el-Sadek. Frankly, I don't envy the CIA's job. A lot of it is just plain grunt work. Digging through rental car records, hotel ledgers, restaurant receipts, etcetera. But the director says she's got two agents who are working around the clock to do all of the crappy detail work. Poor bastards."

"Mr. President," asked Kori, "just out of idle curiosity, did she happen to mention who those two agents are?"

"Um … Moore and Watson I believe are the names. Why, Agent Briggs? Do you know them?"

"No, not really, sir." Kori squirmed in her seat trying to avoid laughing out loud.

"Well, anyway," the president continued, "the fact of the matter is that I'm afraid we'll never be able to catch everyone who was involved. There are still some crazy people out there. But at least Efron Carlisle is no more.

Once again, I cannot express my gratitude sufficiently. Especially to you, Agent Briggs."

"All in a day's work, sir," Kori replied. "And I had some valuable help."

"Indeed. You cannot imagine how happy I was to hear that our man Kovalev has a daughter who has become every bit the agent he was and more. I'm sure she'll continue to be of great value to the security of this country."

"I'm sure, sir."

"And that brings me to the real reason I invited you all here today. I guess I'll just come out with it. After much careful and deliberate thought, I've made an important decision. I'm shutting down Rampart."

The agents sat in silence, none of them believing what they'd just heard. A million things ran through Kori's mind. Shut down Rampart? Hadn't they just saved the lives of perhaps millions of people?

Eaglethorpe was the first to speak. "Mr. President, with all due respect—"

"Richard, you know the inherent problems we have with your agency. This case underscored the danger in no uncertain terms. I almost single-handedly compromised your mission with my desire to want to appease the agency's benefactor. Years ago, I gave critical information away to Grover Carlisle, information that almost scuttled this entire operation. That fact is, so long as Rampart is a part of the executive branch—indeed, so long as Rampart is a part of the government—it will be subject to compromise and open to political pressures. This was not the original purpose of Rampart. The original purpose was to have a top-secret agency that would be above the fray. A small group, working for itself for the protection and security of this nation, answering to nobody, but following, instead, its own mission to keep the world safe. It needs to be independent."

"But, sir, to shut down the agency … " said Eaglethorpe, his voice trailing off.

"It needs to be independent," the president repeated. "And so, because it is currently part of the executive branch, I'm shutting it down." Then he paused and leaned forward, lowering his voice. "Now, should it open back up again on its own, well, then, obviously that's out of my control."

"Open back up?" said Eaglethorpe. "But funding—"

"Funding," interrupted the president, "should not be a problem. Here." The president smiled and handed Eaglethorpe a leather notebook.

"Sir? What's this?"

"For the past two weeks, I've enlisted the help of the FBI's top forensic accountants. They have literally scoured the world's banks and financial institutions for anything tied to Efron Carlisle. It wasn't that difficult, once we knew he was still alive all that time. He'd been accessing his money, which made it easier to trace. In that notebook, you'll find a list of account numbers and respective balances. See the total?"

Eaglethorpe gawked at a number he could scarcely believe. The rumors of Carlisle's wealth were not only true, they had been gross underestimates.

"Now," continued the president, "we're going to call all of that money in. Confiscate it. Carlisle has no heirs and we can clearly demonstrate that the money was used in the commission of a crime. The thing is, different agents worked on compiling that list and each one reported to me directly. I made sure that none of them saw the complete ledger. Nobody outside of this room knows the total. If, say, half of it were to go missing before we call in the accounts, well, nobody would know. The United States government would still get a nice windfall, an amount nobody would question. And a certain agency, a favorite of mine, I might add, could continue on its mission unencumbered by the tethers of politics and without having to worry about funding ever again."

"Wow, sir," was all Eaglethorpe could muster.

"Wow, indeed, Richard. You'll be completely independent now. Answerable to no one. Future presidents will still learn of your existence, of course. After all, you'll still need the executive branch to mobilize the other resources of the government if required; someone to order CIA or FBI records of some criminal perhaps. Or someone to call, for instance, the president of France, if the situation warrants. Or, for that matter, someone for the president to call upon if a national security issue requires the talents of your group. But all decisions for that group will be made by you and you alone. And all your secrets will remain your secrets. What do you say, Richard?"

Eaglethorpe looked at his fellow agents, all of them wide-eyed at the promise of an even better organization and a completely secure future. "Well, sir, it's a lot of trust to put in us. A *lot* of trust."

"Maybe," said the president, holding each agent's eyes for just a moment, "but I know you people. I have had the honor and privilege of working with you throughout both my terms of office. And I know you will always do the right thing."

"Then on behalf of my colleagues, I say yes, Mr. President. And thank you."

"Don't thank me, Director Eaglethorpe. After all, the new and improved Rampart comes courtesy of our old friend, Efron Carlisle. The irony is rich, is it not? I can't think of a better guy's money to spend on the security of our country!"

Then the president rose and the agents followed suit. The president shook everyone's hand and said, "Godspeed to you all. It goes without saying that we never had this meeting and I never handed you that notebook. Incidentally, we'll be calling in what's left of Carlisle's money seventy-two hours from now. I trust that will give you the time you need to hack into the accounts and get what you need."

"Yes, sir," said Eaglethorpe.

"And don't be shy."

"Yes, sir."

"Again, let me say it's an honor to know you all," the president concluded. "I will sleep much better knowing that you're out there. No offense, however, but I hope I don't need to see you again anytime soon, if you know what I mean."

"We understand, Mr. President," smiled Eaglethorpe. "I think we're all looking forward to a little downtime."

That evening, Kori sat across from her mother in a booth at Martin's Tavern in Georgetown, finally having the dinner she'd promised. Joan was working on the shrimp fettucine while Kori was devouring the chicken Milanese, still thinking about the events of the day. And the events of the past two weeks.

"Well, so, tell me, dear," Joan said, "tell me more about that meeting in Colorado."

"Well, like I said, it was fine, Mom. Team-building exercises. Kind of fun, but the whole thing went on a little too long. It's good to be back. What's been new with you?"

"Well, I'm taking Baxter to the vet tomorrow."

"Oh?"

"Yes, I'm not totally sure what's wrong. He keeps pawing at his ear. I think maybe he's got an ear infection."

"Aw, I'm sorry to hear that, Mom. Hopefully, it's nothing serious."

"He's had them before. The doctor will probably just prescribe some ear drops."

"Good."

"This is nice, isn't it?" Joan smiled, looking up at Kori. "You and me having dinner?"

"It's wonderful, Mom," Kori smiled back, holding her mother's eyes. "It's really great to see you. It's been too long."

"We should do it more often."

"Absolutely. You'll get no argument from me."

"Maybe now that you won't be traveling so much. You won't need to go off anywhere else for a while now, will you?"

"Well, truthfully, Mom, there's one more trip I need to make."

"Really?"

"Yep. There's an international conference in Germany and I'd better be there."

"Oh, but you just came back from a trip!"

"I know. No rest for the weary, huh? Well, this one's going to be more like a vacation. Not much business. Just a few meetings and product demos. There'll be enough time to do some sightseeing. The conference is in Heidelberg."

"Heidelberg?"

"Yep. They say it's what you think of when you think of old Germany. It's supposed to be a charming town on a river with brick streets and little cafés. There's a big castle there and everything."

"Ooh, sounds nice. Very romantic."

"That's what I hear."

"Well, that's good dear. You know, maybe you'll meet a nice man over there."

"Yeah, maybe," Kori said, Captain Shane Scott's blue eyes popping into her head. "You never know, I guess."

"Well, at the very least, you could use a vacation. You work awfully hard, Kori. That conveyor company doesn't know just how blessed they are to have you working for them. If anyone deserves a vacation, it's you, dear."

"Thanks, Mom," smiled Kori, finishing up the last bite of her chicken. "I was thinking the same thing."

— *The End* —

Did you enjoy *The Dark Tetrad*?

Let others know! Please consider leaving a review on Amazon, *BarnesandNoble.com*, or wherever you purchased the book.

Coming in the spring of 2022:

We'll Quit When We're Dead:
A Kori Briggs Novel

by AP Rawls

Visit *www.KoriBriggs.com* for updates, promos, news, and merchandise.

UWS
Upper West Side Press, LLC

CPSIA information can be obtained
at www.ICGtesting.com
Printed in the USA
BVHW071949031021
618016BV00003B/12